FORTUNE'S CURSE

WITCHES OF LONG BEACH
BOOK ONE

J.C. YEAMANS

RSP

*For my daughter, who is the strongest woman I know.
You inspire me every day.*

Published by Reed Shore Press under the Imprint Broomstick & Lace.

This is a work of fiction. Names, characters, places, and incidents either are the product of the author's imagination or are used in a fictitious manner. Any resemblance to actual persons, living or dead, business establishments, events, or locales is entirely coincidental.

Fortune's Curse

ISBN: 979-8-88652-022-4

Cover: Charles W. Clark, Reed Shore Press. The design uses Rosarivo font (designed by Pablo Ugerman) and Photoshop brushes by Brusheezy.com.

Content/Line Editor: Sarah Faeth Sanders

Proofreader: Reed Shore Press

PREFACE

This series takes place in the same world as The Bearsden Witch Series. Each series can be read independently. Future books in Witches of Long Beach may contain visits from characters in The Bearsden Witch Series.

Although this series takes place in the city of Long Beach, street names have been altered to avoid any coincidental similarities of fictional businesses and residences in the books.

Please note that British English is used by characters from England, Wales, and Scotland, whether human or fae, despite the story taking place in the United States. These are not typos. However, if you find what you believe to be a typo, please contact the author at jcyeamans@reedshorepress.com.

CHAPTER
ONE

"Shit!" Amber rays splay from my fingertips, burning holes through the top of the dome tent. My suppression band must have fallen off my wrist when I dozed off. You'd think I would have learned vigorous sex renders me unconscious within minutes.

I throw off the blanket in a panic and sit up on my knees, naked, shaking my hand like I'm trying to fling off a spider. With merely the glow from my fingers to light my search, I rummage over the floor and through my pile of clothes in the dark. There it is—the tarnished copper cuff bracelet with a Thorn rune symbol etched into the surface.

Rhys of Dyfed pushes up from the sleeping bag and strands of his waist-length golden hair spill onto his firm chest. "Fuck," he says in a soft Welsh accent. "Fortune Whittle, you burnt holes in my tent roof again. For a descendant of a famous witch, you're none too competent." He glares at me, his cobalt blue eyes grasping my attention.

"Sorry, and stop saying that. Who knows if it's true?" I slip the light green hunk of metal over my hand and my magic recedes.

"I didn't plan on passing out. The thing has always been too big. It slips off unless I shove it up my forearm. I can't keep myself from casting spells while I dream. I mean...I'm asleep." My grandmother made the charmed jewelry for me when I turned seven, the first time my witchcraft skills presented. Unfortunately, the family curse accompanied my familial inheritance. I find my cell phone and check the time—2:15 a.m. "Damn. I have to get home." I pull on my panties and sports bra.

Rhys's hair falls behind his back, exposing an ivory complexion and slightly pointed ears—previously hidden by presenting in human form. "Why not stay, cariad?" He pulls me to him and kisses me fervently, his soft, scruffy beard tickling my skin. The musky aroma of our escapades permeates the air. "It's been months since the last time we...socialized. I missed your sun-kissed complexion and gorgeous baby blue eyes." He slides his hand onto my muscular thigh and squeezes. "And your other features."

"You missed the sex," I say, throwing him a glower. "I hope you enjoyed it, because this was the last time." Never mind that six-foot five-inch body full of glistening, ripped muscles draws me to him like a magnet. At five-foot-eight, I fit well against him. I throw on my t-shirt, shorts, and hoodie, shoving my feet into my sneakers before I stand.

The light from my phone reveals his mischievous smile and growing appendage. He grabs my right calf above my tattoo—a Thorn rune identical to the one that's etched on my copper bracelet. "You said that the last time. Yet here you are."

"If you want me to sleep with you again, you'll have to glamour me."

"I told you. I never glamour humans. It's against my personal code of ethics."

"Still, I have to move on." Though it will take every ounce of willpower not to return. He knows how to please me. A woman has needs. "We both know the reason you wanted me in the first place is because you were attracted to my blond hair. You're a Tylwyth Teg fairy. Your attraction to me is superficial. If I had known you were fae when we met, I would have never slept with you."

When we met, I believed he was a younger man in his late thirties—turns out he's over a thousand years old in the Otherworld, the realm where the supernatural live away from us humans and witches.

He becomes flaccid. "You certainly didn't complain the first night you followed me to my tent. Or the many times after."

"You lied to me." I slide on my backpack and grab my bike helmet. "You said you had fallen on bad times and were looking for work. Once the Tylwyth Teg began revealing their true identities and you divulged your secret, you could have at least found a better cover than being a random homeless person."

"Bloody hell. Is that why you want to end our rendezvous? You humans assign too much significance to stations. In my world, I'm a leader. That should be enough for you. I prefer the homeless cover. No need for false names and the tedious paperwork to create a human persona."

"It's not about stations. I'm not rich. I've worked hard for what I have. My grandmother inherited our house over forty years ago or we wouldn't even own a home. This was fun, but it was never going to last."

I shake my leg to loosen his grip. As I attempt to pull up the tent zipper, a lime-green glow snakes around my hand, trapping it in place. Suddenly, thunder rumbles above. I turn my head around to find a mischievous grin occupying Rhys's face.

"Stop, Rhys," I say, frowning. "Snagging the zipper and messing with the weather won't keep me from leaving. I'll be forced to cast a spell, which could fry the rest of your tent. It's also not a smart use of weather manipulation here. We just entered

June; it's hardly a bastion of thunderstorms." The lime-green snakes dissipate and I drag the zipper to the top.

"I was merely playing with you, Fortune. We were going to celebrate your forty-seventh birthday. For a human your age, you're still as hot as a nymph. You'll be back." His enticing eyes glimmer in the dark like the bioluminescence of the sea. But his allure isn't enough anymore.

"No, I won't." I stare him down and his gaze falls. "You'd better move when the sun comes up. The cops will sweep this area. Avoid the iron railings around here. They'll burn you. Goodnight, Rhys." Iron can repel, injure, or even kill the fae, but I don't want him to get hurt. He was good to me.

Since the Tylwyth Teg divulged their existence to witches, the Selkies down in Seal Beach have revealed themselves bit by bit. I've even heard of the Tuatha Dé Danann crossing over. How many other beings have entered our world? How many are yet to come?

As I exit the tent, the headlights of a passing car bounce off the Long Beach sign. A cool ocean breeze sparks a shiver that overtakes my body, but I inhale the salty air and zip up my hoodie. As usual, the nightly marine layer has rolled in, dragging humidity with it—damn June Gloom. But the crescent moon's luminescence cuts through. I twist my layered long hair and put on my helmet, stuffing my bangs and short strands inside. After hopping on my racer, I head for the Shoreline Bike Path.

After cutting through the outlets, I catch the path that winds around an assortment of chain restaurants and past the marina, glimpsing the 1850s lighthouse and the majestic Queen Mary through the thick, white haze. Although it is safer to cycle through downtown, it's easier to ride the beach trail where I don't have to compete with cars at night, the drivers often drunk as a skunk by this time of the morning.

The city is vibrant and welcoming during daylight hours. As night falls, criminal factions creep out like cockroaches searching for their next meal. But from the beach, the palm-tree-framed modern and historical high-rise buildings reach to the sky, gleaming with building lights that form a pattern of vertical checkers—far from scary.

By the time I reach the beach, I can't see more than twenty feet ahead of me—I begin to regret my decision. Eerie music rides the gusts of wind, nearly luring me from the path, and the fog is so thick even the beam from my bike headlight doesn't break through the murky air. Unknown predators hoot and holler at me, hidden behind the misty veil. "Hey, beautiful!" "Come here, sexy mama!" "Bring that booty over here!"

What did I expect in the wee hours of the morning? I had hoped taking the beach route would avoid this predatory shit. A blurry figure with a pair of luminescent dots dashes through the white cottony haze blanketing the coast. I pedal furiously, my heart thumping like the foot of a rabbit with a severe case of ADHD. Although the parking lot isn't visible, it's not far ahead. I pump my pedals and fly down the bike path as if I'm riding a witch's broom.

Footsteps pitter-patter toward me, but I can't discern where they're coming from. Are they approaching from the left? No, behind me? Suddenly, a man in baggy jeans and a black hoodie appears directly in front of me! In a panic, I veer off to the right, leave the concrete path, and fly like the witch I am over my handlebars. But with no broom! "Aghhh!"

My cuff bracelet takes flight, and amber essence sprouts from my fingers, buffering my fall. But I faceplant on the sand. My arms sink in up to my wrists, camouflaging my magic for the moment. Despite not invoking a spell, magic seeps out when I'm stressed. This family curse blows. I spit granules from my lips as I raise my head.

"Madam?" the man yells in an English accent, dashing toward me.

I scramble to find the copper band that inhibits my wonky magic and push it back over my wrist before the unknown runner finds me. The man is probably an Unremarkable, a human who isn't *in the knowing* of all things supernatural. But if he's got any predatory ideas in mind, I'll fling this bracelet off and defend myself.

When I roll over, the stranger aims a flashlight at me. I bat his hand away, spitting out more sand. "Get that fucking thing out of my face!"

"Oh, I'm dreadfully sorry." He shoves the handle of the flashlight into the sand so the light points upward.

I get the first glimpse of my obstructor, his face highlighted by the spray of the light. An attractive man, most likely in his late forties, he has a rectangular face with a firm jawline and tousled, thick brown hair. His eyes resemble the color of cognac. Something shiny hangs from his neck as he looks me over—a badge.

"I'm Detective Oliver Prescott of the Long Beach Police Department. Are you hurt?"

"No. Just a few scrapes." I glance at my bicycle, crashed on the sand a couple of feet away. "But my front wheel may be damaged."

"My sincere apologies. I didn't see you coming." He gestures behind him. "The fog."

I roll onto my side and the detective helps me to stand. He's taller than my five-foot-eight frame, probably around six feet, and appears to be quite lean. His dress is far from the regulation suit and tie. He must be undercover.

"Well, if you're a police officer, you should know not to run on the bike path," I say, brushing the soft granules from my skin and clothes.

"You're absolutely right," he says, grabbing his flashlight. "I was investigating this area and heard the predatory speech from those unsavory men up ahead. I thought you might need my help. Clearly, I wasn't paying attention to which path I was on."

"Apparently," I scoff. "I can take care of myself."

His eyes roll as he hooks his flashlight to his belt. "What is your name, Madam?"

"Why do you need to know? Are you going to arrest me for almost running you down?" I ask, sneering at him.

"I daresay you failed quite miserably, if that was your intention." He curls his mouth, revealing the sexiest smile I've ever seen.

My heart skips a beat. "No. I'm an experienced cyclist. If I wanted to run you over, you'd have tire marks down your back."

He chuckles. "I imagine so. A bright light appeared when you flew off your bicycle. What was that?"

Fuuuck. "Oh, must have been my phone." I pull out my cell and press the button on the side to highlight the screen, averting my eyes.

"It seemed brighter. The fog was playing tricks, no doubt. Allow me to examine your bicycle."

My professed rescuer walks to my bike and picks it up. I follow him, relieved he isn't rebutting my explanation. As he inspects my front wheel, the flashlight passes over my right ankle, and he stops.

"That's an odd tattoo. What is it?"

Enough of this small talk. I'm tired, and this incompetent cop caused me to damage my racer. "Can I have my bike?"

"Why don't you let me drive you home? I'll put the cycle in my unit."

"I want to get back and go to sleep," I say in a huff. "The wheel is good enough to ride."

"Certainly," Detective Prescott says, passing the handlebars to me. "Again, my apologies."

"Sure. I suggest you look where you're going next time."

He frowns as I hop on my racer. I take off down the bike path toward Toyon Avenue, cutting through the white mist and cool breeze.

In the distance, the police officer's voice rings out. "Madam, you never told me your name! I'd like to offer you money to fix your bike."

I chuckle as I continue on the path, but the cash would have been nice.

When I arrive at my Victorian home in Carroll Park, an antique hurricane lamp illuminates the front window. Under the spray of the nearby streetlight, you can barely appreciate the beauty of the early 1900s house, painted in contrasting colors of sage green, white, and pink, the yard bordered by a picket fence. My grandmother, Elizabeth "Betty" Whittle, inherited the property from her sister, my Great-Aunt Miriam, who also never married. She begged Nana for years to move to the West Coast to live with her.

Born out of wedlock, my grandmother inherited the family surname—supposedly our ancestral claim to the famous Anne Whittle of the Pendle Witches of Lancaster, England. I never put much stock in the family's assertion. An ancestor changed her last name after researching historical birth documents, supposedly proving she had descended from Anne. Conveniently, she lost her copies. All we have is an unsubstantiated tale.

I call my grandmother Nana, unless she pisses me off, which has happened a fair number of times over the years. That's when I toss a couple of Bettys at her to shut her up. She will have a few words tucked away in her robe pocket for me in the morning daylight.

After rolling my bike up the driveway, I store it in the garage.

As I approach the porch to the back door, the sconce casts eerie shadows, and coyotes howl close by. But they don't frighten me. My magic may be unreliable, but I can still cast protection spells. It's just messy.

Once inside, I remove my sneakers and tiptoe through the kitchen to the dining room. I pass Nana's bedroom door, hoping to avoid my nemesis—the evil creak in the center floorboard. Too pooped to cast a spell of silence and risk waking her, I clench my teeth, stifle my breath, and step. *Phew.* Missed it.

After I turn off the hurricane lamp in the parlor, I maneuver up the stairs in the dark. I'm too tired to wash up after my night's frolicking and collapse onto my antique oak bed. A bag of rune-stones creates a dent in my pillow. My magic assistant Norman's passive-aggressive way of pushing me to use them. My mother was competent at casting runes, but Betty, not one bit. I toss them aside.

The moonlight filters through my porch patio door, re-energizing my familiar as he sleeps in his dog bed. Having chosen the persona of a diminutive morkie, a cross between a Maltese and a Yorkshire terrier, he's always there protecting me while I slumber. But he snores like a grizzly bear. Must have smoked too much pot tonight.

As exhausted as I am, you'd think I would pass out. But I can't get my encounter with the detective out of my brain. He definitely saw my unruly magic unfurl when my bracelet slid off. I slide the band of tarnished copper up my arm, shimmy under the sheets, and grind my head into the pillow until I find the perfect spot. Why worry about some random cop, anyway? I'll never cross paths with him again.

But he sure had the sexiest smile.

TWO

etective Oliver Prescott approaches me dressed in a tight *T-shirt and weathered jeans. Is the bulge in his pants obscuring a gun? Or is he happy to see me? Standing a mere inch from me, his breath reeks of pot. Figures. But he probably needs stress relievers like any hardworking professional. He grins, that irresistible smile tugging at me, and tongues the side of my face.*

I open my eyes to catch my morkie familiar licking my cheek. "What the fuck, Norm?" I scoot him away. "I told you not to wake me like you're lapping at your water bowl." My hands land on wet sheets—a damn night sweat. Could I really be in perimenopause?

He laughs like a hyena as he shuffles back to me, speaking in a man's tenor voice. "Peee-yew. Your breath has the odor of five-day-old trash." He waves his paw at his nose. "And you reek of midnight sex at the LA River." His mustache quirks as his mouth spreads into an awkward grin, his tongue protruding and rolling up at the end, resembling a lizard's.

"Oh, shut up." I sit up and rub my temples.

My familiar's face resembles an old man with round chocolate-brown eyes that melt your heart. Then he opens his mouth, and vulgarity spills out. Only fellow witches can hear his human speech unless he chooses to expose himself. To an Unremarkable, his musings present as barks. I sniff his dog hair, a mixture of white and tan with sprinkles of black on his stubby tail.

"You don't smell like roses either, Norm." I pinch my nose.

"Well, I won't remain here and take these insults," he says, taking a step toward the footboard. "And stop calling me Norm. I prefer to be addressed by my proper name, Norman the Conqueror."

I hop off the bed, snorting. "What have you ever conquered except shitting on the neighbor's front yard without getting shot?"

"More than you, my cursed witch." He sticks his puny tongue out at me. "Your mother's bag of runestones remained untouched in that bottom dresser drawer. Many moons have passed since you used them. You shoved them aside as usual."

Ouch. "Can't argue with that," I say, frowning. "Without control of my inner witch energy, they're useless. I'm unable to cast simple spells using herbs or candle magic, the basics of a level one neophyte, and you want me to perform divination with Ivy's runestones."

In our little corner of the world, we must achieve competency in the first-level skills before moving on to higher ones. Intermediate witches on the next tier can also cast spells to manipulate objects, perform healing magic, and use their intuition to sense the coming of danger. At the third-echelon, or proficient, they perform any type: they can summon their inner energy to defend themselves or attack an enemy, bring life back to plants and animals, predict the future, conference with the dead, and cast hexes.

"I'd be happy if I could take a shower without my bracelet." I grimace at him. "Why did you transition from a German shepherd to a morkie if you wanted to be so revered? Now you act like you have a Napolean complex."

"Look at this face," he says, gesturing with his paw. "The ladies can't resist it." He sits on his hind legs and yawns. "You were with that Tylwyth Teg again. Betty won't like your hanging out with him. Not one bit."

"Yeah. Well, she can deal. I am a grown-ass woman. You'd think she'd at least be happy I'm not sleeping with an Unremarkable."

"Doing the mambo with a fairy is hardly a step up in her mind. Could spark an entirely new debate. Although Unremarkables remain at the top of that shit list. You know, because of the whole 'you can't procreate with one' thing."

"Thanks for being so supportive," I say in a snarky tone. "I'm done with him, anyway."

He bursts out laughing, spitting saliva on me. "You're repeating yourself, Fortune. No one believes you anymore."

I throw him a side-eye and search for my cell phone but remember it's in my backpack. "What time is it?"

"Ten in the morning on this glorious day, my witch."

I glance out the bedroom window. "The marine layer is blanketing the coast. Far from spectacular." A foghorn blares in the distance.

"You're alive, aren't you? I celebrate every day you wake." He bats his eyes at me.

"Don't try to suck up now, familiar. Gotta pee and get ready so I can open the store at noon."

"I guess I'll venture onto the porch and raise my leg." He snickers as he leaps to the wooden floor.

"Try not to cause too much trouble. Or you'll find Betty scooting your fluffy ass out of this house. Familiar or not."

He shakes his stubby tail at me as he struts away, farting magic rainbow bubbles out of his ass—his version of flipping the bird at me. I snatch the burgundy pouch of runestones and pull one out —the Thorn rune on an amethyst crystal, associated with protection, conflict, and change, signaling I have an obstacle to overcome. No shit, Sherlock. I don't need a magical mind to interpret that one. I stuff it back into the bag and shake it.

After clearing my head, I concentrate on a question for a full minute. What path should I follow? I dump three stones onto the mattress. Two are upside down; the other displays a downward F —the Ansuz. Communication, wisdom, and truth. It could mean a divine message may arrive from the god Odin, or on the flip side, it could point to deceit, a misunderstanding, or manipulation. Apparently, Ivy could decipher their messages without a second thought. I've got nothing, not even a sliver of an answer. I stuff the stones back in and return the velvet bag to the bottom dresser drawer.

As I rush to the bathroom, footsteps pound on the floor below. Yup. Betty is steaming. I love my grandmother and understand why she worries, but I have never failed her. I've avoided pregnancy with an Unremarkable all these years—all to eliminate passing on the family curse. But sometimes I dream of what my life could have been. After showering, I slip on a thin tee over a worn pair of jeans and head downstairs to face the inquisition.

Betty Whittle lived a hard life. She worked at a florist's shop until she retired, all while raising me. I never met my grandfather, and neither did my mom, Ivy. He was a fly-by-night witch who planted the seed and fled the next day. Nana was a bohemian in those days, but her lifestyle wasn't unusual for a green witch.

Even now, at ninety years of age, my grandmother walks three miles a day, lifts thirty-pound bags of soil, and tends to the gardens. Her witchcraft skills are boundless. Something I can only hope to achieve someday with my deficit. She's also as stubborn as a mule. I swear, Betty is waiting for me to hit menopause before she croaks, just to make sure I don't conceive a child with an Unremarkable.

When I enter the kitchen, Nana is putting dishes in the ivory cabinets and wiping down the marble countertops. Dressed in a loose blouse and capris, she has clipped her long white hair behind her head, a style she applies every single day. Her locks resembled the color of cinnamon when I was a small child, but her russet-brown eyes remain. Too many years of gardening without sunscreen took a toll and left her with weathered skin.

"Good morning, Nana," I say, opening the fridge. "How are you feeling today?"

She throws the sponge into the sink. "Where were you last night? I didn't hear you come in, which means it was after my nightly 2:00 a.m. trek to the toilet. I worry when you're out late. They found a man dead on the beach again. It was in the Long Beach Gazette."

"I'm forty-seven years old on my next birthday," I say, retrieving oat milk, yogurt, and fruit from the fridge. "I don't need to answer that question. If I avoided the beach because of every drug incident, I wouldn't have a life. Homelessness and mental illness are rampant in this economy. It's sad."

She leans back against the counter, scowling. In an instant, I'm seven years old again.

"Fiiine. I was with Rhys. But before you scold me, I told him it was the last time." I drop the remainder of my smoothie ingredients into the blender.

"Fortune Whittle, I told you it was a bad idea to keep engaging in backseat bingo with that Tylwyth Teg." A member of the Silent Generation, Betty always pulls out these zingers.

I chuckle. "Oh, Nana. Rhys doesn't own a car. All he has on this side of the world is that tent." *And a rock-hard body.*

"Don't sass me, girl," she says. "You know damn well you can still get pregnant. Who knows what could result from mating with the fae with your deficiency?"

"At least I wouldn't pass on the curse."

I push the button on the blender to high and its roar echoes throughout the kitchen, triggering tinnitus in my right ear. The glass pitcher reflects my baby blues, turned steely after the years of dealing with this family curse. I pour the mixture into my smoothie bottle.

"Also, I nearly ran over a cop who was running on the bike path. Scared the shit out of me. I rode off the concrete and damaged my racer." I refrain from sharing my magic fiasco.

"Well, he should pay for the repairs, then," she says.

"It was late, so I hopped back on and rode home. Nana, I was careful like I always am. No one understands more than I do that this affliction needs to end with me. It's why I never settled down and had children. Besides, menopause will hit in a few years. I think I had my first night sweat."

Since my mom didn't live past her twenty-fifth birthday, I have no idea when that momentous time will arrive—the day I can fuck anyone I want without the worry of a dreadful consequence.

She shakes her head. "You likely have a decade left. I don't know why you didn't marry that witch you went with. The curse wouldn't have appeared in your babies."

"Well, for one, he turned out to be a prick who cheated on me with a Tylwyth Teg hooker, and two, the curse would still be present. Not having offspring eliminates the issue forever."

"Great-grandchildren would have been a blessing from the gods." A sigh passes through her lips. "If you had a night sweat, why didn't you throw black cohosh or red clover in your smoothie? Or recite an incantation to cool your body."

"I know you push the use of herbs, Nana, being a green witch. But they both make me nauseous. I may try hormone therapy if things get bad. What good is reciting an incantation when I can't control my magic?"

She waves her hand, surrendering. "Suit yourself, Fortune. You're off to the store?"

"Yeah, I have to get there early," I say, screwing the lid on the bottle. "I asked Cam to meet me."

"Cameron Huxley? That young male witch who was kicked out of a coven down in Orange County?"

"Yeah. It wasn't fair, but they have their rules down there. Glad I've never been part of it. Following a solo path like you was a better decision for me, considering my secret. Plus, I've never had enough success to even choose a direction. Do you need anything before I come home tonight?"

"No, dear. I'll pick up groceries while I'm out on my daily walk."

Norman scuttles in and leaps onto a kitchen chair. "Shit. Did I miss the fight? I guess I took too long pissing off the second-floor balcony and shaking my dick."

"We didn't fight," Nana says, pursing her lips. "And it's none of your concern, familiar."

He snarls at her. "My witch is always my business, Grandma."

Nana glares at him while chanting a spell under her breath and his tail rises off the seat, leaving him hanging in the air like dirty laundry. She snickers and exits the kitchen. He splats onto all fours when he hits the tile floor.

"That wasn't funny, Betty!" He rubs his hairy butt. "Sometimes she really pisses me off."

My mom chose Norman against Nana's recommendation. He's a mess, but Ivy must have seen something in him. I grab my thin hoodie and purse.

"Keep it up, Norman. One of these days, she'll turn you into a cat."

He shudders, his hair standing on end. "Spare me the terrifying notion."

"Stay out of trouble," I say, heading to the door. "I have to practice the craft after dinner. Do some spell prep for a change or clean up the magic area in the garage."

"What?" His ears perk up. "Expose myself to spiders and lurking coyotes? Are you fucking mad?"

I frown at my familiar. "Bye, Norman."

I head out into the potent sun of SoCal, how some of us locals refer to Southern California. As I meander around the curvy roads in Carroll Park, I recall my mother's face, merely a blurred image with the passing of the years. But the memories of crying myself to sleep in the days and weeks following the accident will never fade.

Deep down, I believe Nana harbors guilt surrounding her daughter's death. When Betty discovered my mother was dating an Unremarkable without her knowledge, she forbade her from seeing my father. They never married, but by then, Mom was already pregnant with me and mourned the loss of her love.

When I was five years old, Ivy tried to rendezvous with my father in secret. She crossed the street to meet him but got hit by a truck. Betty pinned Mom's death on my dad when she told me the history, but I believe she actually blames herself to this day.

My father introduced himself to me on a playground when I was seven, but I don't remember his name or much else about him—only that he was really tall. Betty screamed at him to leave, and I never saw him again. Every once in a while, I fantasize about crossing paths with him once more. He'd be seventy-two years old.

I understand Nana raised me the only way she knew, according to her ancestors before her. But Mom might be here today if Betty had let her love the father of her child and said *fuck it* to the family curse.

THREE

When I reach Retro Row, a local shopping district, the sidewalks are bustling with locals weaving in and out of the foot traffic. People are walking their dogs and meeting friends for lunch. Or perhaps they're searching for contemporary art, clothing, jewelry, furniture, and vinyl records from years gone by. Storefronts mimic the past with their vibrant, hip ambiance. Buildings plastered in primary colors and geometric shapes or garish décor. Windows shining with vivid neon signs of pink and blue.

Interested in art films from the 1930s? Skateboards and roller skates? Independent bookstores? You'll find them here too, along with an assortment of locally owned restaurants and coffee shops. Because residents support our mom-and-pop shops. It's a designated bike-friendly business district, too.

When Nana and I moved into the Victorian house in Carroll Park, we discovered her sister collected antiques and other paraphernalia. I learned to appreciate old things as well. After I graduated from college, she encouraged me to start my business by stocking it with Aunt Miriam's collections. With her guidance, I established my eclectic store, offering vintage clothing, jewelry, home décor, and odd pieces of furniture.

I gaze at the purple sign on the mint-green building: Fortune's Attic Finds. Underneath, I find Cameron Huxley leaning against the door, scrolling on his phone and waiting patiently. Cam has a head of thick, dark brown hair he keeps trimmed close on the sides, but the strands party on top like there's no curfew. In the fall, he'll be a junior at California State University, Long Beach, my alma mater. The students and locals refer to our highly respected university as "The Beach," and its mascot, Elbee, is an adorable shark with a mischievous grin.

Cam glances up from his phone screen. "Hey, for a minute, I thought you might bag it today." He moves aside, allowing me to unlock the entry door. "You asked me to show up an hour early."

"Sorry," I say, grimacing. "Don't worry. I'll pay you. Gabby will help later when she arrives." Gabriela Lopez is my Unremarkable employee and knows nothing of our supernatural world, but she's a kind, reliable woman in her early seventies. "I didn't get home until the wee hours of the morning and passed out. When I got up, Nana grilled me. I can't believe she expects me to report to her at my age. Worse...I always cave and tell her. Fuck me, right?"

He spits out a laugh. "It's not just you. I cave to my Grammy sometimes, too."

I motion for Cam to enter, and I follow, turning the lock after the door shuts. "But you're twenty years old. I'm middle-aged and still can't say no to her."

"Yeah. That is pretty bad, Fortune." He hangs his backpack on the wall behind the counter.

"Exactly. But what the fuck do you know anyway, Gen Z?" I say, snapping like a turtle. "It's not as if you found your balls when your parents pressured you to leave UC Irvine for Cal State."

I squeeze my eyes shut, cringing, and pop them open. My trusted employee and witch friend gapes at me, blinking.

"That was mean," I say. "I'm a bitch when I don't get enough sleep, and I can't blame perimenopause for this one. You wanna hit me?" I point to one of my high cheekbones. "Take your best shot."

Cam rolls his fingers slowly inward, forming a fist, and bumps my shoulder. A chuckle breaks free. "Eh, you're not entirely wrong. I didn't feel like I belonged there. Not my vibe. I'm excited about starting in the fall. Besides, the coven down there asked me to leave after…"

"Accepting the delivery of a mummified fairy from your brother? I'm sure that went over really well. You got rid of the carcass in the end. My behavior was uncalled for; it's not how a friend should react."

"We all have bad days," he says, shoving his phone in his back pocket. "I'm glad you speak your mind. Fortune, if it weren't for you, I'd have given up on witchcraft. The skills came so easily to my brother, Spence."

"Stop that—comparing yourself to him. Some witches don't have the same proficiency as others. It doesn't make us unworthy. We're just misfits." I hug him and pat his back. "You'll find your path with more training. I'm still searching."

An obnoxious banging on the entry door makes me flinch. A petite woman possessing long black hair with bright red stripes peers through the glass, her forehead pressed against the surface. I recognize the witch in an oversized T-shirt, cargo pants, and bright green hi-top sneakers. It's my best friend, Rylee O'Brien, who is younger than me by two years. Because she most resembles her Japanese side, she likes to dye some strands to honor her father's Irish ancestry. Personally, I think she does it to mess with people who don't believe she is what she says she is.

"Speaking of witch misfits." I rush to let her in.

"Yo, peeps!" She barges in, bursting with the energy I wish I had today.

"Hey, Rylee?" Cam asks. "Don't you have to be at the studio soon?"

"Pfft. It's right next door. Juan doesn't care when I show up."

My best friend is a talented artist specializing in sustainable art. She works at Garcia's Custom Framing to pay the bills while she builds her career. Juan is an amazing painter and started the business to provide a steady income for his family.

"What's up, Red?" I ask. "Thought you had to work?"

"I do, but I wanted to remind you about the gallery opening tonight. You are coming, right?"

"Of course. I wouldn't miss one of your art exhibits. This one is special."

She shakes her arms all about. "I'm so nervous. The exhibit last year didn't fare so well. Normally, Erin would go with me, but—"

"You broke up," Cam says. "That's hard."

"You know, life sucks and then..." She wiggles her eyebrows. "You get even! Bwahahaha!"

He chuckles. "Please keep me in the dark. Fortune, what would you like to do first? Sift through the box of clothes you bought at that estate sale?"

"Yeah, that would be great. You go ahead. I'll help in a minute."

"Later, Rylee. Good luck with the show." He shuffles to the storage area.

"Thanks, dude!" My best friend inspects the baubles hanging on a display at the counter. "I tried to call you last night. You didn't pick up."

"I was with Rhys. Before you say anything, it was my swan song. I needed to get laid with no strings attached. And I have to avoid—"

"Sex with Unremarkables. Yeah, I know. But seriously. Is Rhys the best you can do? A damn shame you're not into girls. You could have had me. I tried, though. You were so alluring that night at the bar."

"We ended up friends instead. A much better resolution."

"For you. I ended up with fickle Erin."

"I'm sorry you're hurting. They say love is fleeting. Friendship is forever." I caress her arm.

"Facts," she says. "Where's your bike?"

"When I got near Toyon Beach on the way home, a cop was running on the cycling path toward me. I rode off the trail into the sand. It was damaged."

"That sucks. Is he going to repair it?"

"I took off without giving him my name. My suppression band flew off and lit up the area like a flashlight. Always happens when I'm stressed out."

"Sheeeit! Do you think he saw what happened?"

"I don't believe so. Doesn't matter now."

The door swings in and a woman in her sixties with warm beige skin, brown eyes, and thick gray hair enters—Pamela Barrera, the local coven leader. The hereditary and eclectic witch integrates several practices of witchcraft openly, like most of us, but Unremarkables aren't aware of the true nature of our magical skills. When I'm running low on materials, I often drop by her metaphysical store, Charmed Alchemy.

Pam is the sort of rich witch who's lost touch with the struggles of us working-class spellcasters, having inherited most of everything in life—her money and her magic. Nana did as well, but there was little cash involved. My deficiency doesn't count for much, either.

Rylee mutters, "You should have locked the door."

"Hi, Pam. How are you doing today?" I ask. "The store doesn't open for another half hour."

She pushes her shoulders back. "The door was unlocked, Fortune."

My best friend points at the glass. "Well, the closed sign is hanging, Pam."

"You're right." I ram an elbow into my friend's side. "I forgot. Can you come back later?"

She huffs and glances at the merchandise. "I was hoping to browse before I open my shop."

"I'm sorry," I say, shrugging. "My employee came in early to work. He's waiting for me in the back."

"Fine." Pam goes to the door but turns around. "The coven is meeting to plan a ritual for the Summer Solstice Festival. You're both invited. Not that you'll come." She exits without waiting for a reply.

"Should we go this time?" Rylee scratches the back of her head.

"You know I can't. They may ask us to perform magic, and the cat would be out of the bag. Besides, after all these years of asking, I don't think she likes me much. She has the idea I believe I'm too good for them because of Nana's Whittle ancestry claim."

"What do you expect? You should come clean. Tell them the truth."

"Sure. An established coven would invite a witch into their circle who's encumbered by a family curse? I don't think so. I feel bad about it. They wanted as many witches as possible to help cast a spell of filtration on the portal in the lagoon to limit nefarious energy from passing through from the Otherworld. As far as we know, their incantation seems to have worked. You could have participated, you know."

"Nah. Not without my best buddy." She slaps my arm with the back of her hand and moves toward the door. "I'd better head to work. Meet me at the gallery?"

"You bet. Later, Red."

"Bye, Blondie!"

As my friend exits, I catch Pam Barrera crossing the street. She must believe I'm a huge snob because of my family's ancestral claim. How far from reality that is. I've walked on eggshells all these years, worried she and the other Long Beach witches would discover my truth.

That I'm a cursed witch who is terrified of performing witchcraft.

I COLLECT the rest of the dishes from the kitchen table and carry them to the countertop. "I can load the dishwasher, Nana."

"No, you'll not have time to practice your craft." She loads a glass onto the top rack and dries her hands on a dish towel. "I believe this ritual you created a few months ago could be the answer. Keep manifesting, Fortune. I have faith in you."

"Thanks, Nana," I say, embracing her. "The last two times, I came close to casting a spell without adverse effects from the curse."

"Please be careful of my sister's old car."

"I will. I understand how important it is to you."

Great-Aunt Miriam's vintage 1975 Rolls-Royce hasn't left the garage but to roll down the driveway once a month since we inherited the place. It's not likely going on the street anytime soon either. Why bother owning the thing if you merely want to admire it?

"Get on out there before that familiar of yours loses his shit. He's the most temperamental and egotistical magic assistant I've ever known. I told Ivy he was a poor choice. I'll never understand why you took him for your own."

"Norman is OK." And he remembers Ivy. His stories about

my mom bring me closer to her. "I don't know when I'll get back tonight, but you shouldn't worry. Rylee will be with me."

"I like her," she says, a wide grin brightening her face. "She's a loyal friend, and a fabulous new witch."

"Yeah, she is. See you in the morning."

I dash down the steps in my yoga shirt and biking shorts toward the garage.

When I enter, Norm appears almost human in his tiny tee as he grinds up mugwort in a mortar with a pestle. He adds garden sage, Nana's pride and joy from her garden, and crushes the herb into the mix. A sprinkled salt barrier lines the perimeter of the table, and a black candle flickers. A collection of grimoires rests on a shelf along with an array of herbs and animal bones.

My morkie familiar glances at me through strands of hair falling from his eyebrows. "It's about damn time, my witch. What took you so long to eat?"

"We'll get through this fast enough. Then I'm off to Rylee's art showing." I search through the basket of crystals and find the selenite wand, shining in its pearly white. "I've been at this for months now. The only way I will ever practice witchcraft successfully is by discovering a spell to remove the family curse. After multiple generations, I doubt I'll form a combination other ancestors haven't tried before. Suppressing it further could help, though."

"What have you got to lose?" He dumps the ground herbs in a bowl, slides it toward me, and lights it with a pass of familiar magic, his hairy paw radiating in yellow. Smoke rises in a spiral as it burns, disappearing into the ceiling. He inhales the scent deeply. "Oh, how I love the aroma of burning mugwort."

"What a shock since it resembles pot," I say, a chuckle surfacing. "I forget. What did we use last time?"

His paws drop to the table, sighing. "Your memory has gotten worse, my witch. Perhaps late nights with sexy fae are a bad idea." He wiggles his nose.

"Oh, shut up. That's not the only reason. Perimenopause has hit me like a brick lately. I'm debating whether to start hormones."

Norm falls to his side, guffawing. "Maybe they hold the secret to nixing the family curse, too."

"You're hysterical," I say, sticking my tongue out at him. "They would replace what I've lost, so no. Let's begin."

He sits up and snorts. "I'm sorry. I am at your service...as I was for your mother. Perhaps you can conference with her one day when you have control of your magic." His dark, round eyes turn glassy. "I, too, would like to see Ivy again."

"Wouldn't that be awesome?" I rub the soft hair on his head, and he pouts.

Despite all of Norman's complaining, he has never failed me. The salt line will help contain my faulty magic while the mugwort and garden sage purify the area. I pick up the selenite wand but hesitate.

"Oh, I remember. I used obsidian the last time. Should I try both?"

"It's your decision, my witch," he says.

I rummage through the basket and pull out an obsidian stone. It can't hurt to suck away more negative energy. I set it on the table next to the candle and lift the selenite wand.

"Norm, I'm not gonna recite anything this time. Instead, I'll concentrate on my intention internally."

"Yes, I will be here at the ready."

I breathe in the bouquet of burning herbs as I pass the selenite wand from my head to my toes, focusing my intention on cleansing my body. My mind floats as the weight of the world fades away. Time stands still. Seconds or hours; I don't recognize either. *Yes.* This is the purist I have ever felt. Then...

Bear-like snoring fills the garage. I flinch. "Nooorm!"

"Ruff-ruff. What?" His head pops up, his ears at attention. "Did I fall asleep?"

"For fuck's sake. I almost had it. I'm not the only one who needs to get quality sleep."

"Apologies, my witch. It might have been the doobie I had earlier."

"You think?" I say, tension lowering my voice.

Norman shuffles closer. "The ritual appears to have gone well. Attempt a small casting—something minor."

"Alright." I grab a withering plant in a terracotta pot and place it on the workbench. "I over-watered this succulent for weeks. Betty's green thumb did not make it into my genes. It's nearly dead."

"Good choice, my witch. I wish you much success." He steps back, paw by paw.

"You don't have faith in me," I say.

"Merely putting safety first, Fortune."

I glare at my skeptical familiar and remove my suppression bracelet inch by inch because I've been on this precipice before. I clench my jaw as I yank off the band completely. *Nothing* happens.

Norman jumps up on all fours. "Well, that's promising."

"We'll see," I say, a hint of optimism rising to the surface. I fetch the plastic watering can, fill it with water at the utility sink, and return to the table. "Here goes nothing."

I raise my hand and chant a simple healing incantation as I pour water onto the soil. "Imbue this liquid to heal this plant. Plump these withered leaves while I chant. Grow and grow with all my will. Thrive now, succulent, and then be still."

As I set the watering can on the table, my fingertips radiate an amber glow and the leaves of the wilted Zebra Haworthia swell.

They expand outward until they pop, their horizontal stripes glistening on the dark green spikes.

Norman jumps up and down. "Fortune Whittle! You did it! You did it!"

I gape at my open hand. "Yes, I did. But how long will this last?"

"You must cancel your plans and remain at home to test your skills this evening. Now's the time to cast the runestones as well."

"No, Rylee is my best friend. I can't miss her showing for any reason," I say, slipping on my Thorn rune bracelet. "I'll check again when I get home. Let's not tell Betty for now. We should wait until we confirm it wasn't a fluke."

"Good choice. I'll clean up, my witch, while you get changed. May the art exhibit go well."

"Thanks, Norm." I head toward the door but look back. "You know, maybe you are Norman the Conqueror."

His ears shoot straight up. "Of course I am."

I rush back into the house, realizing my time is slipping away. As I pass through the living room, Nana is in her corner chair next to the fireplace, reading.

"How did the ritual go, Fortune? Any success?"

My seven-year-old inner me can't lie to her. "A bit more than last time. I have to get moving. Don't wanna be late."

"Keep trying, my dear. Something is bound to work, eventually."

"I agree." A broad grin puffs up my cheeks like two pomegranates as I dash up the stairs. As usual, Nana was right.

But I'm not telling her.

FOUR

With no time to celebrate my newfound success, I slip on my pink sundress, apply some eyeliner, and head out the door, grabbing my aqua sweater and purse on the way. I sprint as fast as anyone can in heeled sandals to the East Village Arts District, where Rylee's oil painting is being showcased in the Fantasy Art Showing at the Whatever Goes Gallery, a local venue supported by an unknown donor.

When I arrive at the gallery, I'm winded, and my usually silky blond hair has developed a case of the frizzies—damn the June Gloom. After a quick brush, I stroll through the lobby into the exhibit area. The scent of fresh lavender permeates the room, reminding me of my mother. Ivy used to cut stalks from Nana's garden and saturate the house with their aroma. When my grandmother and I moved to Long Beach, I would do the same. But the next day I would find them in the garbage.

I spot Rylee standing in front of her painting, but I can only make out the vibrant colors on the canvas. As usual, my friend presents a professional yet artsy appearance, wearing a colorful, geometric collared shirt over black attire, including military-style boots. She's engaged in conversation with the director, William Smith, a middle-aged English expat dressed in a tailored blue suit. As I approach, he moves on. She waves her hand violently at me.

"Hey, lady," she says, eyeing me up and down. "I love that sundress on you, and those beige sandals...wow."

"Thanks. As usual, you look awesome. Very artistic." My back is toward the painting, since she likes to make a grand presentation of her work to me. "I didn't peek, but you better show it to me ASAP or I'll cheat."

She rubs her hands together, an elated grin broadcasting her excitement. "Close your eyes."

"Okaaay?" I do as I'm told and she spins me around, scooting me back to the perfect position.

"Tell me what you think?" she asks.

When I open my peepers, my jaw lunges down, gasping at the magnificent four by five oil on canvas. But my shock isn't a response to my friend's talented strokes. It's the subject of the artwork, and my gaping mouth does not go unnoticed. Rylee yanks my arm.

"You don't like it?" she asks, grimacing. "I was sure you'd be giddy about this one."

"No, I mean, yes. I love the painting. It's one of your best so far." I absorb the exquisite beauty of the winged being on the canvas. "But Rylee," I whisper. "You painted Rhys of Dyfed in all his glory. Wings and..." My eyes drop to a visible bulge, hidden by a swath of cloth. "...everything. Did he pose for you?"

"What?!" Her shouting prompts the glare of angry eyeballs nearby. She lowers her voice. "Nooo. I went by memory of the evening we saw him strolling along the ocean under the perfect moonlight, naked as a stripper. Snapped a photo in my head. I know you noticed because the next night...you know."

"Oh, that ridiculous didactic memory of yours. I wouldn't

have slept with him if I had known he was a Tylwyth Teg fairy. I believed he was some random homeless guy down on his luck."

She snickers. "That's better?"

"Well..." I stand back and admire the vision of Rhys, focusing on his pelvic region. She certainly got the details perfect. "What if someone recognizes him?"

"Like who?" Rylee tilts her head and smiles at the canvas of Rhys.

The director gestures for my friend to join him and a white-haired woman dressed in designer clothes.

"I wonder what he wants? Don't leave. He probably wants me to escort her to the bathroom."

While Rylee is off serving a patron, I gaze at the picture of Rhys of Dyfed, recalling the striking definition of his pectorals, abdominals, and thighs. He certainly is a beautiful man—well, fairy. If only he had true feelings for me and not the obsession of a Tylwyth Teg. I find myself in a trance, ogling his gorgeous face, physique, and wings, my mind swimming through memories of our time together...

"You certainly clean up well." The familiar English voice jars me back to reality.

Shit. I'm face to face with that Long Beach Police detective. In the brightly lit room, his face is more chiseled than I remember. Alluring crow's feet fan out around his cognac-hued eyes, haunting under the ceiling lights, as if they've witnessed a lifetime of trauma yet exude compassion. Close up, he appears to have a runner's body. A slightly sunburned complexion points to a run earlier in the day.

The detective's thick brown hair is tame this evening, not having to fight the winds of the ocean. He must be off duty because he's dressed in a polo shirt and jeans. No way he recognizes me. My hair was stuffed inside my helmet, and I was wearing biking attire. Plus, it was foggy and nearly pitch black.

"Are you talking to me?" I ask, tapping my upper chest. "We've never met, dude." I avert my eyes, feigning ignorance.

The police officer leans into me and I catch a whiff of his musky cologne. "It's alright to admit you were out and about at an obscene hour of the night." He gestures at my ankle, sporting a haughty smile. "That tattoo is unique."

I stand frozen, my jaw hanging on for dear life. How do I get out of this predicament? I raid my sleep-deprived brain for something intelligent to say, but all I find is cobwebs.

"Since you obviously don't remember our encounter in the wee hours of the morning, I'll introduce myself again." He offers his hand. "Oliver Prescott. But my friends call me Ollie. And your name is?"

Oh, what the hell. I clasp his palm. "Fortune Whittle."

"How beautiful, and so unusual. Your mum must have been blessed with the foresight that you would develop a timeless charm."

"Sure." I pinch my lips to contain an explosion of laughter. I've heard better pickup lines in downtown LA. "Since when do cops like art?"

"Actually, my mum is an artist back home in England. She's a widow but keeps busy."

"You must miss her. Why come here to work? Don't they need cops in England?"

He rubs the back of his neck. "I moved here with my ex-wife. She was an American."

Way to go, Fortune. I tug at the front of my dress. "Why not return to England?"

"I love it here. Long Beach weather is brilliant. Beats the rain in the UK any day of the week. Don't you agree?"

"Yeah," I say, a faint smile erupting. "But we have June Gloom to make up for it, and sometimes No-Sky July and Fogust."

"You forgot May Gray." He turns to admire my best friend's

painting. "Exquisite hues in this artwork." He focuses on the top of the canvas. "I know this is fantasy art, but the fairy's face seems quite familiar."

Rylee's voice rings out from behind. "Because I use faces of people I've come across." She nudges me. "Are you going to introduce me?"

"This is Olliver Prescott. He's the Long Beach detective who ran me off the trail last night."

"Oooh!" Her head jerks back. "Well, I hope you don't want to buy my painting because it's sold!"

"What? That's fabulous, Rylee!" I wrap her in a jubilant hug. "Who bought it?"

"No fucking clue. Anonymous buyer. I don't care. They're paying double so I won't make copies."

Ollie shakes her hand. "Congratulations, Rylee—"

"O'Brien. I know, I know. I don't look Irish, but half of me is." She pats her head. "I've got the red hair and everything."

"You're a funny woman and an extraordinary artist," Ollie says, chuckling. "It was a pleasure meeting you. Nice to put a name to your face, Fortune Whittle. I hope to run into you again. But the next time without sending you on a journey through the air—like a witch on a broom." He winks at me. "Have a wonderful evening, ladies."

He nods at us and strolls toward the sculpture room. My best friend guffaws and her laughter echoes in stereo.

"Shhh," I say. "That was embarrassing."

She muffles her boisterous laughter with a hand. "The dude must have a sixth sense. You haven't heard the last of him."

"He was joking, Red. He doesn't even know where I live. Besides, the guy is an Unremarkable."

"Didn't he offer to pay for repairs? You could still hit him up for the green stuff."

"I was hoping never to see him again." I glance at Ollie

Prescott as he exits the room. "Enough about some nosy cop. That's awesome someone bought your painting."

"Super cool but weird I don't know who it is."

"I need to tell you something." I grab her arm and drag her to an empty alcove. "Those rituals I've been performing the past few months? I finally had some success tonight. I cast a simple spell to revive a dying plant. It worked, and I didn't trash the place."

"Yes!" She cringes and attempts to whisper. "Sorry. I'm just so excited for you. Why aren't you home trying to cast more spells?"

"Because I didn't tell Nana. I don't want to put her on the hope train because it's probably temporary."

"Will you sneak into the garage and attempt more spellcasting when you get back?"

"No, but I won't be able to sleep if I don't attempt a spell one more time. I'm thinking of going to the lagoon. I've never tried to summon fish. Would be so cool if I could. That's like a level three incantation. The trail should be empty and dark enough to obscure my spellcasting."

"Want me to go with you? I can blow this off early. I am sold!"

"Are you allowed? I'd feel more confident if you were with me."

"Hell, yeah. I'll tell the blue suit I've gotta go. Meet you out front in an hour. We'll drive there in my car. Meanwhile, enjoy the show."

"Thanks, Red."

THE RIDE to the horseshoe-shaped lagoon in Rylee's scarlet sedan takes about fifteen minutes thanks to the non-stop traffic lights on Fourth Street. After finding a spot in the small parking lot, I throw on my sweater and we dash across the road to the causeway.

A salty odor hangs in the air, but nothing relaxes me more than a whiff of the beach. The partial moon peeks in and out through murky clouds, its beam zigzagging along the trail. Great blue herons slink through the water as the trill of a killdeer pierces the night.

"I haven't taken a walk here in a long time," I say. "I miss the palm trees lining the road that used to wind through here."

"They were pretty, but they didn't belong here," Rylee replies. "Restoring the area to a salt marsh was the right thing to do. I loved eating at the picnic tables, though. Where do you want to… *poof*." She wiggles her fingers in the air.

"Somewhere on the other side. Thankfully, no one is around. Later would be safer, but I'm pooped."

We arrive at the end of the causeway and turn right onto the sandy gravel path. I have to admit I prefer this to a hard blacktop road. But my heeled sandals would like a word. As we approach the bend in the trail, the water shimmers under a moonbeam in the distance. Rylee puts the brakes on her boots and points.

"There's someone up there near the lagoon's edge."

"Well, that blows," I say, eyeing the dark figure. "What are they doing here at this hour of the night?"

"Up to no good like us." She tugs at my sweater. "They'll leave when they notice we're approaching. Come on."

As we move closer, the moon retreats behind a clump of gray, darkening the sky, but the surface of the water continues to glimmer with wavering light—eerie. The stranger throws their dark jacket hood over their head, hops over the short fence protecting the sage scrub plants, and darts down the trail. When I look back at where they were squatting, the odd shimmer has disappeared. A pungent stench attacks us as if it's defending the lagoon.

"Dang," Rylee says, pinching her nose. "Where did that smell come from?"

"Must be something in the water," I say.

I inch toward the man-made path where the plants sowed in the restoration have been worn down by traffic. After I step over the fence, my best friend creeps behind me. When we arrive at the water's edge, the moon throws a spotlight on the rippling surface. Dead fish are floating everywhere!

"Did that asshole dump chemicals in here?" I squat and inspect the water, but I can't see shit. "I guess they were checking out the origin of the odor, too."

Rylee chuckles. "You won't be summoning these fish?"

"Actually…" I slide my copper bracelet over my hand, stopping at my fingertips.

She squats next to me. "Are you gonna do what I think you're gonna do? Maybe that's not wise."

"Why not? They're dead already. It's not like I can kill them."

I slip the metal band off—no seeping magic. The suppression ritual continues to hold.

"Wow," she says. "How will you do it? You don't have any materials here for a spell."

"I'll attempt a simple incantation of renewal. Probably won't work, but I can try." I face my palm toward the lifeless fish. "Creatures of the sea, you've left us far too soon. Arise from your death, and face the beaming moon." My hand illuminates the surface, but the sand bass and halibut float aimlessly.

"You need fire," Rylee says as she searches for dry plant debris. She pulls a lighter out of her pocket. "Don't worry. I'll burn a small amount on the sand."

"Alright." I scan the area for late-night insomniacs. "Be careful."

As I set my copper band on the ground, she ignites the pile of leaves. While my right hand radiates, I repeat the chant. "Creatures of the sea, you left us far too soon. Arise from your death, and face the brilliant moon." The eerie eyes of the fish carcasses stare back at me, as if they're laughing. "Maybe I need to touch them?" I place my gleaming fingers on the cool, rippling water...

Fuuuck! Streaks of yellow bounce off the surface and the small area bursts into flames! Amber beams resemble lightning strikes as they continue to boomerang across the lagoon. I attempt to draw back my witch energy, but the control I had earlier has disappeared.

"Fortune! Do something!" Rylee faces her palm at me as she chants a protection spell, but it fails.

"I'm trying!" I poke around for my bracelet on the sandy edge, my hands still glowing. It's missing. "Help me find my copper band."

"As soon as I take care of the blaze you started. Unfortunately, I didn't bring a broom." My BFF rushes through the plants to gather long stems and fastens them together with strips of eelgrass from the lagoon. She chants while using the makeshift broom to fling water into the air. "Rain, I call on thee to soak this fire. Do it now before this shit grows dire!"

After a few repetitions, the pitter-patter of raindrops falls on the water, smothering the flames until smoke rises in swirls of black. She scrounges through the pickleweed succulents, but raises her head toward the lagoon and points. "There it is."

"Oh," I say, reaching for my bracelet.

Rylee slaps my arm. "No fucking way you're dipping your hand in there again."

"Sorry. I wasn't thinking. Hurry!"

I draw back the flailing amber while my best friend buries her hand in dead fish to retrieve the tarnished copper. After picking off eelgrass, she shoves the bracelet at me and I thrust it over my wrist. But my right arm glows like molten lava, seeping through my suppression band.

My heart beats as though an ape is pounding on my chest. I rip off my sweater and frantically wrap the thin knitted garment around my right hand, but it's as effective as covering a naked body with translucent gauze. Trust me, I've been there—don't ask.

The moon has covered itself in a blanket of clouds, leaving only the spritz of light from a distant lamppost. In my peripheral vision, someone or something whooshes past me in the dark, a faint splash of lights flashing. I spin around and search for the sneaky invader, gasping.

"What are you looking at?" Rylee asks, stomping on the smoldering pile of leaves.

"Did you notice anyone running past here?" I spin around, scanning the area.

"No, did you?" She kicks the evidence of our magical shenanigans into the lagoon.

As I survey again, the marsh appears still except for the whispers of the sage scrub plants rustling in the wind and the faint sound of a musician playing a violin. "I guess not. But I swear something ran past me. Was it simply a rush of air? I'm paranoid."

"You should be. We'd better get the hell outta here. The LBPD could show up. And look."

In the distance, a few residents are emerging from their homes on the other side of the lagoon. We sprint toward the causeway like criminals leaving the scene of a crime—well...

"Someone may have seen us," Riley says, panting.

"Only if a busybody in one of those houses witnessed the blaze. Slow down. I can't run in these sandals."

I stop to adjust my poor choice of footwear. Someone yelps in the distance, and a faint figure runs through the marshy area away from the path and causeway.

"What was that?" I ask, panting. "Shit. I hope no one saw us."

"Too late now, and we don't have time to figure it out."

We continue on the path, crunching with each step until...

Bam! I trip over a soggy log on the trail and land on the gravel. My pink dress is a goner.

"Are you alright?" Rylee asks, huffing and puffing. "What is that?"

"A rotten log, I think." I push up on my knees and poke the squishy mass—and gasp. "Oh, fuck. It's a body." I tumble back onto my butt, tachycardia seizing my chest.

"What?! Like a corpse? Shit."

Rylee drops to the ground and rolls the person over—a young man. His eyes are glassy, and white frothy foam seeps from his nose and mouth.

I tug at my friend's shirt. "We have to get out of here."

"Shouldn't we call the cops?" She pulls out her cell phone.

"What?" I gesture at my wrapped right arm, a faint glow shining through my sweater. "He must have been strung out on drugs and drowned. I bet a friend pulled him out of the water and fled. We have our own problems."

"Right. Let's go." Rylee grabs my arm and drags me across the causeway.

"My bracelet always contained my faulty magic when it misfired. Would you drive me home and help me figure this out in the garage?"

"I don't know how much I can do, but I'll try. I'm a level two practitioner. Could Norman assist you?"

"Well, any skill tier is better than my scrappy skills," I say, gasping for air. "I've trashed so many things over the years practicing the craft with this curse. And Norm? Who knows? Depends on whether he's high."

We arrive at Rylee's car and leap into our seats. As we head toward Carroll Park, I contemplate my situation. How will I hide this from Betty?

FIVE

Rylee peels into the driveway and we dash to the garage side entrance. I grab the doorknob with my left hand and jiggle it. Shit. Nana locked up for the night. I gesture at the potted rosemary next to the door.

"Can you dig into the dirt for the key?" I ask. "Betty hides one in there."

My friend blinks at me. "Dead fish. A human corpse. Now dirt. What's next?" Her voice rings in the backyard like an announcer at a boxing match.

"Shhh..." I glance back at the house. "We don't want to wake her. Please?"

She gives me the side-eye and impales her digits into the soil. "Ah, found it."

As she opens the door, the sound of creaking wood boards originates from my bedroom balcony. Norman's fluffy head pops between the porch railing balusters, his hairy face lit by the lantern.

"What the hell are you up to at this hour, my witch? I was

curled up and dreaming about the Cocker Spaniel in the Craftsman bungalow three doors down." He snickers like a hyena.

I raise my right arm, radiating in amber yellow up to my elbow. The Thurisaz symbol flashes in and out like a neon sign. I shout in a whisper, "Shhh. Can you help? Or are you too stoned?"

Norm's ears perk up. "On my way, Fortune."

My morkie familiar scuttles to the side of the house, slides down the gutter like the local firefighter to the porch underneath, and runs down the back steps. He dashes into the garage, and we rush in after him. I flip the light switch and shut the door.

"What the fuck did you do?" he asks, jumping from the chair to the table. His hair is matted and he's still wearing his satin pajama shirt.

"I tried to revive a bunch of dead fish in the lagoon. I was fine until I touched the water. My magic ping-ponged all over. I used a renewal spell. I don't know what happened."

"Did it not occur to you to check with me before casting spells in public?" He flips through a few pages in Nana's grimoire.

"It wasn't your decision," I say. "I felt confident when I removed the suppression band. The ritual was still holding. I'm sure of it."

"I was there, Fluffy. She was fine," Rylee says. "There was something in the water. It caught fire."

"What?!" The grimoire drops from Norman's paws. "Did anyone notice you?"

"I don't know. She snuffed it out. Can we worry about that later?" I wipe the sweat off my face. My arm shakes as if it's cut off ties to my brain. "We need to do something about my problem now."

Norm picks up the family spellbook and turns page after page with his paw. "I can't find a spell to regenerate your bracelet.

You're gonna have to wake up your grandmother. She must have combined some to create the charm."

My head quivers. "She'll freak out. Can you try something? What about a special containment spell?"

He slams the book shut. "Fine. But I take no responsibility for the outcome."

"Of course you won't," Rylee says, grabbing the mortar and pestle. "What can I do to help, Norm?"

"Collect these herbs from the hanging baskets on the wall. Lavender, St. John's Wort, and a stem of sage. Grind them together. Quickly."

My friend grinds up the herbs and pours them onto the table while my half-stoned familiar pours salt around the pile to create a circle. He motions for me to lay my hand inside. I place it in the center, the tremor still there, taking care to encompass the bracelet within the boundary. Norm's paw hovers above, radiating in a brilliant neon-green.

"Here we go, ladies," he says. "Prepare yourselves." He mutters the chant over and over, the words inaudible in his morkie ruffs. The Thorn rune symbol transforms into a green hologram, rising off the shiny metal...then snaps back like a rubber band.

Rylee jumps. "Shit!"

"Aghhh!" I try to rip my hand from the circle, but it's stuck to the table like glue.

"Oh, my witch," Norman says, pulling his paw back. "Your hand should be free now."

As I lift my arm, my magic recedes, fading into nothingness. "Yes! Thank you, Norm!"

"I wouldn't count your chickens yet," Rylee says. "Take off your bracelet."

"My magic always seeps out a little when I remove it," I say.

"As long as I don't perform any spellcasting, I should be fine." I peer at my familiar. "Right?"

Norm's eyes turn into miniature eight balls. "Maybe? What the fuck do I know?"

"There's one way to find out," my skeptical friend says, stepping back farther.

"I'll be under the table." Norman hovers to the floor on a halo of green and scuttles beneath. "Purely a precaution."

"Thanks for the vote of confidence, friends."

I slide my suppression band over my fingers, hesitating with every inch. When it nears the tips, I rip it off. An amber beam shoots from my hand and ricochets off the ceiling onto Nana's vintage Rolls-Royce. I gasp. The bolt shoots toward a ceiling light hanging from a joist. The bulb shatters, exploding like fireworks, and sends shards of glass flying everywhere. A burning chemical odor pervades the air.

My bracelet tumbles out of my hand as the stray enchanted shaft takes on a life of its own, bouncing from one surface to the next without an end in sight. Norman shields his head with his paws while he crouches under the table. Rylee covers her face with her hands and runs behind the front of the Rolls-Royce.

"Put your bracelet back on, Fortune!" She peeks over the hood of the car. "Before you destroy the garage!"

"I'm trying!" I grab my suppression band and force my fingers through the molded copper. My magic draws back, but the Thorn rune symbol glows as brightly as before we began. My left hand is oozing amber now, too. "Oh, shit."

A door slams in the distance and footsteps clop, clop, clop on the porch stairs. My heart races like a roadrunner. I lay my left hand over the deficient charmed metal, as if that will work. Who am I kidding? I'm cooked.

"Ah, fuck us all," Norm says. "Here comes Betty."

I hide my hands behind my back before the side door swings

in. My grandmother enters, wearing her cotton nightgown and robe. Rubber-soled slippers adorn her feet. "I heard someone scream. What in all the universe is going on out here?"

The three of us glance at each other, but our lips won't move. There's no way to hide this. Nana eyes the black soot around the socket of the shattered light bulb.

"Shit!" She glares at me. "Are you gonna spill the beans or do I have to beat it out of these two with my witch's broom?"

Rylee's eyes grow wide. "I didn't do it."

Nana turns her gaze to Norman. "Well?"

He sits on his hind legs. "Now, Betty—"

"Don't you 'now, Betty' me, you seven pounds of fluff," she says, twisting her lip. "You have a paw in this calamity, I'm certain. I didn't live to be an old crone by letting a second-hand familiar pull the wool over my eyes."

Norman crosses his paws. "That's a bit harsh."

"Stop, Nana. What happened is all my fault." I unclasp my hands from behind my back, exposing them and my bracelet, less vibrant but still radiating. "I asked Norm to help. Rylee was here for moral support. I'll tell you everything. It started with the ritual after dinner..."

I spend the next few minutes confessing, from the successful results of the cleanse to the incident at the lagoon, and ending with the witchcraft mishap in the garage. Betty stands there with her fists on her hips and a "you-should-know-better" expression spelled with the wrinkles of her skin. Yet she remains silent.

"Say something, Nana." My suppression band threatens to blow like Mount Shasta any minute. "I get it. You're pissed. But if you aren't going to help, then go back to bed."

"Hmph." Betty pushes past me and grabs a basket. She tosses an array of herbs and animal bones into it. "Stay in here. When I'm ready for you, I'll yell." She turns around and heads into the house.

Rylee straightens her back. "Is it safe to come out?"

"I think so. My magic appears to be contained for now… thanks to Norm."

He fluffs his hair. "Well, thank you. At least someone appreciates my efforts."

I stroll toward the door. The clanking of pots and pans rings through the screen. Hues of yellow and orange flash through the windowpanes while she chants incantations of old—vaguely familiar from my childhood.

"What is she doing?" Rylee asks, flinging her hands in the air.

Norm scuttles across the table. "She's creating a new charm."

"Yes," I say, my heart searching for a steady rhythm. "I hope so. But for what? I'm wearing the band."

We all pace the garage for the next hour while Nana completes her work. I've been here before. A memory transports me back to the day my magic first presented. My grandmother had scattered Ivy's ashes a few weeks before in the nearby forest where she and my father had met. I was on the playground hanging on the monkey bars and got the brilliant idea to sit on the middle one. Rocking back and forth, I lost my balance and fell backward. My left arm broke my fall but also split in two. What a sight that was —my bones spelling an upside-down V.

Nana screamed my name, and her distraught voice echoed in the park—it rings in my head even now. She scooped me up and took me home to the house we left in Milton. Being the skilled witch Betty Whittle was, she healed me by setting my arm and casting a spell instead of taking me to the emergency room, always fearing anything might trigger my magic to appear. As intelligent as she was—is—it never occurred to her that using spells to heal me would spark the curse to emerge.

If she had let medical doctors treat me, my magic might have remained suppressed. I could have led an Unremarkable life— perhaps one with a husband and children.

"Get in here now!" Nana yells through the back porch door, startling me. "I'm tired and my mattress misses me!"

Norman runs off ahead. I hide the bright glow on my hands the best I can as Rylee and I bring up the rear. When we enter the kitchen, it appears as if Nana has used every pot and surface. Stems of herbs lay in random piles and several spellbooks rest on the countertops, their pages flipped open. Her matching yellow and white checkered oven mitts sit untouched on the table, except for the marking of a Thorn rune drawn on each with a black marker. Norm jumps up and sniffs the symbol.

"Fresh ink. Is this what you came up with, Betty?"

Nana shakes a finger at him. "Don't you dare question my choices. It was the best I could scrounge up in an emergency. It's not like I can contact the local coven, you know."

I stare at the mitts. "Please tell me you didn't charm these."

"They're kinda cute, I think," Rylee says, picking them up.

"Then you wear them." I step toward my grandmother. "For fuck's sake, Betty. You expect me to wear those? Indefinitely?"

She crosses her arms. "I wasn't the one who got cocky and went all *I-can-do-magic-anywhere* now. No, they're temporary while I recharge your suppression band. It will take me about a week to complete the process...with Norman's assistance. If he's willing to work with me."

Norm straightens his pajama shirt. "At your service, Betty."

My friend shakes the mitts in front of me. "Ready to try them on, Blondie?"

A lengthy sigh slips out. "I guess I have no choice."

My BFF slips a checkered mitt over my left hand without issue, but she stops when I lift my right. "How are we going to do this? Fortune has to remove the bracelet first."

"I suggest you open the mitt to trap any uncontrollable rays," Norman says, scuttling to the edge of the table.

"Yes." Nana moves next to us. "I'll pull it off. Rylee can slide the charmed mitt down. Fortune, don't move."

"Sounds like a plan." My friend readies herself. "Norm, count down from three."

He stands on all fours. "Here we go. Three—two—one!"

In one motion, Nana slides my copper band off, and Rylee shoves the mitt down, catching a roving beam of amber inside. I stand there, donning yellow and white checkered oven mitts, ready for the LA County bake-off. Norm lays a paw over his mouth, snickering. My friend bites her lip, but she can't hide the laughter wrinkling her eyes.

"What the fuck, Nana? How can I go to the store like this? What will I tell the customers?"

"Not my problem. I'm going to bed." Betty yawns and heads toward the hallway leading to her bedroom, disappearing when she turns the corner.

"I love ya, Fortune, but I'm with Betty." Rylee drags her feet to the back porch door. "I've gotta get to sleep, too."

"Thank you for helping. I'm so sorry about tonight. At least it's over."

"What are friends for if they can't help their cursed buddies from time to time? I'll call you."

I wave my mitt at my friend as she leaves, and my dependable familiar shuts and locks the door.

"Well, let's go to bed, Norm."

"As you wish, my witch. I'll turn down the sheets for you."

He dashes ahead of me to the stairs, the pit-a-pat of his paws echoing in the stairwell. On the way up, I recall the incidents at the lagoon. Who was the person in the hoodie? Did they dump a toxin into the water?

And who was the poor dude who overdosed?

SIX

For the next three days, I'm trapped in these ridiculous charmed oven mitts. Brushing my teeth and using the toilet has taken ingenuity I didn't realize I had. I haven't showered since the day of Rylee's art exhibit, and I must go to my shop. Cam and Gabby have kept the store operating, but they need my input for the new displays.

I've been living in the same T-shirt and shorts since the night I set fire to the lagoon. My hair has created a new definition for stringy, resembling a mop of blond cinnamon sticks. But there has been a silver lining—no bra. I strip down to my birthday suit and wrap the gallon-size plastic bags over the mitts, using my teeth to slide the closure, and step into the clawfoot tub.

After half an hour of fighting with the handheld showerhead, I'm finally done. "Nooorm!" I stick my head around the edge of the shower curtain.

"The towel is ready, my witch. I swear I won't peek." He turns his head, squinting.

"Why are you acting so weird? You've seen me naked since I was a kid."

"Trying to be respectful, Fortune. As your mother would have wanted."

I wrap myself in the towel. "I appreciate it. Can you remove the plastic bags? And then I'll need you to comb my hair. It'll have to air dry."

He jumps up onto the chair and leaps to the vanity sink, grabbing the wide-tooth comb. I sit, and he begins the arduous task of sifting through my knotty strands. He presses his nose against my hair and sniffs twice.

"I love the aroma of your lavender shampoo. Much better than the BO. It was getting so bad, I imagined I'd have to camp out on the bedroom porch."

"You're a riot. You should perform stand-up." A whiff of the fragrance passes my nose. "I feel so much better, though. Unfortunately, it doesn't remove these damn mitts."

Norman finishes and tosses the comb aside. "Your grandmother continues to work on your suppression band. Give her time. I'll meet you in the kitchen once you've dressed." He leaps onto the floor and darts through the bedroom door.

After a major struggle with my bra, I finish dressing in a loose blouse and a pull-on skirt, and head to the kitchen. I'll have to wear flip-flops to the store. When I arrive, a peanut butter and jam sandwich sits on a lunch plate on the table with a napkin. Nana has cut it into four triangles.

"I usually take a smoothie with me," I say, sitting. "You know that."

"A sandwich took less time." She sets a cup of peppermint tea on the table. "To help you rid your body of negative energy."

Gee, I can't imagine why I would have bleak thoughts? "Thank you, Nana." I stare at the PB and J on the plate and glance at my mitts for hands, sighing. With no other solution, I bend down and bite into the sandwich like a dog.

Norm hops onto the chair next to me, chuckling. I wrinkle

my nose at him as I chew and sift through the online news on my phone using a stylus.

"I ate my lunch, so I'm going to work on your bracelet. This is taking longer than I expected to recharge the symbol. Norm, can you join me in the garage?" She chants an incantation and floats a plate into a slot of the dishwasher using a wave of her hand. "I may need your assistance, but remain here until Fortune has left, in case she needs your help."

My morkie familiar's ears rise to attention. "Understood. I'm happy to assist."

"Fortune, I would stay in the back of the store as much as possible. Hide your hands behind the counter. If someone sees them and asks, say you're trying a new skin treatment I made for dryness." Nana exits through the porch door.

"Really? Skin treatment? Gabby will never buy that."

Norm levitates onto the kitchen table and sits. "Do not tell Betty. I have an idea. You could say you got your nails done and you don't want to chip the finish." He waves his paws in front of me.

"That's not viable either. I got a manicure once this year. Gabby is gonna be a problem. I'll figure out something." I return to my phone and continue scrolling through the news articles, biting my lip.

"Are you looking for a particular report, my witch?"

"Yes, I am." The glassy eyes of that dead man pop into my head. "Norm, I've gotta tell you something. When Rylee and I were running back to the car the night at the lagoon, I tripped over a corpse. Probably a drug overdose, but I didn't share with Betty."

"We were all preoccupied that night. Better not to mention it."

"Scared the shit out of us. I've been checking the news ever since. Nothing."

I slide the stylus one more time and stop. The headline reads: Dead Man Found Near Causeway. "Fuck my luck."

"What, my witch?" Norm's eyes wander back and forth, glued to my phone screen.

"Let me read." I skim the news article, skipping the general information until I get to the cause of death, and gasp.

"What's wrong, Fortune?" he asks, his hairy head tilting.

I peer up at my trusted familiar. "He didn't OD on drugs. Someone drowned him."

Norman's ears stiffen like a surfboard. "Do you think anyone saw you there?"

"I don't know." My stylus plops into my teacup.

<hr>

WHEN I ENTER Garcia's Custom Framing, the owner waves at me. "Buenas tardes, Fortune."

"To you, too, Juan. I hope you're doing well."

"I can't complain. Business is good." He glances at my hands wrapped in a light gray hoodie. "Are you hurt? I noticed you weren't at the store for the last couple of days."

"No, taking some time for myself," I say, avoiding his prying gaze. "The low body fat from cycling doesn't leave me much insulation. It may be warm out, but the air is cool. Isn't Rylee working today?"

"Ah, yes. She's in the back matting a large print."

"Thanks. Do you mind if I talk to her? I won't be long. I have to get to work."

"Of course. Down the hallway, second door on the right."

I rush back in my flip-flops, the rubber soles slapping against my feet. After I enter, I nudge the door shut with my toes. Rylee turns around, her gaze immediately dropping to my bundled mitts.

She snorts. "That looks ridiculous. You might as well walk around with them showing."

"What else can I do? Forget about my shortcomings." I turn and push the button lock on the door with my elbow. "Did you read the news in the Long Beach Gazette about the dead body found near the lagoon?"

Rylee drops her mat cutter. "No, but I expected it would show up eventually."

"So, you didn't read the article. That guy did not die of a drug overdose. Said he was drowned."

"Oooh, shit. I really hope no one saw us that night. Should we go back and make sure we didn't drop anything in the pickleweed? Ask Cam to come."

"Do you think that's smart? Besides, I can't go like this." I toss my hoodie and shake my charmed oven mitts in her face.

"OK, OK," she says, chuckling. "So, in a couple of days? When will Betty have your suppression band recharged?"

"She said a week, but who knows? I don't dare ask her. She'd snap at me and say I broke her concentration." I pick up my hoodie and swaddle my hands in it. "After I've spoken to Cam, I'll call you." I open the door but hesitate. "We need to settle on a story."

"Stop your worrying. It was dark as a pile of shit that night. If anyone got a glimpse of us, they'd be guessing."

"You're right. Talk to you later."

I say goodbye to Juan on the way out and dart to work. After an awkward pull on the door with both hands, I enter Fortune's Attic Finds. Cam is standing at the register eating sushi takeout while a young woman with platinum blond hair and a pink complexion attacks the clothing racks. But she isn't a random shopper. It's Anwen Beddoe, that shifty Tylwyth Teg prostitute who slept with Jonathan. She has a reputation for earning her dinner—and everything else—in the bedroom.

"I'm really sorry you didn't get your lunch hour, Cam," I say. "I had hoped my grandmother would have solved my issue by now. Is Gabby here?" I peer at the back of the store.

"Not yet," he replies, mumbling as he chews. "She'll be here in an hour. Good thing, too. I have to meet a professor on campus." His gaze wanders to my hoodie cocoon. "Are you still stuck in the oven mitts?"

I glance out the door to check for inquisitive window shoppers and remove my hoodie, not caring about Anwen. I model the yellow and white checkered monstrosities for him. Cam spits out his sushi.

"It's the best Nana could do last minute." I rush behind the counter and lower my hands out of sight. "It was late when we got to the house. We woke her up from a sound sleep, so she wasn't in tip-top shape."

He wipes the counter with a napkin, chuckling. "I bet she did it on purpose."

I twist the side of my mouth. "You know, I wouldn't put it past her. Even at the age of forty-six, she still finds ways to punish me as if I'm five."

"If it's any consolation, my parents treat me like an elementary schooler, despite the fact Spence nearly burned down the house when he was in high school."

"Oh, my gods. How did that happen?"

He snickers. "Practicing witchcraft. That's when he confessed to me he was a witch. He started teaching me after that, but I never had the success he did."

"You'll improve, Cam. Rylee and I will keep working with you. Even though I can't perform much myself, I can mentor you through the spells. Now that you're going to school here, perhaps you could squeeze in more sessions."

"Yeah. I'd like that. Do you think you can hold down the fort while I go to the bathroom? I've been holding it for an hour."

"Sure. It's always dead around here now. I'll hide my checkered hands behind the counter."

"Gabby should be here any minute," he says, glancing at his phone screen. "You'd better have a story ready to explain the mitts." He laughs as he darts away.

What am I going to say? Norman suggested a manicure as an excuse for my oversized accouterments. Or I could use Nana's recommendation and announce it's a skin treatment. Neither is believable. Anwen struts toward me and throws three blouses and a mini skirt onto the counter.

"How are you today?" I pick up the scanner with my two mitt-covered hands and ring up the clothing. "Do you need a bag?"

"No, I'll carry them out." She waves her index finger at me. "Why are you wearing those?"

Her Welsh accent is less noticeable than Rhys's—all the *socializing*. I refuse to answer because it's none of her damn business. I total the purchase.

"That comes to twenty-three dollars."

"Fucking LA County sales tax." She throws a twenty and a five on the counter. "You aren't going to tell me, are you?"

"Do you have a credit card?" How am I supposed to get money out of the cash register?

"You know damn well I don't have credit cards, IDs, or anything else. Just give me my change."

I open the drawer and use two pencils to grab a couple of one-dollar bills and place them in front of her. "There."

She sprinkles lime-colored fairy magic from her fingertips, aiming at one of my mitts, but I jerk my hand back. "You really shouldn't do that in public. Someone might see you. Enjoy the rest of your afternoon, or should I say...evening?"

Anwen sneers at me and scoops up the clothes with swirls of

lime-green. "You witches are so fucking weird. All that magic at your disposal but you never use it."

She exits the store, her butt swaying from side to side. The last thing I want her to know is that I'm magic-challenged. The next passerby stops and presses his face to the window glass display. It's Rhys, a bit more cleaned up and less scruffy. He blows an air kiss at me and points toward the beach. Then he gestures down, grinning seductively. I mouth the words, "No. Go away." He stares at me, expressionless, and continues down the street.

An air of relief expels from my lungs as I squat behind the counter and attempt to straighten the paper bag pile. I end up knocking half of them onto the floor. I pick them up one by one between the mitts and slide them onto the pile. This is going to take an hour I don't have. The door chimes and steps approach. Shit. I didn't decide which white lie to tell Gabby.

I rise reluctantly, hiding my mitt-covered hands below the counter, and flinch at the man who's standing there—Detective Oliver Prescott. He's wearing a white collared shirt and tie, tan dress slacks, and a navy-blue sport coat. My heart decides it's time for a sprint without inviting my feet.

"My apologies," he says, clearing his throat. "I didn't mean to startle you. Ollie Prescott. We spoke at your friend's art exhibit."

Suspicion has joined my heart for the run. "Did you search for me in the police database to find where I worked? Because that's creepy."

That broad, alluring smile sneaks up on me. "For five years, I have walked Retro Row, passing a business with a unique, enticing sign: Fortune's Attic Finds. After running into you at the art exhibit, I pondered. How many women in Long Beach could perchance have the name of Fortune? Not more than one, I wagered." He leans over the counter. "I am a detective. I detected."

Apparently, he's a good one, and I'm a suspicious bitch. My

face flushes. "I apologize. Seeing you show up here was a surprise. That's all."

"I'm a cop. As you can imagine, my presence is rarely desired." He pulls an envelope out of the inside pocket of his sport coat and offers it to me. "This is for the damage to your bike."

I stare at the envelope, my lips parting. "You didn't have to. It was an accident."

"No, it was my fault for being on the wrong path. There should be enough to cover the repairs, but let me know if this doesn't cover everything."

"That's so nice of you." I reach for the envelope with both hands and freeze, my cloth-covered extremities hanging over the counter in all their yellow and white checkered glory. *Shit.*

Ollie's brow furrows. "Are you baking back there, Miss Whittle?"

Fuck my luck. Or my stupidity. "I...uh...no." Alright, Betty. You win. "I'm trying a new skin treatment for my hands. They get really dry. I have to keep them covered for twelve hours. My grandmother's suggestion."

"Brilliant to use oven mitts. Your grandmother must be a wise woman with years of knowledge." *Dude, you have no idea...*

"She is," I say, nabbing the envelope between my mitts. "I'll store this until I can remove these. Again, I'm sorry I was so bitchy. I really appreciate you covering the cost of the repairs. The business doesn't always bring in enough to cover more than living expenses. I have a couple of employees to pay, too."

"Times are difficult for many residents in our community." Ollie loosens his tie. "Fortune, I left my personal telephone number in there in case that amount is not enough. Also..." He straightens his jacket. "I'd love to buy you a cup of coffee sometime, or tea, if you prefer. Please don't feel obligated. I won't be offended."

My pulse races. My knees are about to give out. *Get a grip, Fortune. Say something.*

Ollie gestures toward the front door, averting his eyes. "I have to get to work. Have a glorious afternoon."

He straightens his tie and exits the store while I stand, clenching my teeth.

Cameron shuffles to the counter, laughing. "That was awkward. All of a sudden cops scare you?"

"No, I wasn't expecting him to come on to me."

"He's an Unremarkable. What are you gonna do?"

"I can't think about him now." I slap my mitts on the counter. "Listen, could you go with Rylee and me to check out the lagoon in a couple of days, after the police investigation dies down there?"

"Sure," he says, cocking his head. "What are we looking for?"

"I don't know. Check for anything we may have left where I cast magic. Inspect the area using an incantation if needed."

He flinches. "You trust me to do that?"

"Yes. You need to build your confidence. But Rylee will be there, too."

"Thanks for believing in me. I wish others would."

"You mean Spence? I'm sure he does, Cameron. That chip on your shoulder is heavier than an anvil. Wouldn't you like to bury it?"

His head bobs. "Yeah. Casting spells came so easily to him. I have to work twice as hard as he does to accomplish what he has."

"Have you ever asked him? You may be wrong about that."

Cam grabs his backpack from behind the counter. "I don't know where Gabriela is, but I have to go. Will you be OK with your baking friends?"

I chortle as my checkered mitts dance on the counter. "Go. She'll be here soon, and we have no customers right now. I'll call you when Rylee and I decide when to sneak around the lagoon."

At that moment, the storefront door swings in, chiming. Gabriela Lopez enters, huffing and puffing. "Forgive me, Fortune. The bus got stuck behind a car with a flat tire. The traffic gets worse and worse in Long Beach every week. I'm so happy you're feeling better."

Gabby's bronze skin has golden undertones that radiate sunshine when she enters a room, even for a woman in her seventies with a few wrinkles. Her presence always peels away my layers of stress.

"That's not a problem," I say, swinging my hands around. "You're here now."

The whites of her eyes spring out. "Fortune, why are you wearing oven mitts?"

Cam chuckles as he heads toward the door. "I'm outta here. Bye."

"Have a nice day, Cameron," Gabby says, continuing to scrutinize my hands.

"You know Nana experiments with homemade moisturizers. She has me trying a new skin treatment on my hands."

"Oooh, let me see." She grabs at the tip of my right mitt and tugs.

"No!" My heart leaps in my chest, nearly thrusting through my ribs. I push her hand away. "She said I can't take them off for twelve hours."

Gabby frowns and backs off. "Well, I would love to know how the cream works." She inspects the backs of her hands. "This crepey skin could use a boost of hydration."

I exhale, inching mine back. "I'll need your help to do inventory."

"Well, I would guess so." She wags her finger at my mitts. "How did she expect you to work with them on?"

"Good question." But I can't answer that truthfully. "Nana does what she wants."

"Set in her ways. Well, let's get moving then before customers roll in."

"You go ahead. I have to put something away."

My trusted employee struts to the back of the store while I lock the register. When I glance down below the counter, the white envelope rests silently, full of cash and a phone number. I stuff it in my backpack.

No Unremarkable man has ever interested me in the slightest. Why does Ollie Prescott fluster me so?

SEVEN

Friday evening, I sit on a stool in the garage, spinning the mangled front tire of my bike around and around while Nana casts the spell on my copper band, her fingers radiating in amber. Garden sage and lemongrass permeate the air. She chants an incantation under her breath, as if she doesn't want me to discern the words.

Seriously, Betty, are you afraid I might actually learn the incantation and not need you? What happens if you get hit by a bus tomorrow? I'm fucked. At this rate, that's the only way she's crossing over because she won't be leaving this earth willingly.

I've become astoundingly adept at functioning with mitts for hands, but I'm done with these checkered protectors. I propel the rubber tube one more time with a snap of my hand and Betty stomps her foot on the floor.

"For the love of all the goddesses, Fortune! You're breaking my concentration! Don't you want me to finish?"

I stop the tire with a quick grab of the spokes. "Sorry. You know patience escapes me."

She hisses through her teeth and turns back to my

charmed jewelry. "Well, I've done several castings to saturate the band with energy to suppress the misfiring of your magic. I can't be certain I remembered the order I used the first time. That was over forty years ago. The charm I cast on the oven mitts will wear off soon. You must try on the bracelet tonight."

"And if the suppression band no longer works?"

Betty shrugs a shoulder. "You should have contemplated the consequences of casting a spell without properly vetting the extent of your success." She crosses her arms. "Why didn't you tell me? I could have been there to help."

The fuck you would. "Facts. You wouldn't have let me go. When will you realize you're not always gonna be here?"

Her eyes glisten with certainty. "Hmph. I'll outlive you, granddaughter." She picks up the Thorn rune bracelet and holds it near my right mitt. It shines in its original copper hue.

"I bet you will," I say, a faint smile rising. "Thank you for polishing it. I'd forgotten how pretty it is. If I rip off the mitt, you can slide it on. Ready?"

Nana nods. I yank the mitt off and she shoves the charmed metal over my hand, amber magic seeping from my fingertips. We wait silently for the shiny band to settle on my skin, but our heavy breathing drags down our hopes. My grandmother passes me a clear quartz wand. I wrap my glowing fingers around its smooth surface and manifest the best I'm able as sweat collects on my upper lip.

The amber glow fades. I remove the left oven mitt—nothing. My charmed bracelet is working again. But for how long?

I wipe the beads of sweat from my upper lip. "Should I worry the spell may stop working?"

"Have you fretted over the possibility all these years?"

"No, because you're the best."

"Damn straight, I am." She chuckles and pats my arm. "Why

haven't you taken your bike to the repair shop? Do we not have money left after paying our property taxes to fix it?"

Now we do, but I can't tell her where it came from. "We're always saving up for the next installment, but we do. I haven't had time to take it to the repair shop, especially with my recent deficit. Tomorrow. Why don't you go inside? I'll clean up the table."

"Thank you, dear." She shuffles to the door but turns around. "Fortune, I've been ruminating on something. Pam Barrera invited us to plan the Summer Solstice Festival this year. I think we should go. We may need to ask them for help in finding or creating a spell to remove this family curse once and for all."

"You always said we didn't need a coven. Why the change of heart?"

"My slumber has not been the most restful these past few months. I've not come across a spell in all these years that would even lighten the effects of the family affliction. I agonize over what could happen to you when I'm gone."

Remove the curse? Is it even possible? "I've lived with this solution all these years. And I was making progress with my ritual in trying to suppress it. I don't want to go, Nana. They'd expect me to cast spells with them. How would I get around that?"

"It's merely a planning session. Pam would hop on her broom for a flight if you brought your friends, too. Would show good faith. I want you to think about it."

"I won't go," I say, crossing my arms. "Please don't ask me again."

Nana frowns and my heart sinks. She bent her solitary practice rules to consider this, but I'd be walking into quicksand. It's a disastrous plan.

"Thank you for recharging my suppression band," I say. "I do appreciate your talent and help. I don't tell you enough."

"You're my only family, Fortune. I need to know you'll be safe when I've left this world. Thank you for tidying up." She continues through the door.

You'd think after forty years, she'd finally realize I get it. But in her eyes, I'm still that seven-year-old baby witch. Damn it. Betty is right again. This setback has proven one thing. I *must* find a fix for this family curse. What if she were dead? Yet joining the coven isn't the answer.

I tidy up the worktable and altar, thinking about the envelope Detective Ollie Prescott gave me. After I finish cleaning, I lock up the garage and dash upstairs to my bedroom, startling Norman when I push the door in with a *whoosh*.

"Ruff! What fuckery is this, my witch? You almost prompted me to piss my bed."

"You're so dramatic," I say, digging into my purse.

"Betty triumphs again. She said she didn't need me for the final touches, so I took a much-needed break."

"Yeah, I smell it. Please relax on the bedroom porch next time."

I remove the cash-filled envelope and tear open the top. Inside, I find enough to cover the cost of the bent rim and a piece of folded paper. I slide the note out and sit on my mattress to read it.

"Ms. Whittle, my sincere apologies for the damage to your beautiful bike. Please contact me if this amount doesn't cover the repairs. My blunder has preoccupied my thoughts since that evening."

Norman levitates onto the bed and scuttles next to me. "What are you perusing, my witch?"

"None of your beeswax." I continue reading as he nudges his head to sneak a peek.

"Considering how we met, I feel it is inappropriate for me to write this. But I fear I may never have the chance again. It was such a pleasure to speak to you the night of your friend's art exhibit, and I

would love the chance to get to know you. Perhaps over a cup of coffee? If you decide that is agreeable, please contact me. If it is not, I will file the moment of our meeting in my cherished memories. Warmly, Ollie."

I drop the piece of paper on my desk next to the bed, recalling my gauche moment at the store. My insides melt into a clump of *why-does-he-have-to-be-an-Unremarkable?*

Norman taps my thigh with his tiny paw. "Another Unremarkable taken by your beauty and charm. How did you manage it this time, my witch? Did you tell him to fuck off?"

"No," I say, scowling. "He asked me to go out for a cup of coffee when he stopped by the store to give me cash to fix my bike."

"Oooh." My familiar waggles his butt. "Inching for some nookie, no doubt."

"Get your mind out of the gutter, morkie. He was very nice."

"What did you tell the *nice* detective?"

"I didn't say anything. I was so taken aback by the question, I stood there with my checkered mitts in the air, staring at him."

Norman rolls onto his side, guffawing. "Well, no worries there, then. He won't be back."

I snatch the note from my desk and pull my cell out of my purse. His phone number has a 562 area code, which means he probably lives in Long Beach. Norm jumps up on all fours.

"What are you doing, Fortune?"

I don't answer. I type in his phone number and float my index finger above the green icon.

Norm's head quivers. "No, no, no, no. Betty won't like that one bit."

"Since when do you care what she thinks? Whose familiar are you?"

"Yours, of course." He sits next to me and leans his head

against my arm. "I'm looking out for your welfare, like I promised Ivy I would, should anything happen to her."

I rub his hairy head. "You were a faithful familiar to her." I stare at the green icon on my cell phone and read his words again: *I will file the moment of our meeting in my cherished memories.* "Don't I deserve a chance at happiness, Norm?"

"Yes, my witch. Indubitably."

I press the green circle and the phone rings. It clicks, and Ollie's voice fills my ear.

"You've rung me while I'm tirelessly fulfilling my duties for the City of Long Beach. Leave a message and I'll get back to you straightaway."

The phone beeps, and I hesitate. "Uh, hello. This is Fortune Whittle. I wanted to thank you again for the funds to repair my bike. I, uh, I'm sorry I reacted the way I did. It's been a long time since a man asked me out. Actually, I'd love to meet you for coffee. Thanks for asking. Bye." I push the red icon and fling my cell onto the bed.

Norman pats his paws together and snickers. "Smooth, Fortune. Fucking smooth."

"Oh, shut up, Norm." My hands are trembling. I jump onto the floor and shake them out. "Why am I so nervous?"

"Because this goes against the rules you set for yourself, my witch. No turning back now, though."

My cell plays a short riff of music—a text. "It must be Rylee. She and Cam are meeting me tomorrow night at the lagoon."

Norm's hairy eyebrows arch.

"I'll explain in a minute." I lift my phone and gasp. "It's him." I tap the notification.

OLLIE

I got your message. I'm working on a case
with a colleague.

OLLIE

However, I am delighted you called. Meet at the Java House tomorrow at 9:00 a.m.?

That would be lovely. 😊

Smashing. I'll see you then.

Norman throws his paws up. "Well?"

"I'm having coffee with him in the morning."

"It's merely injections of caffeine, my witch. Hardly anything to get nervous about."

I swallow hard. If Betty finds out I'm seeing an Unremarkable, she's going to burst her fucking spell jars.

EIGHT

I tap the heel of my sandal on the pavement outside Java House, a local café down from my store on Toyon Avenue, and stare at the mural painted on the side of the white brick building—steam rising from a gigantic coffee cup. A rainbow flag flaps in the ocean breeze above the awning over the front entry. What the fuck am I doing? This is an abysmal mistake even for me. I adjust my light blue blouse over my skinny jeans and pull on the red-framed glass door.

Java House has a warm, inclusive ambiance and is as busy as ever on this Saturday morning. No matter who you are or whom you love, you are welcome here, or anywhere in Long Beach. Although I doubt the owners of this coffee shop were thinking about the fae in that inclusivity. How would Unremarkables of any persuasion react if they knew beings from the Otherworld lived among us?

I scan the golden-framed chalkboards displaying handwritten menus as the heart attack level pastries scream out to me through the glass case. When I glance to the right, Ollie is waiting for me, sporting a broad grin. He's dressed in a casual short-sleeved shirt and jeans. They suit him more than the tie and jacket he wears for work.

"I thought you had changed your mind," he says.

"No, I was outside having a debate with myself over whether I should come in. I haven't done this in a long time."

"I'm chuffed you did. It's been a bit for me as well."

Joseph Hernandez, a barista of medium height with dark brown hair and eyes, calls out. "What can I get you, folks? Your usual, Fortune?"

"Yeah, a green latte. Thanks, Joey."

"Black coffee for me," Ollie says.

He smiles at my date. "Your usual. Sure thing, Detective Prescott."

Joey is a member of the local coven. He's in his late thirties and turns the heads of most patrons, both men and women. You'll never meet a nicer guy and witch. Like many people, he juggles two jobs, teaching yoga classes when he's not brewing coffee. While he works on filling our orders, his gaze wanders between us but lands on me with a boatload of questions.

"I hear Pam invited you to the Solstice Festival planning session. Please, can you come this time, Fortune? It would be so much fun with you there. Or do you not like her?" He pouts and sets a disposable cup full of tea on the counter.

Shit. I wish he hadn't mentioned this. "I'm sorry, but I'll have to pass again. It has nothing to do with Pam. My schedule is too packed." I hate lying to him, but I can't tell him the truth.

"That's sad, but I hope you change your mind. Bring Cam and Rylee too when you come."

"I'll think about it." I peer at Ollie and catch him staring at me. Ugh. I sense an interrogation coming.

"Here ya go, detective." Joey winks and sets the second cup on the counter.

Ollie taps his credit card on the terminal, blushing. How

refreshing to meet an attractive man who has no pretensions about it.

"Would you care to take a stroll to the beach?" he asks. "I didn't get my run in this morning, and it's a brilliant day."

"Yeah, I'd love to get some steps in, too." I wave to our server. "Later, Joey."

"Beautiful day for a walk to Toyon Beach. Enjoy."

Ollie holds the door open for me as we exit, catching my glance as I walk through. Those expressive eyes melt my insides.

"Did that bother you?" I ask. "Joey's coming on to you?"

He rubs the back of his neck. "No. It's happened before. He said he fancies me. I told him I was flattered but not interested. He is a friendly bloke." He glances at the flirty barista through the window glass and chuckles. "Now I think he is pulling my leg."

"No, he's reminding you what a handsome man you are."

"That's kind of you." He smiles but says nothing as he hits the pedestrian push button at the crosswalk.

Damn. Why does he have to be so sweet? Do something to piss me off. Tell me I act like a bitch or slurp my tea like a goat— anything to reduce the attraction. As we continue down Toyon Avenue, I take a sip of my latte. He smiles intermittently between tastes.

"You know, you didn't have to pay," I say. "I can afford to buy my own tea."

"I invited you. It was my obligation. You're welcome to pay next time."

I tilt my head. "There's going to be a next time?"

"Well, I certainly hope so," he says, a slight smile erupting. "I did not expect to hear from you. When I invited you at the store, you didn't reply. I left feeling like a bloody idiot."

"Yeah, I'm sorry. I was in a state of shock. Also, I was a little preoccupied that day." Hiding unruly magic is a stressor, but I can't tell him that.

He points at the backs of my hands. "The oven mitts worked. Your skin looks fabulous. Your grandmother must know a thing or two."

I chuckle. "You could say that." Betty wouldn't laugh at the situation at all, though.

"Tell me more about yourself, Fortune Whittle. I know you own a vintage shop, you live with your grandmother, and you take risky rides on the beach at all hours of the night. Or are you harboring secrets you can't divulge?"

Dude, you have no idea. "My mother died when I was five, and Nana raised me. I never knew my father. She inherited the house in Carroll Park from her sister. We moved here from the East Coast when I was seven. That's about it." I mean, what else can I tell him without him thinking I've checked out of reality? "And you?"

"Let's see. I told you why I moved here and about the divorce. You're aware I'm an LB detective. I hail from Lancaster, England. My mum still lives there and is an artist, as I shared at the exhibit. I love art, movies, hiking..." He stares at me for a moment, a glint in his eyes, and I shift uncomfortably. "And apparently running down gorgeous women while on duty."

I erupt in laughter. "Well, I did spit sand at you after. I would say we're even. I am so sorry I was such a bitch to you. Fatigue had set in. All I wanted was to get home and go to bed."

"I imagine so," he says, curling his mouth. "Why were you riding your bike in the middle of the night? 2:00 a.m. is rather late for a ride, not to mention...dangerous."

"Yeah..." *Fuck my luck.* How do I answer this without lying to him? I sure can't say I was screwing a Tylwyth Teg fairy behind the Long Beach sign. Telling him I was humping a homeless man I had the hots for wouldn't garner a positive response either. "I fell asleep in Golden Park."

He takes another sip of coffee, his brow crinkling. "That's not a safe place for a woman to snag a nap, Fortune. Lots of homeless men have moved there recently."

"I assure you. I can take care of myself, Ollie."

He tips his head. "So it appears."

We arrive at the bottom of the winding section of Toyon and cross to the pedestrian section of the beach trail. As we head up the path toward the pier, the ocean breeze plays with my blond locks and toys with his hair. The salty air relaxes me as we chat about the variety of restaurants in the city and how much we love living here. My copper band slips and I slide it back up my forearm.

"You've worn that bracelet each time I've seen you," Ollie says. "Is there something special about it? The symbol on it matches the tattoo on your ankle."

I stiffen. I have to tell him something. "My grandmother made it. The symbol is a Thorn rune. It's associated with the Norse god Thor. I am a pagan and wear it for protection. I hope that doesn't put you off."

"No, not at all. I'm an atheist myself, but you're welcome to believe whatever you want. It's part of who you are."

A small crowd has formed on the beach ahead near one of the trenches that facilitates the storm sewer drainage from the bluff to the ocean, yanking Ollie's attention. One police officer hammers stakes into the ground while another ties crime scene tape to them. A forensic team is taking pictures and collecting samples. But of what?

"What's going on up there?" I ask.

He glances at me. "Couldn't tell you." He checks his phone and discovers a text. "It's my partner, Manny. He's there actually, but he told me not to come. He knows I had a date."

"Do you need to go? I understand if you do. It's your job."

His jaw tenses. "I should check in with Manny...since I'm here. Could you wait?"

"Yeah. That's absolutely fine."

Ollie increases his stride as I hurry my pace to keep up. As we approach, two officers are encouraging the onlookers to disperse. When we arrive, the details of the crime scene come into view. A body is face down in the ditch. An attractive husky man in his forties with short brown hair and tan skin dressed in a black T-shirt and jeans is inspecting the body with a forensic examiner. When he glances in our direction, he waves to Ollie to join him—must be Manny.

"Stay on this side of the tape." Ollie touches my arm. "I'll make this as brief as I can."

My date joins his partner and slides on blue nitrile gloves. After examining the victim, he straightens and wanders up the ditch, climbing over the sand mound to track footprints. Probably not much left if the sand has dried. His chest deflates, as if he's expelling frustration from his lungs. He returns to the body and chats a bit with Manny, shaking his head. Dare I say it's alluring for a man to show so much concern and compassion for a stranger he has never met?

As the two detectives plod through the sand toward me, I catch part of their conversation.

"Why the fuck are you even here, man?" Manny asks. "I told you not to come."

"We were already here for a stroll. Who discovered the body?" Ollie asks.

"A couple of teens came across it. That totals three if you count the one you found on Toyon Beach the other night."

He's talking about the night Ollie ran me off the trail. *Fuck my luck.* That could have been me! They bend over and pass under the crime scene tape. Ollie blushes as he introduces me.

"This is Fortune Whittle. Fortune, my partner Manuel Lopez. He's also a mother hen."

"Someone has to keep you in check." Manny shakes my hand. "Great to meet you. Ollie talks about you...a lot."

My date blushes. "Give me a minute?"

"Sure. I'll be talking with forensics. Nice to meet you, Fortune." His partner heads back.

He steps closer. "I need to stay. I'm dreadfully sorry."

"It's alright," I say. "I had a wonderful time. How many people can claim their first date included a visit to a crime scene?"

A faint smile emerges. "Fortune, I would love to see you again. Would you be open to having dinner with me some evening?"

"Sure. I'd like that. You have my number."

"Despite this horrendous incident, I hope you have a smashing day. I'll call you later."

"I'd say the same, but I don't think yours will be."

Ollie nods and makes his way to Manny, and I start my trek back to Toyon Avenue. On the way to the store, I mull over the murders in my head. The first one was too close for comfort.

What if Ollie hadn't run into me that night?

NINE

By the time Tuesday rolls around, I've given up on Ollie Prescott. I haven't received a phone call or a text. Screw him. Another "fake" nice guy to add to my list. What was I thinking? But at least he paid for the repairs to my bike, and I can ride again.

I have more important things on my agenda. The inventory got backed up in the store while I was "recuperating," and I have to go to the lagoon with Cam and Rylee later. I almost decide not to bother with it. The LBPD has scoured the area for sure. But we need to investigate ourselves. Why did my magic spark a fire on the water?

While I sift through the items I purchased at an estate sale, Gabby tags them. She's dressed in comfortable clothes today—a short-sleeved blouse and cotton pants. My Thorn rune band keeps snagging the knit shirts, so I shove it up my arm. After four decades, you'd think I'd gotten used to it. *Nope.* My dedicated employee glances at me.

"Fortune, why don't you take your bracelet off? It obviously bothers you."

I straighten my light-blue V-neck shirt and tug on my loose jeans. "I'd feel naked without it, Gabby."

"After wearing it every day, I understand. Where would you like me to hang these?" she asks, shaking a pair of gold lamé pants at me. "Are we carrying a line for prostitutes now?"

I chuckle. "Don't you remember the seventies and eighties? Disco? Women still wear them to parties. Hang them with the formal wear. I promise you. They won't last long on the rack."

She clips the fancy pants onto a hanger and stuffs them next to a pair of satin slacks. "I forgot to mention how wonderful your hands are after that skin treatment. You should sell some of your grandmother's special ointment here in the store. Can you imagine what her talent could offer women on a budget?"

"I doubt she'd sell it cheaply. Takes her hours to mix the ingredients." Not to mention the use of witchcraft. We can't sell charmed items in the store. It wouldn't be ethical. "I'll tell her you were impressed, though."

The door opens, chiming, and Pam Barrera waltzes in, wearing a black dress and a cheery smile. Why is she so happy? Her usual expression could kill the joy in a puppy's wagging tail.

"Hey, Pam," I say, hanging a blouse. "Are you here to browse, or can I help you find something?" I bend down to pick up a pair of acid-washed, high-waisted jeans from the eighties.

"Oh, I didn't come to shop today. I wanted to stop by and thank you for coming to the next coven meeting to plan the Summer Solstice Festival. I'm thrilled you accepted our invitation after all these years. Betty said your friends may attend with you."

I jump up, snapping at the waist like a robot. "Uh, when did you speak to my grandmother?" *Fuck you, Betty.*

"This morning. She called me on the phone. I understand you probably had reasons for keeping to yourself, but I'm elated at your change of heart."

My faithful employee continues to hang clothes on the rack, but an ear reaches out to snag our conversation.

"You're welcome, I guess," I say, forcing a grin. Oh, Betty, you are so going to pay for this.

"Well, I'll see you tomorrow evening. Have a great day." Pam exits the store with giddiness in her stride.

Gabby smiles as she hangs another pair of jeans. "I hope you enjoy your new group. Are you excited to go?"

"I'm flabbergasted at the thought." It's the best I can state without lying through my teeth.

Cam darts in and rushes behind the register. "Sorry I'm late. The meeting with my advisor on campus took way longer than expected. You can go to lunch, Gabby."

"No worries, young man." She grabs her purse from under the counter. "Buenas tardes." She waves as she darts out.

A female customer enters immediately after Gabby leaves and browses the clothing rack near the back of the store. I dart to Cam.

"You're still on for tonight?" I whisper.

"Yeah," he says. "I figured we'd go together."

"Great, Rylee is gonna drive. Listen, can you cover the register for thirty minutes while I run home? Betty told Pam Barrera that we're going to the next witch's circle to help plan the Summer Solstice Festival."

Cam snorts. "I'm gonna guess your grandmother didn't tell you?"

"Oh, you haven't heard the best part," I say, crossing my arms. "She told her you guys are attending, too."

"What? That's fucked up, Fortune. I don't have enough confidence in my magic to join another coven yet."

"No need to worry." I snatch my purse and cell phone. "I'll take care of this right now. Be back as soon as I can."

I dart out the door and head home, running in my sneakers.

The intensity of the California sun beats down on me and sweat beads on my face. When I arrive at the house, my grandmother is on the back porch drinking a cup of tea, dressed in an old lady housecoat. Norman is lounging next to her in a matching wicker chair.

"Betty, we need to talk," I say, huffing and puffing.

Norman sits up and rubs his paws together. "Oh, this should be good."

"Stay out of this, Norm." I glare at her, the anger bubbling over as I wipe the sweat from my cheeks. "I think you know what I'm upset about. What the fuck, Betty?"

"Pam must have stopped by the store." She sets her teacup on the side wicker table. "I knew you wouldn't go without a push. I did what was best. We need their help."

"Wait," my familiar says. "I'm confused. Go where?"

I growl like a dog and twist my blond strands into a knot. "It's not bad enough you said I would attend the witch circle. You told Pam my friends would attend."

"Whoa, Betty." Norm hops on all fours. "That's bad even for you."

She glares at him. "Shut up, familiar. This is not your business."

"If it involves me, it concerns him," I say. "Whatever, I'm not going, and neither are Rylee and Cam."

She pushes out of her seat. "If you don't go, they'll be angry. We may never get another invitation. You can say goodbye to any assistance in ridding yourself of this family curse."

"Too fucking bad." I turn around and head down the steps. "Norm, be ready around nine. We may need your help to assess the lagoon."

"Fuck yeah!" His tail wags like the fluttering of a humming-bird. "I get to leave this abode. What should I wear, Betty?"

"I don't care." She picks up her cup and enters the house.

"That was rude," he says, sitting on his butt. "After all the help I gave her."

"Ignore her. She's pissed I stood up to her this time. I don't know what she was thinking."

Norman scuttles to the door and peers in. "Betty must be desperate, Fortune. If she's willing to cave and join a coven, she is worried about you living with this curse after she has passed on."

"Or she doesn't trust me to keep it hidden and under control." I run my hands through my hair. "It's not like I didn't give up all possibilities of living a normal life—one with an Unre-markable—to end this curse."

"Oh, woe is me," he says, laying a paw on his forehead. "I sacrificed my entire life."

"Stop mocking me, Fluffy. Whose side are you on?"

"As always, yours, my witch. But the declaration is far from the truth now after your little date."

"Shhh." I peek through the screen door into the kitchen. "She could have heard that."

"At least be honest with yourself. You've been less than careful recently. Am I wrong?"

I turn my nose up at him. Of course he's right. "Well, the detective never called me. I guess he changed his mind. So, that ship has sailed. I truly believed I had control of my magic after the last ritual. That's why I want you to come tonight. You need to test the water. There has to be something in there that sparked a negative reaction."

"That is concerning. I'll be ready when you arrive. I'm sorry things didn't work out with the detective."

"Thanks, Norm. Keep an eye on Betty," I say, heading down the steps.

"When will you call Pam Barrera and give her the bad news?"

"Tomorrow. I'll make up some reason so I don't insult her. Later, Norman."

"May your day be productive, my witch."

RYLEE PARKS her sedan on the street near the side of the lagoon where I attempted to rejuvenate the dead fish. While she and Cam exit the car, I open the door to prepare my morkie familiar. I grab the dog collar and leash and get out.

Norm shakes his head and puts his paw up. "You don't expect me to wear that, do you? It's not like I'm going to run off."

"Come on," I say. "You know the city has a regulation. I have to keep you on a leash or I could get fined."

He sits on his hind legs and refuses to move. My friends join me on my side of the car.

"What's the problem?" Rylee asks.

"Norm doesn't want me to put a collar and leash on him."

Cam waves him on. "Walk with me, Norman. If a cop wanders along, I'll tell him you're my dog."

"Don't act stupid," I say. "Or I will shove this collar on you."

My arrogant familiar jumps out of the car and lands on all fours. "Thank you, Cameron." He swoons, swiping a paw across his forehead. "You're my savior."

Norm sticks his slobbery tongue out at me and struts ahead of us on the trail, wiggling his butt as he goes. Cameron darts to catch up with him while Rylee and I follow closely behind. A cool breeze carries the salty air to our nostrils as I zip up my thin hoodie. The moon is nearly full, casting a stream of white across the soft ripples of the lagoon, and the marine layer hasn't moved in yet. Not ideal conditions to perform magic.

"Don't worry about the dog law. It's almost ten," my best friend says. "The objective is *not* to run into anyone. Remember?"

"We planned that last time, and look what happened."

She chortles. "That doesn't count. He was dead. Hey, I forgot to tell you. The director of the gallery told me I was invited to a special fundraiser at the Casa de Playa. It just sold, and the new owner moved in over the weekend. I think it may be the same person who gave a shit ton of money to the art gallery—that nameless donor." She rubs the tips of her fingers together.

"Wow, that was fast," Cameron shouts back. "A bougie place."

"Best part is I can take a guest. Please attend with me, Fortune. It's next Saturday night. Sorry, Cam."

"I've always wanted to go inside," I say.

"Awesome. Hey, you can pretend to be my date. I'm really not ready to get hit on."

A creepy shadow appears from around the curve in the trail and Norm stops. "Someone is coming, my witch."

Cam reaches for my morkie familiar. "I'm going to pick you up. Don't complain."

"You better not drop me," he says. "My paws are tender."

I raise a finger to my lips. "Shhh, Norm. Or I won't take you out again for a long time."

When the late-night trail invader appears under the light, my heart puts on the brakes. It's Ollie. He's dressed in dark gray slacks, a blue polo shirt, and a sport coat. His brow crinkles as he approaches us. Rylee leans into me.

"Wow, bet you weren't expecting to run into him."

"Nope." I remain calm, but this is going to be awkward.

When he gets close, he pauses. "Fortune, um, what are you doing here? It's rather late."

My eyebrows reach for the sky. "And that's your business, because...?"

Rylee interrupts as usual, always saving me from myself. "Hi, Ollie. I didn't expect to run into you again so soon." She gestures to Cam. "This is Cameron Huxley and"—she rubs my familiar's head—"Norman the Conqueror." Norm sticks his tongue out, panting.

"A pleasure to meet you, Cameron. I'd shake your hand, but both of them are occupied by this adorable creature." Ollie leans over to pet Norm, but my familiar growls and snaps at him. "Your dog has a bit of a vicious streak in him. He should be on a leash. The city has an ordinance in case you weren't aware."

"I'm sorry," I say. "He actually belongs to me and can be unruly." I squint at him, muttering the word stop.

"Fortune, would you mind speaking to me privately for a moment?"

I hiss through my teeth. "For a couple of minutes, I guess."

We walk back on the trail a little way and he turns toward me. "I apologize profusely for not calling as I said I would. The case I'm on has engulfed my life recently. It's why I'm out here tonight. I was going to call you tomorrow."

Riiight. "Did you find any clues?"

"No, sadly. It's befuddling." He shoves his hands in his pockets. "But that's no excuse for letting my work bleed into my personal life."

I can't berate him for trying to be a good cop. "I understand, and I accept your apology."

His shoulders fall. "Fantastic. Well then...I would love to have you for dinner."

I snort. "Can you prepare food instead?"

His face flushes and that alluring grin emerges. "Of course. Is there an evening that would suit you?"

"I'll have to confirm with Cam and Gabby about covering the store. Does Friday work for you?"

"Perfect. I'll text you my address." He peers past me toward Cam and Rylee. "It's a tad late for a stroll around the lagoon. Please keep your senses vigilant."

"No need to worry about us. Besides, I've got a vicious morkie with me. Remember?"

He smiles. "It would be best to put him on a leash, though. I will send you a text by Thursday. I promise." He moves closer, his eyes twitching. "Be careful, Fortune. I can't explain it, but I sense things in the city are awry. Goodnight."

Ollie proceeds on the trail toward the street while I return to my friends. Norm is off to the side, peeing in the pickleweed.

"Well?" Rylee asks. "Spill the tea on the detective, Blondie."

"He invited me to dinner at his house."

Cam cocks his head. "I thought you were done with him?"

Norm joins us, shaking a leg. "Sounds like the ship has returned to the harbor, my witch."

"He was caught up in these murders. He deserves a break."

Cam closes his eyes, his head lolling around as if in a trance. I slap him. "Don't fall asleep on us. Let's get this over with so we can all go home."

"Sorry," he says, shaking his head. "I guess I should have gone to bed sooner last night."

Norm jumps through the fence and we witches hop over it. I scan the homes across the tranquil lagoon to confirm no neighborly busybodies are out front or peering at us through their windows. Cam checks out the area to the right.

Rylee squats next to the water's edge. "Pee yew. They haven't removed all the dead fish."

Norm scuttles to her. "I will examine the water without inserting my paw. I'd rather not get wet. Taking another bath this late at night is not my idea of a good time. I must remind you, I have your mother's earth connection since I was called to be her familiar."

"Spare us your fear of the wet stuff, Norm," I say. "Check it out, please."

"Energy of the nature realm, I call on you to aid my helm."

My morkie familiar lifts his paw over the soft waves of the lagoon, forming a faint dark green halo. "Elements of the water, speak to me. Send your message. What is wrong with thee?"

The ripples bend, attempting to form a spout, but dissipate and return to their normal state. Norman lowers his paw.

"It is as I feared," he says. "I cannot manipulate the water enough to receive a response."

I squat next to him, mesmerized by the ripples. My mind wanders, but I shake it off. "That fucking blows."

"At least you tried, Norm." Cam pats his head.

"But with your and Rylee's help, the boost of witch energy may allow me to glean something from it."

My best friend doesn't comment as she stares at the dead fish.

"Red?" I ask. "Can you help Norm?"

Her head pops up. "Yeah. We've only practiced enough to reach level two in our magic training, but I'm game. You ready to rumble, Cam?"

He nods. "Yeah, that's why I came. I hope I don't screw up."

"Thank you, guys," I say. "You know I can't join you, but I can draw a pentacle to help you channel your energy." I grab a twig from a nearby shrub and scribe the five-star symbol within a circle in the sand.

Rylee and Cam kneel on either side of Norm, laying their hands on his back. He summons his magic again, repeating the incantation. The green halo shines on the ripples below as he lowers his paw to the water.

My friends call on their magic, one hand resting on the symbol, the other on Norman. "Energy of the nature realm, we call on you to aid our helm."

They close their eyes, manifesting their desire and goal. The five-star symbol transforms, burning a bright golden yellow, and the energy passes from my friends to my trusted familiar.

"It's working," I say, smiling. "Try now, Norm."

He nods and lowers his paw, barely pressing into the water, and sparks fly in all directions, whistling in the air. One reaches as far as the causeway!

"Fuck!" I pull Norman from the water, knocking Rylee and Cam to the ground in the process. The pentacle goes dark and silence ensues, except for the faint sound of music in the distance.

"What happened?" Cam asks, pushing off his butt. "Did I do something wrong?"

My best friend pushes up and scatters the symbol with a foot. "I don't think that was supposed to happen. Was it, Norm?"

My morkie familiar stands on all four paws. "No. But I gleaned one answer from the interaction. The water in this area of the lagoon is devoid of salt, and the portal is not far away, if not within it."

"What?" I ask, dusting off the sand from my jeans. "You mean like nonsaline?"

Cam's head jerks. "Wait. How can there be fresh water in the lagoon?"

"Great fucking question," Rylee asks. "Do you have an answer to that, too?"

Norm points his paw at the surface. "Someone has manipulated the water with magic here. In addition, it may have tampered with the spell the coven placed on the lagoon's portal to filter out negative energy. Could be witch or fae."

"What does that mean exactly?" I ask. "Why would someone want to remove the salt to create fresh water?"

"No idea, but we have an obligation to tell the coven. Betty wins again, my witch."

Our eyes lock and I puff like a dragon in heat. "Fuck my luck."

TEN

Rylee pulls up to the curb and parks in front of the three-story Craftsman home of Pamela Barrera. Built in the early 1900s, her house is massive—six bedrooms and five bathrooms. It has garnet-red clapboard siding with cream trim and a gray stone porch. From what I've heard, she inherited the historical structure, having passed down to her through multiple generations.

"This house is ostentatious," Nana says, peering through the window. "No one needs a home this big."

Cam scans the front of Pam's property. "I think it's beautiful. And only a block from the beach!" He runs around and helps Nana out of the car.

I open the passenger door. "Sheesh, Betty. We don't live in a small house either, and we inherited ours the same as Pam. Good thing, because we couldn't afford the property taxes on it if we bought it now."

"At least you own a house," Rylee says, locking the car. "I'm going to be renting forever unless I sell a lot more of my artwork." She picks lint off her shirt. "I hope we're dressed OK."

I motion toward the house. "If T-shirts and jeans aren't acceptable, then we don't belong here."

We stroll up the concrete walkway to the porch and stop in front of the etched glass door.

"Maybe we should have come in the Rolls," Nana says.

"Does it actually run?" Rylee rings the doorbell. "I figured it was stuck in the garage."

"Oh, the vintage car runs," I say. "But I'm only allowed to back it down the driveway to make sure the engine works once a week. I get gas like once every four months."

Cam bursts out laughing. "That's one way to save money."

The door swings in and Pam motions for us to enter. "Please come in." The exuberant grin on her face could light up a football stadium.

Nana enters first. "You have a lovely house, Pam. Thank you so much for the invitation. We should have taken you up on the offer years ago. You can count on us to attend more circles and events in the future." She scans the decor in the foyer. "I don't think I've ever seen such beautiful wallpaper, and the stained oak woodwork shines like glass. Your ancestors would be proud of how well you have maintained the family home."

Damn, Betty. Could you lay on the compliments any thicker? Also, no one promised to attend future planning sessions or circles.

Cam, Rylee, and I follow her in, and *wow*. Nana wasn't exaggerating. The grand foyer has a coffered ceiling, columns with half walls, and a built-in seat guarding the turned staircase. The wallpaper displays intertwining vines of sage and basil, white peonies splattering the greenery throughout. An elegant marble-top walnut table rests in the center of an antique Persian rug, hosting a large vase full of lilies. Voices travel through the living room to the foyer.

"Your home rocks, Pam," Rylee says.

"Ditto." Cam stares up at the stained-glass chandelier. "It sparkles."

The coven leader shuts the front door. "Thank you. I'm so glad you're here."

Don't be rude, Fortune. Say something. "You've done a wonderful job making your home a welcoming place." She has, and now I regret not coming before.

"You're here," Pam says. "That's what matters. The others are waiting in the side room in the back. I believe you all know everyone except for one new member. Follow me."

We walk through the living room, past a magnificent oak fire-place mantel with a beveled mirror, and enter the area behind it. Only three of the local city witches are in there, drinking iced tea. It's hardly a full coven. The walls are painted a dark berry hue, creating a cozy atmosphere. An instrument case leans against a chair.

Zara Harris, a tall, slender woman in her mid-thirties, waves. "Hi, all. It's great to have you join us finally. If you ever need help with anything, just ask."

This extremely competent witch has flawless skin with a sepia tone, like you find in photographs from the late 1800s. Her eyes are the color of chestnuts, nearly translucent, and she has shoul-der-length brown hair styled in ringlets. She is a local psychologist and therapist who has offered her services to me more than once at the store. Either she needs the work, or she senses I've got issues. I'm wary of her.

"I told you they would come." Joey Hernandez sets his drink down and darts to us. "You know everyone here, right?"

A young woman of medium height in her twenties, dressed from top to bottom in black and covered in tattoos, steps forward. She's sporting thick, short brown hair the shade of molasses, fair skin, and blue eyes resembling Caribbean waters. "Except me. I'm Heather Thompson. I hear you're supposed to be a descendant of the famous Anne Whittle of the Pendle Witches. You must be powerful. You could show us how much tonight since you graced the coven with your presence."

Pamela flinches at Heather's bold admission. She must have spread that gossip.

I toss the idea back at her. "We don't know that for sure. The stories were probably fabricated generations ago."

"Why would you say that?" Nana asks. "Don't mind Fortune. It embarrasses her."

My best friend interjects, saving my ass from Betty as usual. "Hey, my name is Rylee O'Brien."

"I'm Cameron Huxley," Cam says. "But most people call me Cam. Haven't I seen you on campus rolling a cello?"

Heather squints at him. "Yeah, I'm a senior. Tough year ahead with a recital. I should've probably waited to join the coven, but Pam's daughter Izzy asked me to when I attended a Samhain event last fall."

I tap on Nana's shoulder. "This is my grandmother, Betty Whittle."

"An old crone," Heather says. "You can probably cast any spell you want with your skills. You're a level three, I assume?"

"Young witch, I'm way past the coven's arbitrary levels." Nana crosses her arms, her head settling to the left.

Sure, Betty. Let's piss off the witches you're trying to butter up. "Where is Isabella?"

Pam's sixteen-year-old daughter enters the room wearing a purple hoodie, stopping when she sees us, as if she's crashed into a brick wall.

"There she is," Pam says. "My mini-me."

The nickname is appropriate. Isabella has the same coloring as her mother in skin tone and eyes. Her hair shines like polished walnut under the ceiling light. She's a junior in high school.

"Izzy, you remember Fortune Whittle and her grandmother, don't you?"

"Yeah. Hello. Mama is really happy you came."

"We're glad to be here to help," I say, bending the truth.

"Mama, how long will this meeting take tonight?" she asks.

"As long as it has to be. That shouldn't concern you."

She pulls her cell phone from her jeans pocket and reads the screen. "I forgot Jessica wanted to practice orchestra music tonight. I can't stay."

"You have an obligation to attend this planning session." Pam glowers at her daughter, clenching her teeth. "You will remain."

"I have to practice, Mama," Izzy says, peering at our awkward stares. "You said I must improve enough to be a top player in the new school year. I can't do both."

"Yes, you can. We all have tasks, young woman. Put the phone away and fulfill your duties. Arrange another evening for practice."

This poor girl. I empathize. Being raised by an overbearing mother sucks. She glances at her phone again and shoves it in her pocket.

Pam takes a breath. "Sit in that chair while we wait for the rest of the coven to arrive."

Izzy moves toward the seat. "No. Jessica is waiting for me." She grabs her violin and darts out of the room.

"I apologize for my daughter's insolence. I'll be right back."

Pam rushes out and a tense discussion echoes in the foyer. Soon after, the front door slams.

Rylee mutters, "Family squabble. That was awkward."

"Izzy is too young to be a formal member," Zara whispers. "She is way too immature and only a neophyte. Pam spoils that girl."

"She's OK," Joey says. "I like Izzy's zest to learn. Her mother will not be happy she took off at the last minute, though."

"So, that leaves the four of you?" Cam asks.

"Five, actually," a familiar male voice blurts out from behind.

My face flushes with rage. *Fuck. My. Luck.* I turn around to find Jonathan Walker strolling in with Pam. A tall, rugged, eclectic witch in his early fifties with silver hair, blue eyes that sparkle with the brilliance of sapphires, and a tanned complexion, he possesses a charm that has swayed many women, including witches like myself. He's a local financial broker who lives on one of the exclusive islands in Alamitos Bay that's full of multimillion-dollar homes on the water. The single thing I miss about him is the boat rides on his small yacht he keeps at the marina.

Even though Pamela is the coven leader, Jonathan has bent many decisions to his liking according to Joey's gossip. He's also my old flame who won Nana's heart. But he cheated on me with Anwen Beddoe, and that was the last straw for me. I'd heard he no longer attended the witch circles, or I wouldn't have come.

"Well, hello, Jonathan," Nana says. "A pleasure to see you after all this time."

"Hello, Betty." He smiles, a touch of arrogance seeping in. "I miss the fabulous salads from your garden."

I think I'm going to vomit. Buttering her up will get you nowhere, sleazebag.

Pam follows him in, a bit flummoxed. "With Jonathan's arrival, we can begin. Why don't we gather around the dining room table to complete the event plans we're responsible for? Covens from Orange County and other parts of LA are tidying up their assignments as well. Since this pagan festival began, each year is another opportunity to educate the residents that we aren't to be feared. But there are always troublemakers. We need to be prepared."

We spend the next hour determining who will handle merchant table setup as well as designating volunteers to help usher the crowds. I've only attended the festival a few times over the years, not wanting to bring attention to myself. Attending this planning session is more than I ever expected to take part in. Yet, here I am.

I catch Jonathan ogling me every time I sneak a glance at him. He shouldn't still affect me this way, but we were together for almost two years. The lying and dicking around left me hardened. After he throws a few blatant smirks in my direction, I need a break. I take a couple of empty glasses into the kitchen and place them on the counter as the floor creaks from behind.

"Jonathan," I say, grinding my teeth.

"Fortune." He smiles, his blue eyes commanding my attention.

"Did you know I was coming? Or did Pam keep it from you?"

"I suggested she invite you, actually. You won't take my calls or respond to texts or email. I wanted to talk to you."

"Why? Do you need a vintage mid-century modern credenza?"

He chuckles. "I miss your humor, your beautiful face. Everything about you." He moves closer and his overpriced cologne pushes me back. "I made a mistake, Fortune. I should have committed to getting married."

"That's kinda difficult when you're fucking every woman who flashes a flirtatious smile in your direction. What makes you think I'd want to date again after you cheated on me with that Tylwyth Teg?"

"That's a matter of opinion. We weren't in a committed relationship as I remember."

"So, talking about getting married after dating two years doesn't count?"

"It was conjecture, Fortune. Nothing had been decided."

"Hmph." I walk past him but spin around. "Apparently, you had." I return to the dining room and drop into my seat.

Rylee whispers in my ear. "You OK?"

"Yes," I mutter back. "He's a dick. If I had known he was still a member of the coven, I would have never come."

"Of course you would have. Because you had to do the right thing."

"So far, I haven't done shit. I hoped Nana would have told them about the problem at the lagoon by now. What is she waiting for?"

"Hey," Zara says. "No whispering among the members. It creates mistrust. We can't have that in our circle if you're going to remain."

"Sorry." I send a dagger-filled glare at Jonathan. "I wouldn't want to do anything to create a confidence issue."

"It's all good." Joey taps the table with a drumbeat. "We trust you, Fortune."

When we're nearly finished, I grimace at Nana. When do we divulge what's going on at the lagoon? She closes her eyes briefly and nods. What the fuck, Betty? I glance at Rylee and Cam. My best friend takes the bait.

"By the way. Fortune, Cam, and I were at the lagoon last week. A small area is full of dead fish."

Pam sits up straight. "That's strange. What caused that?"

"Sewage. Chemical runoff. Decaying organic matter." Joey throws his hands up. "Take your pick."

"No," Cam says. "We tested the water. Well, Norman analyzed it."

"Who the fuck is Norman?" Heather asks, grimacing.

Jonathan leans back in his chair. "Fortune's uppity dog familiar."

"Norm is an adorable morkie," Joey says. "He just has personality."

"He's not uppity." I glare at my former beau. "He just thinks you're a piece of shit."

Cam snorts and the room goes silent as a morgue. Zara scans our faces and stands.

"I know we aren't running tonight's meeting as an official circle. But if these four are going to join the coven, we should review the rules with them. This isn't acceptable behavior."

"You need to chill, Zara," Joey says, rolling his eyes at her. "You are way too serious. If you don't learn to go with the flow, you're gonna have a stroke someday."

Pam motions for our resident witch psychologist to sit. "Fortune is new to the structure of a coven, being a solitary witch. I'm certain she'll adapt once we join hands to cast spells."

The fuck I will. I won't come back, no matter what Betty promises you all.

"Sit down, Zara," Jonathan says, peering at me. "I'm sure Fortune will adhere to the coven's rules. Her declaration was directed at me personally, and I deserved the remark in her eyes. We should move on."

"Fine." She sits and crosses her arms. "Someone has to keep us on track."

Betty nudges me. "Yes, let's stay on topic. Norman is eccentric, but he is a competent assistant."

Folds form on Pam's brow. "What did he find?"

"The fish died because that area of the lagoon is full of fresh water," Cam says.

Heather flinches. "How is that possible when it's comprised of saltwater?"

"Norman believes magic changed its composition," I say.

"You mean witchcraft?" Heather asks.

Rylee glances at me. "Or maybe fae?"

"Norman couldn't identify the exact source. He doesn't interact with the water element well." I tap my chin, thinking she could be one hundred percent correct. Could Rhys have done this? If so, why?

"Do you think the transformation affected the negative energy filter we placed on the portal?" Pam asks.

"Norman seemed to think so," I say.

Jonathan leans back in his chair. "Pam and I will visit the lagoon and investigate."

"Yes," the coven leader says. "Thank you for bringing it to our attention. I'm curious, though. What prompted the three of you to go there and check?"

Rylee and Cam lock eyes with me and Nana kicks my leg under the table. I can't divulge the truth, so I do the next best thing—lie.

"Norman doesn't leave the house much, so I took him for a walk. Rylee and Cam wanted to get some steps in. Good thing Norm jumped in the water or we wouldn't know."

Joey chuckles. "Lucky you had him with you, then. I hope our work wasn't ruined."

"Jonathan and I will soon determine that." Pam stands, facing her palms toward the ceiling. "Thank you all for coming. I'm hoping for a special Summer Solstice Festival with the four of you joining us this year, and hopefully, many more to come. It is done."

We say our goodbyes and dash out as quickly as we can, which translates to me tapping my feet on the floor while Betty layers a few more compliments on Pam before we head outside. Joey approaches me before I join the others inside the vehicle.

"I'm really sorry I didn't tell you about Jonathan. I found out a day ago he was returning." A teasing smile curls his lips. "But that cheating SOB shouldn't matter now, right? You seemed pretty cozy with Detective Prescott at the Java House." He wiggles his shoulders.

"Shhh," I whisper. "My grandmother doesn't know I'm seeing him."

He shimmies closer. "Oh, you have more plans? Why don't you want her to know? Does she hate cops?"

I glance at Nana through the car window. She's waving for me to get in. "I have to go, but we're good. I'm not mad."

After I settle in my seat, Rylee pokes the bear. "What did Joey say?"

"He apologized for not telling me Jonathan had returned to the coven."

A mischievous grin morphs Betty's face. *Oh, shit. She's plotting again.* "Well I, for one, am delighted he's returned to the coven. You didn't have to be so rude to him, Fortune."

Rude? I'm just getting started.

CHAPTER

ELEVEN

I examine my choice of clothing—a light-blue shirt with a deep plunging V-neck and clingy skinny jeans. Ollie said to dress comfortably, and I am riding my bike to his house. A sundress would have been overkill and a pain to pedal in. Better to go without appearing too interested.

It's Friday the 13th, a lucky time for witches, and named after the Norse goddess Frigg, the wife of the god Odin. Her domains are marriage, motherhood, fertility, and fate, and we celebrate the day in her honor. But now I question my choice of evenings for this date. Maybe I shouldn't push it? Norman is lounging on the bed, his belly facing up and a paw resting behind his head.

"That's the third set of clothes you have modeled, my witch. You've never spent more than five minutes deciding what to wear in all the years I've assisted you."

"Is this outfit too casual? I'd rather not appear too eager, but dressing like I don't give a shit wouldn't be great, either. What do you think?"

He sits up on his hind legs. "You surely do not want to know what I think."

My head drops. "I wouldn't have asked if I didn't."

"Since your breakup with Mr. Walker a year ago, you have slept with an abundance of witches, young and old, with abandon. Then you moved on to a few selkies. What was the last one's name?" Norman's ears twitch. "Oh, yes. Maaal-colm." He bats his eyelashes. "What a stud he was. Am I right?"

I cross my arms and huff, but he continues, hopping onto all four paws and strutting on the bed.

"After those many rides to Seal Beach, you returned to Long Beach, determined to find yourself an Unremarkable to share your folly with, despite the possible repercussions. You thought you'd outwitted Betty when you laid siege to the unusually attractive homeless man you found tenting on the sand. But even with him, you failed—as he turned out to be a Tylwyth Teg. At this point, you might as well bed this Unremarkable and be done with it. Self-sabotage is strong with you, my witch."

I gape at him. "Is that what you believe? That's not at all what I'm doing!"

His whiskers twitch. "Isn't it? Then why are you pursuing this Unremarkable?"

I clasp my copper bracelet. *Oooh, shit. My outspoken familiar is right.* "I've never been happy with any witch I have dated. Even with Jonathan, I was grasping at straws. He wasn't ever going to settle down, and he proved it by dragging me along with promises of marriage. I started thinking, if Ivy found my dad..."

"Bingo!" He jumps onto the floor and approaches my dresser. "I knew you'd figure it out."

"You think I want to date Ollie Prescott because I miss my dad?" I grab my purse from the bed. "I never even knew him, Norm."

"That hasn't eliminated the wanting for him, has it?" He taps a paw on the bottom drawer where I keep the mementos of my mother. "Perhaps it's time to take out the runestones again."

"They fill my head with unfulfilled promises of a vague future. Ivy was competent with them, you said. Without control of my magic, I've never had any real success interpreting their meanings. A reminder of my shortcomings." I check my cell phone screen. It's nearly five.

"Nonsense." Norman opens the drawer and grabs the burgundy velvet pouch. "It is time you try again. Let's not forget the success you experienced in the garage before the incident at the lagoon. Time heals all wounds, Fortune. An Unremarkable once said that. Yours will too. Then we begin once more."

"Leave them on the dresser. I'll reacquaint myself with the stones when I return." I head toward the door and turn. "Don't I deserve to be happy, Norm?"

My loyal familiar mutters an incantation and levitates onto the mattress. "Of course, my witch, but what are you willing to sacrifice for such happiness? Ivy lost her life."

"Why do I have to give up anything? Catch you later. Don't get into trouble."

"Me?" He snickers and nestles his body into a pillow.

***

THE RIDE to Ollie's place is a short five-minute jaunt up Toyon Avenue from my house in Carroll Park. When he sent his address, my heart skipped a beat. How has he lived so close and I've never met him before now?

When I arrive, I discover his house is an adorable Craftsman bungalow with a light shade of blue-gray wood siding and trim painted in a crisp white. A black SUV sits in the driveway. I hop off my racer and roll it up the concrete walkway, pushing it up the steps. Fearing the local porch pirates and the recent bike thefts, I lock the frame to a metal chair to the right of the door. A matching seat and small side table complete the set. I imagine Ollie sipping his coffee and waving to neighbors in the morning.

I remove my purse from the basket, tap on the dark-stained wooden door, and wait. After a few minutes, I knock a little harder, but he doesn't come. Could he be stuck on the toilet? Oh, screw it. I turn the knob and enter. "Ollie? Are you in here?"

The bungalow is quaint and shows signs of a tasteful modern renovation, including gleaming oak wood floors and freshly painted white walls in an open floor plan. A beige sofa full of comfy pillows rests on one wall opposite a set of modern leather seating, with a walnut mid-century coffee table sitting between them. The dining room has a long, rugged pine table surrounded by Wishbone chairs. Ollie must be in the kitchen.

I shuffle in to find maple shaker cabinets and shiny white quartz countertops covered in food prep. The backdoor flings open and my date rushes in with an empty metal pan. He's wearing a tan linen shirt and worn jeans. When he lifts his head, a broad grin erupts.

"Fortune, I see you found your way. I'm chuffed you could come." He gestures with a thumb at the door. "I put the kebab on just now. Would you like a beer while I monitor the barbecue?"

"Sure, I'll have one. But I should drink water, too."

He reaches into his stainless refrigerator and pulls out both, placing one in each of my hands. "For the two-fisted drinker."

I chuckle. "Actually, I don't drink much alcohol. I prefer to remain in control of my faculties." And my magic.

"Shall we?" he asks, motioning toward the door.

He holds the backdoor open for me and I walk down the steps of his back stoop to a vision of nature's beauty that would impress even Nana. The yard is the best combination of immaculate and inviting. There's an outdoor kitchen section with a nearby dining table, an area for lounging, and a firepit. Blue yucca, lavender, succulents, and an assortment of sage shrubs hug the fence while a magnificent magnolia tree provides shade.

The garage sits to the right in the back, but the second story appears to be an ADU, an accessory dwelling unit. Ollie attends to our dinner on the grill while I lean against the smooth concrete countertop. I set my water down and take a sip of the cold beer.

"Your yard is beautiful. It's not what I expected."

He flips a kebab and squints. "Thought I'd have my own personal prison back here, did you?"

I chuckle. "Well, I haven't seen the inside of your ADU yet."

The gate next to the garage opens and Anwen Beddoe darts through. She waves to my date but sends me a side-eye. "Hey, Ollie. How they hanging? Fortune." She tramps up the stairs and enters the ADU.

"You know Anwen?" he asks, tipping his head.

"Yeah, she comes by the store frequently to buy clothes." And she slept with my old boyfriend. I shouldn't tell him that, though. "Have you noticed she brings home a lot of men?"

"And a few women," he replies, curling his mouth. "I'm very aware of her shenanigans, but I have more important things to investigate than a woman down on her luck."

Dude, she's a lazy Tylwyth Teg who doesn't want to go through the hassle of getting a real job. Plus, she enjoys every lascivious minute of it. It's not like I have any room to talk. How I wish I could tell him about her, though. He might think differently.

"I didn't expect you to be a cop who looked the other way."

"Times are tough for lots of people in Long Beach. When Rachel left, I wanted to retain this house. I had completed most of the renovations myself, but I couldn't afford the mortgage on a detective's salary alone. So, I converted the attic of the garage into a rental. It meant giving up a bit of privacy, but I got to keep my home."

I down a little beer and muster up the nerve to ask. "What happened there? Was it mutual?"

"Not at all," he says, flipping another kebab. "Apparently, my late nights left her lonely. She found comfort in the arms of my former street partner, who was oh so happy to keep her company after I was promoted to detective."

"Wow, I'm so sorry." I mean, what else can I say? And I shouldn't, but my M.O. is sticking my foot in my mouth. "What a bitch."

He flinches and turns his attention back to the kebabs. "Actually, Rachel is a wonderful woman. I'm not completely blameless. It takes two to make a marriage work."

"True." What do I know about the subject? "Even if you were working too much, whatever, she could have told you. Everyone deserves to know the truth."

"Agreed. And I'm chuffed to hear you say that. I've had a difficult time reconciling what happened. Frankly, trust issues have affected my other relationships. It's said that everyone lies. How does one move forward?"

"I suppose it depends on the lie." A slight buzz from the beer makes me dizzy, so I set it down and break open the water. This conversation isn't helping.

"Is any lie acceptable?" he asks with a tilt of his head.

"To protect someone you love would be a damn good rationale." But can I say that about Nana and not get pissed?

"Sometimes people think they're protecting those they love, but really they're only protecting themselves." He scoops up the kebabs and places them on a large plate. "Why don't we go in and eat in the dining room? Bring your drinks."

I help him gather the rest of the food—a salad and some rice —and we settle in at the table. It's comfortable sitting across from him, as if I've been here before. I am certain I've never met the detective before crashing into him on the beach trail that night. Yet every fiber of my being tells me I belong here. Betty is wrong.

We spend the next hour enjoying the delicious meal he prepared and sharing stories of our childhoods, me in Long Beach, him in Lancaster. What a fool his ex-wife was. He's charming, attractive, and a decent cook. I keep waiting for him to pick his nose or cut the cheese. No one is this perfect.

He eats another slice of grilled pepper and sets his fork down. "You attended Cal State Long Beach then?"

"Yeah. It made the most sense. It's a fantastic college, and I could commute. Nana didn't have much money to help me with tuition. She wanted to mortgage the house, but I wouldn't let her. I got a small scholarship and worked part time. How about you? Did you go to school to become a cop?"

"Yes, actually. I attended a university in London. I needed to get away from home."

"Is that why you have a posh accent? What do they call it? The Queen's English?"

"Yes, and I worked rather hard to acquire it. I wanted to remain in London. I hoped it would open up more opportunities to move up in the ranks. Then I met Rachel. She missed Southern California, so we moved here. The Queen's English has the opposite effect working here."

"You mean the other cops give you shit for it?"

"Some do. A few have accused me of making detective because of my British English. As if that has anything to do with competence. I worked hard to attain it. At the expense of losing my wife, I might add."

He gazes at me for a stretched moment and my heart races into overdrive. *What are you doing, Fortune?* You shouldn't be here. I peer up at the wall of framed photographs—an assortment of landscapes and people. Three empty spots long for replacements.

I stand and examine a photo of dingy brownstone buildings with cobblestone streets. "Is this Lancaster?"

"Yes. The buildings are quite old. I miss the pubs and the afternoon tea."

Ollie joins me, standing rather close. His aftershave has a scent of musk and leather. My heart dances the rumba. I moved from the table to avoid this.

I shift to the right to view a picture of a sandstone fortress with towers. "Which castle is this?"

He slides next to me, and the hair on my arms springs up. I've never reacted this way on a date. I should leave, but my sneakers are glued to the floor.

"That's Lancaster Castle. It has an amazing history, including the Pendle Witch trials." An eyebrow arches. "One supposed *witch*"—his emphasis on the word makes it clear he's a skeptic—"who was accused of murder by witchcraft has your last name. Maybe she's an ancestor of yours."

A lump surfaces in my throat. "There are lots of Whittles in the U.S. Hard to say."

He chuckles. "I was trying to be cheeky. That would be a fluke, no?"

"Funny." I force a grin and change the subject because this is too close to home. I turn and face him. "You have empty spots on the wall."

"Yes," he says, stepping closer. "I hope to fill them someday." He shifts even more and edges his face toward mine, as if he's going to kiss me, but he hesitates. "Is this alright?"

Don't be stupid, Fortune. Say no. "No...I mean, yes." I am so in trouble.

"Are you sure?" he asks in a breathy voice.

I lift my chin, transfixed on his warm brown eyes. "Yes."

He kisses me, barely grazing my lips, but wraps his arms around me and presses harder. I open my mouth, inviting his tongue, and he accepts. I embrace him around the middle and urge him on, but he pulls away. My hands slide to the front.

"I liked that. How about you?" I ask, catching a breath.

He adjusts his pants around the zipper in his jeans. "Isn't it obvious?"

I laugh and caress his chest. "I'm sorry. It can make a man so uncomfortable." I want so badly to rip off his pants right now and ride him like a horse. But I can't. I should go before I lose myself.

"Would you fancy a cup of coffee? I brewed a pot for after dinner. We could sit around the firepit and chat a bit more."

"I'd love some."

We take the dishes to the kitchen and make our way outside with mugs of caffeine. After chatting for about thirty minutes, Ollie's cell phone rings. He glances at the screen.

"Oh, I have to take this. Work." He gets up and listens as he takes a few steps. "How is that possible? But it explains the dead fish. No other leads?" He pauses. "So, forensics don't agree the cases are related. What about the nosy woman who lives across from the lagoon? Was she able to identify the people she witnessed there?"

My heart thumps like a thief who got caught with her fingers in the cookie jar.

He nods. "Thanks, Manny."

I stand and approach him, clasping my bracelet. "What was that about? Is it related to the murders?"

"No, something bizarre actually. There were dead fish in the lagoon, so we had the water tested. Somehow, fresh water seeped into the area. They can't explain it. Has nothing to do with the deceased men." He stuffs a hand in a pants pocket. "You understand, I'm not permitted to discuss the specifics of the cases with you."

"Yeah." I gesture toward the house. "It's getting late. I should get going."

"I'll walk with you."

We drop our mugs in the kitchen on the way to the front porch. I unlock my bike and Ollie rolls it down the steps for me. He hasn't acted weird since he asked his partner about the resident across from the lagoon. She couldn't have identified us.

"I had a fabulous time," he says. "Thank you for coming here for dinner. Restaurants can be so noisy. They don't provide a proper atmosphere for conversation. I'd love to take you somewhere next time if you're agreeable?"

"Sounds like fun. Long Beach certainly has an extensive list to choose from." I take my bike from his hands. "Before I go, I do have one question. Did Anwen tell you I owned the store?"

He adjusts his collar. "You got me. I'm a detective. I used the resources available to me."

"That was hardly much of an investigation," I say, frowning.

"I asked her where she bought her outfit in passing one day. However, it is true that I passed your store every week. I wish I had succumbed to my curiosity and stopped in. I would have met you sooner." He leans over the bike and kisses me on the cheek. "Be careful riding home, Fortune. We don't know if these murders are related, but the city has an underbelly like most cities, and it's showing its vile face recently."

You don't even know the half of it, dude. "I'll be fine. Thank you for dinner. Ollie, I had a great time." I hop on my racer and head down Toyon Avenue, a shit-eating grin plastered on my face.

When I enter the house, Nana has already retreated to her bedroom to read for the evening. At least I can avoid her nightly interrogation. She could give Ollie a few pointers. I send a text to Rylee on the way upstairs.

I'm back. He grilled shrimp kebabs.

RYLEE

Niiice!

OMFG. That Tylwyth Teg, Anwen Beddoe, rents his ADU. 😬

RYLEE

Probably a relief he doesn't have blond hair!

He's a do-the-right-thing kinda guy. He'd never sleep with her.

Since you brought it up. How was he? 😜

FFS. We kissed one time. He was so nice.

You are sooo in trouble, Fortune.

I know. I'll share more tomorrow night on the way to the party.

OK, Blondie. Later. 😘

When I enter my bedroom, Norman is curled up against one of my fuzzy throw blankets. His head pops up.

"You're back so early, my witch. Let me guess. The detective wasn't as good in bed as you imagined?" He snickers, his tail wagging.

"What? Shhh." I close my door, holding the knob until it meets the jamb. "Betty is still awake, Fluffy." I plop onto the mattress and drop my purse to the floor.

Norman scuttles over and lies next to me. "My apologies. I assumed your social interactions went well, as they always seem to. My assumptions were decidedly false."

"No, he cooked a delicious meal, and the conversation was... normal."

His ears perk up. "Then why the sad expression, Fortune?"

"Because I'm lying to myself thinking a relationship with this man is possible."

"You're beginning to sound like Ivy." He rubs his head against my arm. "A good reason to work on the runestones again, don't you think?"

I push out a long, frustrated breath of I-give-up. "What did my mom like about my father so much?"

"That he knew nothing of the supernatural world. It's what she longed for. Like you said—normal."

I pat his hairy head. "But eventually, he was *in the knowing*. Is that what ruined everything?"

"I do not know, my witch. You'd have to ask Betty."

"Pfft. As if she'd ever tell me the whole truth."

"That's the conundrum, isn't it?" My morkie familiar sits on his hind legs. "What will you do regarding this Unremarkable, my witch?"

"I don't fucking know."

TWELVE

I make my morning smoothie while Nana loads the dishwasher, humming an old English tune as she works. After rinsing each plate and pan, she mutters an incantation, sending it into a slot in the dishwasher with a wave of her hand. She's in a chipper mood. And she has yet to ask me where I was last night—definitely sus. Norm is lying on his dog bed in the corner, juggling magic bubbles with his paws. I screw the lid on my bottle and head toward the door.

"Bye, Norm. Plan on a session in the garage tomorrow, a ritual and practice with the runestones. But first, I want you to assist me in training Cameron. He's functioning at level two, definitely not a neophyte. He needs to boost his confidence. I can't help him much with my condition, but maybe you can."

His bubbles pop one by one. "At your service, my witch." A comical grin curls his whiskers.

"Nana, if you can garner some patience, I'd love you to show him a few things."

"That's a wonderful idea. Thank you for asking," she says, lifting her chin.

"Have a good day. Don't work too long in the garden. And please put on sunscreen. It's a miracle you haven't developed skin cancer."

"Not a miracle, granddaughter—magic. I cover up with loose shirts and wear a hat, but I'll do as you ask." She shuffles toward me. "I'm happy you have returned to the rituals. They were helping. Work with the runestones. The interpretation will come."

"Don't get your hopes up. I'll see you later for dinner."

Nana's mouth falls open, but she hesitates. "Fortune, I want you to do something for me."

Ahhh, here it comes. "What, Nana?"

"Pam and Jonathan are going to the lagoon tonight to assess the spell they cast. She asked if you could meet them there to point out the exact location where your encounter took place. It will save them time."

"I can't. I'm going to a fundraiser with Rylee tonight at the Casa de Playa. The Whatever Goes director asked her to go. She thinks the same person who donated to the gallery bought that estate, too. We have to arrive around nine. I won't get home until late."

Her eyes widen. "Ohhh, swanky." She shimmies her hips. "You could go right after sunset. That would give you plenty of time to meet Rylee there."

I stand there, clutching my smoothie. If I say no, an argument may ensue. I don't have the energy to fight her because it's still packed in my bottle. "Fine. I'll stay for fifteen minutes. The traffic from the lagoon to downtown will be a bitch on a Saturday night."

"Thank you, Fortune. We need to offer as much support as possible if we're going to ask for their help with the family curse." She exits the kitchen and turns toward her bedroom.

Norm snickers. "You told her."

"Oh, she's right. We may need them and the coven." And I hate admitting that fact. "Later, Norm."

Clouds, puffy like cotton balls, litter the blue sky, but it's a gorgeous sunny day for a quick bike ride to the store. When I roll my racer in, Cam is stocking the shelves while Gabriela rings up a customer.

"Gracias," Gabby says, handing the young woman her shopping bag. "And have a wonderful afternoon." The shopper exits the store.

Cam waves. "Hey, glad you arrived. I've got questions about a box in storage."

"Let me park my bike in the back," I say.

"Good afternoon, Fortune." Gabby shuts the register. "Cameron says you are helping the local pagan group with the event on June 20th. I'm thinking of going and taking my grandchildren."

"Yes, but they are a coven. Not all pagans are witches, but these ones are. It should be a lot of fun. They're going to have community rituals, but participation is completely voluntary. There will be food and store vendors, too."

"I know what they profess to be." She pauses, the cogwheels turning in her head. "I've never asked you because everyone should practice their faith as they please without criticism. Do you believe in all that hocus-pocus? Participate in their little rituals?"

I can't lie to Gabby, and I am shocked she's asking now after working for me for two years. "Lots of people celebrate the summer solstice. It has little to do with witchcraft."

"Very true, but do you cast spells like the people in this local coven?"

"I can truthfully say no to that." Because I'm fucked. "We're volunteering to help with the celebration—extra hands." I roll my bike, pointing as I pass Cam.

"I'll be back in a few minutes, Gabby," he says.

"Take your time. It's been slow for a Saturday." She takes out a cloth and dusts the counter.

I park my racer and hang my helmet on the handlebars. Cam heads to the box.

"I found these old music boxes and a mess of spiders. Scared the shit out of me when I opened the flap. I had to grab the bug spray. They're coated in chemicals now. Sorry." He pulls out a typical mini grand piano and attempts to turn the knob, but it doesn't budge. "Why haven't you put these out?"

"Oh, that's my Great-Aunt Miriam's collection. Most of them are broken if I remember correctly. They may just need cleaning. People don't really buy them. I wanted to get them out of the house when I opened the store because seeing them on display made Nana sad. So, I stuffed them in a box and brought them here."

"I know a little about the mechanics. During my freshman year in college, I worked as an assistant to a clock repairman who also repaired items like this. When the store is slow, do you mind if I tinker with them? I mean, someone could wander in and buy some."

"Sure, but don't tell my grandmother if we sell any. I'm hoping she forgot about them. Speaking of Nana, would you like to come by the house tomorrow and do some training? She said she'd teach you a few things, and Norman will assist. If we have to attend another coven meeting, they're going to press us to take part in a circle and cast a group spell."

Cam's face lights up like a stage on Broadway. "That's lit! I love working with Norman." He sets the music box down, grimacing. "I'm kinda worried about training with your grandmother. She can be critical."

I lay a firm hand on his shoulder. "If Betty gets out of line at all, I'll send her into the house. I promise."

"Because you've been so successful in the past?" He chuckles and closes the flaps on the box.

"I asked for that," I say, frowning. "I choose not to confront Nana. But I will fight for you because my friends matter. She seemed really excited to do it. Give her a chance. I can't help you very much in my state."

"What will you do if they ask you to join in a spellcasting?"

"That's my problem. I'll figure it out."

"Alright. Can Rylee come? She could act as a buffer."

I chuckle. "When Betty gets on her high horse with witchcraft, you'd need titanium armor for a buffer. But I'll ask her to come. Let's get back to the front. The door has chimed three times since we came in here. Gabby is probably swamped."

As Cam walks out, I slide my bike against the wall. A muffled, high-pitched laugh echoes behind me, and I spin around. No one has entered the storage room. Gabby's voice must have trickled in. I stare at Great-Aunt Miriam's collection. A single open flap of the box beckons me. I kick the flimsy cardboard to check for spiders. No more arachnids, thank the stars. I push the flap down and dart back to the front of the store.

***

AFTER A LATE DINNER WITH NANA, I get dressed in a black sleeveless cocktail dress and spiked high-heel shoes. A gold necklace and dangling earrings finish my over-the-top ensemble. My copper bracelet clashes, but oh well. I'm not one to kowtow to wealthy investors, but I'll do it for Rylee. This benefactor could send her art career into something more than matting prints at a local frame store. I apply eyeliner, brow pencil, a swipe of pink blush on each cheek, and my favorite candy-red lipstick. How do women do this every day?

I grab a light cardigan and the gold sequined clutch I found at an estate sale and head to the bus stop. The Long Beach transit drops at a corner in front of the lagoon, opposite the Simunye Restaurant, a frequented eatery that serves amazing cuisine. The sun has set, but slivers of pink and burnt orange streak the sky. I have to tramp across the causeway in these damn heels, so I begin my arduous trek.

By the time I arrive at the gravel trail on the other side, the sun has finally relinquished its grasp. Except for the beam from a gibbous moon and the spray from a few lampposts, the lagoon appears at rest for the night. A few steps on the pebbles remind me my shoes won't survive. I slip them off and carry them in my hands.

Far up the path, I discover two people near the freshwater area—one standing, the other kneeling at the water's edge. Shit. As I approach, I notice one of them is dressed in a dark hoodie, the hood pulled up over their head. Their stature is familiar somehow. Although I'm in my bare feet, I crunch on the stones, alerting them to my presence. The hooded person takes off down the trail in the opposite direction.

The other is a young man. He appears small in the shadows until he stands, revealing a rather tall physique. He's wearing a tight black T-shirt and worn jeans. His long, dark-brown hair is wet. An object hangs at his side. As I approach, the musician raises what's in his hands—a violin and bow—and performs a tune, his body swaying in motion to the rhythm. The music is familiar and soothing, and I find myself meandering up the path to its melody. When I draw near, he locks eyes with mine and lowers his instrument.

"Good evening, love. I haven't seen you here before." His eyes trail down my body in the moonlight. "What a shame."

These guys have to come up with better pickup lines. "Do you live around here?" I recall the late-night practicing session the night of my mishap. "Wait. Are you the dude who plays after people have most certainly gone to bed?"

"Perhaps," he says, a mischievous smile rising. "It's my most productive time."

"That's pretty rude, don't you think? No matter how well you play, people can't go to sleep with you practicing during bedtime hours."

He steps closer, his facial features becoming sharper under the splay of a nearby lamppost, and I gasp. *Damn. He's gorgeous.* After carefully setting his violin and bow on a clump of plants, he removes his T-shirt to expose a well-defined torso. I'd say a swimmer's body. A faint glow emits from my copper bracelet. *Fuck my luck.* I wrap my sweater around my wrist.

"I was about to take another swim." His voice is deep and alluring. "Care to join me?" He unbuttons his jeans.

I stand there, frozen and about ready to yank his zipper down. Screw the busybody neighbors on the other side of the lagoon. It's been a while since my tryst with Rhys. A little one-night fling with a random musician wouldn't amount to anything. Stones crunching in the distance bring me back to reality. *Get a grip, Fortune.*

"No, thanks. I'm waiting for a couple of friends. Personally, I'd suggest another night for skinny dipping. You're bound to get arrested."

"Fortune?" a man's voice rings out in the dark. It's Jonathan.

"Noted," the stranger says as he picks up his shirt and violin.

I stroll toward my ex and stop. He's dressed in a lightweight blue suit and a white collared shirt but has shed the tie. And he is alone.

"Where's Pam?" I ask.

"Something came up with Izzy." He ogles me up and down. "You didn't have to dress up for me."

"It's not for you. I'm attending an art fundraiser with Rylee."

"Interesting. I hadn't heard about it. Pam said you have limited time, so let's get started."

"I don't think so. Some dude is practicing his violin at the site." I gesture with a nod of my head.

He peers past me. "There's no one there, Fortune."

"What?" I turn around. A wide moonbeam illuminates the ripples as a great blue heron steps gracefully through the water. "I guess he took off. He lives near here. The night I came here with Rylee, his music traveled across the lagoon. Hmph. Musicians."

I step over the fence, groaning as the pointy needles of the California buckwheat dig into the soles of my feet. Jonathan follows, because pointy dress shoes still beat bare skin any day of the week. When we arrive at the water's edge, I gesture at the area where my mishap occurred. He squats and raises his hand but pauses to scan the trail and the homes on the other side.

"You're safe," I say. "I don't notice anyone around, and none of the residents are outside."

He chants so low I can't discern the words, and a warm amber glow emanates from his hands. Hydromancy, divination through the use of water, is a forte of his, among other skills. He's been a level three witch for as long as I've known him. He tosses a flat stone across the surface and it skips several times, sending rings outward. After interpreting the signs, his magic dissipates, and he stands.

"Norman's analysis was correct. Someone tampered with the spell of filtration we cast on the portal."

"Should we be concerned about malevolent beings crossing over? I mean, we didn't have a problem with it before you cast the spell. Cam said his brother's coven had to close their town's portal. But they had to sacrifice a human to do it, albeit a nefarious one."

"Our coven would never agree to such a solution. Supernatural beings who cross over freely will always present an issue.

Closing this one does nothing when there are others everywhere, including the one at Seal Beach. We must learn to live with them."

I check the time on my cellphone and pick up my shoes. "I have to go. Rylee expects me, and the bus ride takes a while."

I head to the trail and set my black shoes on the gravel while I slip on my cardigan. A cool breeze plays with my hair and Jonathan brushes the strands off my face. He grabs my upper arms and pulls me to him, kissing me hard—his typical alpha male ego. I push him away.

"What the fuck are you doing? We're done, and there's no going back."

"You used to enjoy kisses on the rough side."

I recall the tender moment with Ollie and smile. "Not anymore."

"I made a colossal mistake, Fortune, and I had a lot of time to think about it. At least let me try to make amends." The longing in his eyes proves his sincerity.

"My life has changed." I grasp my copper band. "Something happened here prior to the night Rylee, Cam, and Norm came here. I can't talk about it now because I really have to leave. Can I still trust you'll continue to keep my secret?"

"Of course. But the coven may expect you to cast magic at the next circle. What will you do?"

"I don't know yet." I check my phone again. "If I don't leave now, I'm gonna miss my bus. See you Wednesday night."

Jonathan squints at me as if he's plotting his next move. "I look forward to it."

He takes off toward the street and I run on the gravel in the direction of the causeway, bitching to myself with each excruciating crunch of stone. As I approach the entrance, someone whooshes past me, almost knocking me to the ground. I glance back to see an individual wearing a black cloak, the wide hood hanging over their face. They roar like a lion and raise their hands over their head. I freeze, drawn to the faceless person like a magnet. The Thorn symbol on my suppression band glimmers again.

I shove my hand under my cardigan. After one more long bellow, the mentally incapacitated creep runs north into the coastal brush past the end of the trail, disappearing into the horizon.

The homeless situation is getting out of hand here, but this takes the cake.

THIRTEEN

The bus drops me off on Beach Boulevard about a block from Casa de Playa. As I walk past the bland apartments built in the 1970s, I can't imagine owning one of the fabulous homes that border them. But ten-foot stucco fences can hide anything.

I turn and stroll down the red brick road to an elaborate iron driveway gate. A man dressed in a black suit and tie peers through the bars. There's a block of white stone to the left with a name and address in fancy script. I can barely see it through the legs of the person lounging on top.

"Whoa, you're gonna turn some heads, Blondie. I was worried you weren't coming." Rylee gestures to the man behind the gate. "That goon hasn't taken his eyes off me since I got here. Do you think my outfit is too casual?" She's wearing a bright red collared shirt with a matching black vest and trousers. Platform boots finish out the ensemble.

"No, you look great. Sorry I'm a touch late. I had to meet Jonathan and Pam at the lagoon. Except he was the only one who showed up. Some excuse about her needing to deal with Izzy about something." I motion to my friend to get up. "That guy is probably the guard who screens the guests."

She hops off the pretentious slab of stone. "I hope so. I don't want to blow my chance of getting a permanent backer. This sponsor must have a stack of money to throw around."

"I hope so, Red. You deserve a break."

"How did Jonathan act without Pam there? Was he a dick?"

"Is he ever not a dick? He kissed me."

Her head snaps back. "What the fuck? What did you do?"

"Told him the truth...that he blew it. But I think he's regretting our breakup now."

"Pfft. His loss. You'd be better off with Rhys."

We approach the gate and the guard opens one side. "IDs, ladies." We show him our driver's licenses and he checks a page on his tablet. "I found O'Brien but not Whittle."

"She's my date," Rylee says, grinning like a gal who won the lottery.

I wrap my arm in hers. "Let's go in, doll."

Rylee and I stroll onto the terracotta circular driveway toward the main entrance, snickering, but stop to *ooh* and *aah* at the elegant water fountain in the center like the common folk we are. This place is massive—close to 9,000 square feet, I bet. It's in a Spanish style with a white stucco exterior and an orange tile roof. Most likely built in the 1920s, the home has retained its original charm.

We pass through another set of iron gates to a courtyard surrounded by a six-foot white stucco fence. A pathway takes us past a koi fish pond and ends at the entrance to the home. The double doors are wide open, so we go right in. The foyer is round with white marble floors. A curvy hallway with iron railings adorned with intricate swirling designs hangs suspended above us.

"This is another class of living, Blondie," Rylee says, gazing at the modern crystal chandelier hanging above our heads.

"Wipe your mouth," I say, chuckling. "You're drooling."

She touches her face. "No, I'm not." She slaps my arm.

"If that's how you treat your dates, no wonder you're single again."

She chuckles. "Fuck you, Blondie."

Boisterous chatter and laughter spill into the foyer from the rooms in the back. The hallway leading to the rear has dark-stained wood beams in the ceiling. They pass over my head as we walk, taking in the array of modern artwork, all depicting fairies.

We enter the expansive living area with oak parquet flooring. Black leather sofas and chairs arranged in a U shape sit opposite a modern white fireplace on the right. A marble dining table with pedestal legs and upholstered chairs fills the space on the left. The shiny grand piano rests in the center, overlooking a long wall of patio doors that runs the length of the house. The view of the Pacific Ocean is overwhelming.

We find it packed—not like sardines, but with fae in their human forms. They toss their fairy magic back and forth across the room, retrieving drinks and food. Everyone is dressed in formal-casual attire, the men in button-down shirts, dress pants, and shoes, the women wearing flowing dresses. A pianist is playing soft music. I get the impression these are well-established elite supernatural, but not necessarily benevolent ones, judging by those I recognize.

I recognize selkies from Seal Beach, Tylwyth Tegs from Long Beach and the surrounding Los Angeles area. Some of the fae are strangers. They're probably Tuatha Dé Danann, but I've never met any. Anwen Beddoe is lounging on the lap of an Unremark-able, and he isn't the only one sprinkled among the supernatural beings here. It appears she has brought a few colleagues with her. A few local politicians who must be *in the knowing* are here, and I doubt they're the transparent kind.

"Do you see what I see?" I ask, scanning the creatures from the Otherworld.

Wrinkles fold on Rylee's brow. "Yeah. But you have to admit. This place is bitchin'."

"But why are we here?" I turn to the left and gape at the wall guarding the dining room table. "Uh, Red, you better look at this." I elbow her.

"What?" As her head turns, her jaw drops. "My painting!" She cringes as the others snap their heads at us. "Sorry. Whoever purchased this house must have bought it. This could be big for me."

"I hope so," I say, grinning. "You deserve it. If the sponsor is some being from the Otherworld, don't ask where the money came from."

"I'll deal with that *if* it happens."

William Smith, the director of Whatever Goes Gallery, is talking with a Tylwyth Teg female I've seen around and a tall, muscular man with blond hair that's styled in a bun. He's wearing a loose white linen shirt and tailored tan trousers, but his shapely backside is all I can view, which I declare is a sight to behold.

Judging by the deference William is showing them, they appear to be the couple who bought this estate. He must be a fairy, too. What the fuck is going on here? The director nods at my friend and motions for her to join him and the new owners.

"OK, I'm freakin' out. What do I say?" she asks.

"Thank you would be a great start. Go ahead, Red. I'll stand here and admire your amazing artwork."

At that moment, the tall blond fairy with the man bun and firm buttocks turns toward us, an impish grin peeking through his neatly trimmed beard. It's Rhys of Dyfed, and he's all cleaned up. My heart takes off like a car in the Long Beach Grand Prix.

Rylee's head snaps back. "What the fuck? Rhys looks fantastic."

"Fuck me." I glare back at him.

She chuckles. "Yeah, that's probably his plan."

"Go talk to him. No need to screw up your chances, whatever he's finagled. But I have to get out of here."

I take off through an opening to the left of the dining room that leads to a hallway and past a set of stairs. After exiting through a patio door to the outside, I descend several steps, nearly tripping over my heels, until I stop at the head of the pool. I catch my breath, watching as the lights under the water create the illusion of tiny stars twinkling in the moonlight. They mesmerize me for the next fifteen minutes while I attempt to gather my thoughts.

Footsteps approach behind me, stopping so close the heat of the body they're attached to penetrates me. They aren't heavy enough to be Rylee's. I peer over my shoulder. Rhys's cobalt blue eyes appear to glow in the dark.

"I nearly popped my zipper when I saw you—stunning as always. Why did you rush out here like a frightened horse?"

I missed his charming Welsh accent. "Oh, I panicked. I avoided being seen with you because you were pretending to be homeless. But I doubt any of your guests will care, considering who they are."

He moves next to me, shoving a hand in his pocket. "No, they won't."

"What are you doing, Rhys? Why this charade all of a sudden?" I gesture at the house and the grounds. "Did you think this would impress me?"

A pretentious smile curls his lips. "It does. Your eyes betray you, Fortune."

He moves closer and bends over me. My heart pounds against my ribcage, and I struggle to keep from clutching at his shirt to kiss him. Once his lips touch mine, I won't stop. I'll spread my legs willingly and enjoy every lustful minute of it.

"It would impress me more if you had actually worked for it. How did you make this happen? Magic or...making deals with the seedy Unremarkables of this city? How many of them are *in the knowing* of fairies living here? And about the true nature of the witches of Long Beach?"

"We can talk about those specifics later." He swipes a finger down my cheek. "I want you, Fortune. Yes, I created this persona for you, since my station mattered so much to you."

"I told you none of that matters. Supporting Rylee like this isn't helping her. She'll know it's a bribe to twist my arm."

"Now who is being arrogant? I roamed through the art exhibit before the opening. When I saw Rylee's portrait of me, I was gobsmacked. She has incredible talent, and I'll support her work no matter what you do regarding me."

"I'm going home." I head up the steps to the house, but he darts after me, stopping on the step below to grab my arm.

"Don't go. Stay for Rylee. There are many fae and Unremarkables here with unlimited funds who would hire her. Are you willing to risk her opportunities?"

Damn him. "Alright, but only if you leave me alone. Can you do that?"

His face is so close, the aroma of his cologne makes my head spin. He brings his lips within an inch of mine, and my heart palpitates. "Whatever you want, Fortune." He continues up the steps into the house.

After I get my shit together, I return to the living area. Several of the guests are singing while the pianist accompanies them. Rylee is off in a corner chatting with a lean, fit woman who has brown hair laced with copper highlights, most likely a selkie, because she emits a light blue haze from her hand when snatching a wineglass from a tray. The eyes of a few fae emit a green essence as they float food from the trays to their fingers.

As I mingle with the guests, I sense the groundwork for a

wicked future is fomenting. Why would Unremarkable politicians be involved with a group of wealthy fae? Wherever crime and corruption converge, nefarious affairs gain a foothold. The hair on my neck stands up.

Unwilling to get into deep discussions, I make small talk and try to steer clear of my former selkie lover, Malcolm Scott, all night, which proves to be tough as nails. His long, jet-black hair and emerald green eyes are enticing. After my encounter with Rhys on the stairs, I'm barely holding it together as it is. I meander through the living room, bouncing from one conversation to the next, and end up on the balcony with Anwen Beddoe, who's nursing a gin and tonic.

"So, are you going to stay the night?" she asks, her Welsh accent seeping through.

"What? Why would you ask me that?" *Like it's her business?* I lean on the balcony and gaze at the moon's reflection on the ocean water.

"I mean, I know you sleep with Rhys. Figured you would want to try out his new bed. I'd stay if he weren't so hung up on you." She sips her drink and shoves her platinum blond strands behind an ear. "Tasty stuff he has. I am curious. Why would you date an Unremarkable, especially a cop? Seems like an odd choice after sleeping with one of us."

Has she told Rhys I ate dinner with Ollie? "Shouldn't you get back to work?" I ask, peering at her.

"You think we're so different, don't you? Fae or witch. We both fuck to get what we want." She sneers at me and goes back inside, leaving me to question myself. *Is she wrong?*

My phone vibrates in my clutch—a notification from Ollie.

OLLIE

How is Thursday for dinner at the waterfront?

> I'd love some seafood. It'll have to be after I close.

OLLIE

Brilliant. I'll pick you up. It's a bit of a walk there from Carroll Park.

No way he can come to the house. Nana will throw an herb jar if she finds out I'm dating an Unremarkable.

> Pick me up at the store at seven. I can't wait.

Chuffed to hear it. See you then.

When I walk back inside, the guests are gathering their belongings and sharing goodbyes with the host. The woman Rylee has been chatting with most of the night types something into her cell and passes it back to her. My friend smiles sheepishly and darts over to me.

"Got her phone number," she says, stuffing her cellphone in her pants pocket. "Her name is Isla Douglas."

"You realize she's probably a selkie, right?"

"Oh, suddenly it's a bad thing to sleep with fairies?"

"No, I just don't want you to get hurt. That's all."

"Well, Unremarkables and witches do a fine job of breaking hearts, too."

We head to the front doors. I managed to avoid Malcolm all night. I'll take that win. As I'm about to leave, Rhys rushes to the foyer.

"Wait, Fortune. I want to give you something."

Rylee points toward the courtyard. "I'll hang at the gate."

When she's gone, Rhys takes out his cell. "Give me your phone number."

"Maybe I don't want you to have it."

"Allow me to rephrase the question. May I have your

number? To send you a text. In case you ever need me for anything. Or Rylee wants to reach me."

I stand there, squinting. No way I should give it to him, but I do it for my friend. I snatch the phone from his hand and enter my number into a text. He types and pushes send. I recall what Jonathan said about the unusual magic he sensed near the portal.

"Something is awry at the lagoon. You wouldn't know anything about that, would you?" With his new status, maybe even the recent murders?

His mouth twitches. "Perhaps we could discuss it over dinner one evening."

Sure. When the Otherworld ceases to exist. "Goodnight, Rhys." As I walk toward the gate, his text vibrates on my phone.

RHYS

Thursday evening? 😕

Fuck my luck.

FOURTEEN

Norman has set up the materials for my ritual on the table, the circle of salt waiting for my intention. He scuttles to the mixture to light it. The pungent aroma travels through the garage as I dump the runestones on the table. The vague symbols fail to reach out to me, their meanings trapped inside the amethyst crystals. *What would Ivy do?*

"You're right, Norm. I have to stabilize my magic again in order to tackle the runestones. I wish my mom were here to guide me."

He lays a paw on my hand. "That makes two of us, my witch."

My cellphone dings and I grab it to turn it to vibrate. A breaking news notification lights up my screen: *"An unidentified person wearing a black hooded cape dragged a female runner into the lagoon, attempting to drown her. The victim is being treated at a local hospital. Her name is being withheld for her safety. The suspect is at large."*

"Shit. That could have been me." I set my phone on the table.

"Your face went pale, my witch. What has happened?"

"Last night after Jonathan and I split up, I encountered a homeless person near the causeway. Their hood covered their face, so I couldn't get a glimpse of them. The creep howled at me like an animal, then took off. That matches the description of the suspect in this article. He tried to drown someone."

"You were lucky, Fortune. You'd think the police in this city would do something about these murders."

"They're short on officers and can't be everywhere. I was extremely impressed with Ollie and his partner the other morning when we stumbled onto the victim at the beach. He cares so much he often puts his work ahead of his personal life. I hope the woman got a glimpse of the assailant's face. No time to process that now." I grab the selenite and obsidian wands. "Well, let's get this ritual done. Cam and Rylee will be here soon. It's been at least a week since Nana recharged the protection and suppression properties in my copper band. The universe willing, I'm back to my baseline of control and can duplicate my success. Here I go."

The aroma of the herbs enters my nostrils as I close my eyes, sending me into a trance-like state. As time stands still, I set my intention to rid my body of obstructive thoughts, more determined than ever to overcome the effects of this family curse. I wave the crystal wands over the smoking embers, siphoning strength from their properties. When I lift my lids, Norman's paws are radiating neon-green and surrounding me in an aura. I drop the wands.

"What were you doing?"

"Giving you a boost, my witch."

"You're the best, Norm."

He fluffs his hair. "I know."

"Well, let's see what happens during the practice session. I feel better, more confident than last time."

A text notification vibrates my phone. It's Rhys.

RHYS

You never replied to me about dinner.

That was intentional.

I may have information regarding the portal in the lagoon. You should come.

Shit. Either he's lying, or he really knows something.

???

Alright, but not Thursday.

Saturday night, then.

Fine. But I won't sleep with you.

My guard will let you in.

Going to that estate alone is probably a huge mistake. But I have to find out. The garage door swings open and Nana strolls in with Cam and Rylee close behind.

"Well, that's wonderful, Rylee," my grandmother says. "Does this mean you'll quit working at the framing store and devote your time to producing more art?"

"Oh, no. I wouldn't do that to Juan. He needs my help. I'll cut back my hours to part-time, though. Rhys of Dyf...I mean, Rhys Davies says he'll pay for me to have a private studio with more appropriate lighting, too."

"That's lit," Cam says. "Sounds like he was hiding his wealth, huh?"

"Maybe you underestimated the Tylwyth Teg, Fortune." Nana grabs a copper bowl from the shelf. "With all that money, you could do worse."

For fuck's sake, Betty. Where did his affluence come from? I don't comment because he's going to support Rylee's career. But I do worry about his motives.

"Something to think about, my witch," Norm pants, his tongue hanging out.

I glare at him. "Really, Norman? Hey, guys." I dump the sage and mugwort into the trash bin. "I hope you're excited about this session. It's not every day Nana is willing to share her witchcraft knowledge."

"I am," Cam says. "Miss Whittle, please be patient with me. I screw up a lot."

She pats his hand. "Don't you fret, young witch. You need proper instruction. Fortune was hardly the answer to that."

Rylee snickers and I bite my tongue. For the next hour, Nana shows them the basics of her witchcraft and philosophy, how to harness the energy from nature and one's inner witch energy. She models how to prepare herbs for spellcasting while Norman runs back and forth on the table to assist her.

My two friends mix the ingredients and chant incantations to manipulate objects. Cam is ecstatic about his success as he wields a garden spade around the garage, placing it on a hook on the far wall. Rylee swings a painter's brush through the air, the house kind, and drops it in a bucket.

"Such wonderful students," Nana says. "And fine witches. You'll make level three before you know it if you continue to work hard."

"I wonder if I could incorporate this as a style in my art?" Rylee taps on her chin.

Cam chuckles. "I want to use the skill to load my dishwasher like Miss Whittle."

"You'll find other uses," Nana says with a chuckle. "Next time, we'll work on transformation."

Cam's face lights up. "So cool. I can't thank you enough, Miss Whittle."

Norm pokes me with a paw. "Your turn, my witch."

"Is it wise to try?" Nana asks, raising her chin. "Have you completed a ritual recently?"

I clasp my suppression band. "I did right before you came, but I didn't remove my bracelet yet. Are you OK if I try?"

"Do it, Fortune," Cam says.

Rylee punches my arm. "Go for it. We're here in case you screw up."

I peer at Nana. The grimace on her face relays she doesn't trust me.

"Oh, Betty," Norm says, leaping next to her. "What's the worst thing that can go wrong that hasn't happened before?"

"Will you allow me to override the spell should things progress poorly?" she asks.

"Yes, Nana. You can help." Ouch. That hurt. I slide my bracelet off in increments until my arm is naked. I exhale with relief. "What would you like me to try? I brought a plant back to life the last time."

She gestures to the leather-bound grimoire on the shelf. "Take that tome and flip through the pages...without touching it, of course."

Manipulation. You would expect that to be much easier than reviving a succulent, but a spellbook has inherent magic sprinkled among its pages. She's challenging me. I don't know whether to be elated or angry. Rylee and Cam step back to give me space.

"Sure, Betty. No problem." But I'm scared shitless.

Whenever I've tried to manipulate objects in the past, they end up burning into a pile of ashes. I set my bracelet on the table and raise both hands, drawing on the energy from the spell mixture my friends used.

"Tome of spells, rise and fly, come to me now, and don't be shy." Snakes of amber seep from my fingertips as I pull on the grimoire. It floats off the shelf and tumbles a foot, but I catch it with my other hand. It hovers over the table and I turn the pages mid-air until I sense I'm losing my grip. The tome falls flat and my magic stretches out beyond my control. I snatch my copper band and shove it on my arm.

"As I expected." Nana crosses her arms. "You have made progress, Fortune. I want to commend you on that. But you'll never become competent as long as the curse lives within you." She lays a hand on my arm. "We need the coven. Rylee and Cam, talk to you at the next circle on Wednesday night. We'll take the Rolls-Royce." She grins and exits the garage.

Sure, try to impress Pam with your vintage car because your granddaughter is a worthless witch. I stare at the grimoire, a fiery glare in my eyes.

"Fortune, you did great," Cam says. "At least you didn't start a fire."

Rylee scowls at the door. "Don't let her bring you down. You've made awesome improvement."

"Listen to your friends, my witch." Norman closes the tome.

"No, she's right. She is always fucking right." I squeeze my copper band. "But once the coven succeeds in ridding me of this family curse, I'm out the door."

Who knows how many days, months, years that will take?

THE COVEN GATHERS in Pam Barrera's backyard under a luminous half-moon, bright stars glittering in the sky above—the perfect setting to run a circle. After reaching eighty degrees during the day, the night remains warm, and most of us are dressed in tees, shorts, and flip-flops. Not Pam. You'd never catch her in such informal attire. She's donning a classic black blouse and skirt. Nana is wearing capris. The sun hasn't seen her knees in two decades.

I have to admit. As much as I detested the idea of joining a coven, it's not all bad. I still don't know what I'm going to do if they want to join hands and cast a joint spell.

All the others are there: Joey Hernandez, Zara Harris, Heather Thompson, and Jonathan Walker, unfortunately. Nana, Rylee, Cam, and I bring the total to nine, but Izzy is supposed to join us this week, too. She's not present, and I agree with Zara's comments from the circle before. The teen is too young to be casting spells with the group. She is a neophyte and doesn't have a handle on basic witchcraft skills yet. But then who am I to talk?

Pam has a designated area with gravel for circles in one corner of her backyard. A permanent altar sits at the head—a source of energy and worship. A large magnolia tree stands majestically to the right, providing shade to a spacious patio during the day. Large hedges surround the property, hiding our witchy shenanigans from inquisitive neighbors. Jonathan checks the time on his phone.

"We should get started. I have an hour to spare tonight, and then I've got to go."

"Isabella is upstairs practicing her violin," Pam says. "She should be here any minute."

The backdoor to the house slams shut and Izzy rushes toward us. She arrives panting. "Sorry. I had to prepare for a performance test."

"I'm so proud of her," Pam says, smiling. "She was having so much trouble until she started practicing with her friend and receiving tutoring sessions from a senior in her high school orchestra. You should hear her now. She's playing so well."

The young neophyte witch blushes as she scans our faces, her gaze dropping to the floor when she locks eyes with me. It's understandable. She doesn't know me well. Rylee taps her foot on the gravel.

"Can we move along now?" Zara asks, air passing through her lips.

The coven leader grinds her teeth. "I call this meeting to order. Jonathan has a report of his findings regarding the spell we cast, and the analysis is not positive. But first, are there any last-minute items that need attention for Friday's festival?"

Joey's hand flies up. "I'll be working at the Java House booth most of the day. Come by for a complimentary cup of hot or iced coffee."

"Nice," Heather says. "I have a request. The trio I'm in will be performing transcribed dances and motets from the Renaissance period. I'd love it if someone could be there in case a gust of wind attacks our sheet music? We'll have clips, but it's hard to turn pages."

"Sure, I can help." Cam grins like a teenager who snagged his first date.

Heather nods. "Cool. Thanks. Talk to me beforehand."

Pam scans the group expectantly. "If there is nothing else, Jonathan will report on his findings. I could not attend due to"—she glances at her daughter and Izzy slides in her chair— "a family matter. However, Fortune met him there."

Jonathan steps forward into the circle. "Fortune's familiar was correct. The spell we cast was tampered with. The change in the water from salt to fresh is baffling but appears to be connected. I could not identify the origin of the magic involved."

"We should do something then," Zara says. "Cast another spell."

Nana interjects. "The inclination to fix what is there is always an admirable goal. Yet we're unlikely to accomplish much lacking the source of the manipulation."

"Then what?" Zara asks. "We allow it to fester without acknowledging what could happen?"

Joey shrugs. "I say, why not? Other than dead fish, what's happened there?"

For the next half hour, we debate the unknown threats of our city's portal, when they exist everywhere. Not to mention, there's another only thirty minutes up Pacific Coast Highway—what we locals refer to as the PCH.

Rylee has been quiet. Miss I-always-have-an-opinion has not uttered a word. Izzy hasn't contributed to the discussion either. In fact, she's been sneaking peeks at her cellphone when her mother's gaze was commanded elsewhere. Jonathan snatches a glance at his phone, too.

"Why don't we finish up here, Pam? I can't be late for this client. He's demanding."

"There isn't time for a full ritual," she says. "Why don't we join hands and chant the incantation of renewal? To celebrate our new members' commitment to our venture."

Oh, fuck. A rumbling of fear spreads in my stomach as the nausea builds. Cam and Rylee shift close to me while a grin straightens the wrinkles on Nana's face.

"Yes! We would love that!"

Betty, have you lost your mind?! The knots in my belly shift upward until I'm sure I'll spew my dinner. She pats my hand, nodding.

"But for a level of comfort, the four of us should stick together for tonight. If that's agreeable to you, Pam."

"Certainly, Betty. We want you to feel welcome. Zara, Heather, and...Cam. Would you get the candles from the altar and place them on the stump in the center of the circle?"

"That's a great idea," Zara says. "To establish a new partnership. Set us on a proper path."

Cam's face lights up as he accompanies Zara and Heather to the makeshift altar. They each pick up a candle: black, white, and red. They set them on the stump and return to the circle. I lean over and whisper in my grandmother's ear.

"What are you doing, Betty?"

"If we're casting as a group, they'll never notice you aren't adding to the energy. It'll be fine." She pats my hand.

Rylee whispers in my ear, "I got you." The whites of Cam's eyes shine in the dark. Apparently, he's not so sure. Neither am I.

Pam grasps Izzy's hand, smiling. "Join hands, everyone. We will recite the incantation and light the candles together. Flames of renewal, awake and rise. Send your embers to the indigo skies. Burn from sparks to a blaze full and bright. We call on our power to cast the flame with our might."

As we repeat the words of the fire renewal, we raise our hands as one. Amber tentacles seep from others' fingers while I pretend to add to our joint venture, my deficiency hidden by Nana and Rylee. I hold my breath, begging the universe to stay with me long enough to get through this. Their magic combines, floating until it leaps to the candles. But the electric-like witchery collapses.

"What happened?" Joey asks. "We've performed that renewal dozens of times."

"Someone didn't cast their magic?" Zara says, peering at the coven leader's daughter.

"Who?" Pam glances across the circle at us. I'm about to puke.

Izzy jumps up. "I have to pee." She darts off toward the house.

"Get back here, young lady!" her mother shouts. "That is not how you leave a circle!"

Joey chuckles. "When you gotta go, you gotta go."

We all burst out laughing, except Zara. She is not amused. Pam stares at the candles, shaking her head. I realize Isabella isn't to blame, but I have to let her mom believe she's the culprit. It tugs at my heart. I know what it's like to feel that kind of pressure to perform witchcraft from a loved one you want so badly to impress.

"We'll have plenty of opportunities for renewal in the future," Jonathan says, peering at me.

Rylee squeezes my hand and I swallow my impending doom.

Pam ambles toward the tree stump and picks up a candle. "We shall meet on Friday at 10:00 a.m. It is done."

Rylee and Cam can walk with Nana. I dash ahead, leaving the yard through the side gate to the car, and catch my breath. As I lean on the Rolls-Royce, I thank the gods I didn't vomit all over the circle. I wave to Joey as he leaves, but Zara rushes to me.

"Hey, Fortune. I know we didn't get off to a good start last week, and I am happy you returned. I was hard on you because I'm leery of solitary witches. They tend to put themselves first. The truth is, we're stronger with the four of you in the coven. I hope you stay after the festival is over. But..." She glances back, as if to inspect who's watching. Rylee, Cam, and Nana are walking in our direction. "I watched your reactions tonight. You have reservations about Izzy, too. Would you meet me for coffee at the Java House tomorrow morning?"

How strange she's confiding in me. What is her angle? "Sure. I can do that. Send me a text. Get my number from Joey."

"I will. Thanks, Fortune."

As I drive us home in the Rolls, we ride in silence while I contemplate Zara's unusual request. I think we're all just relieved everyone believed the incompetent witch was Isabella. After parking the car in the garage, we drag our feet to the back porch.

Norman jumps off the bench onto the top step. "How did it go?"

"We recited an incantation of renewal," Cam says.

My morkie's ears stand at attention. "Oh, let me guess. That did *not* go as expected."

"No, it did not," I say, grasping my bracelet. "The candles failed to ignite, so everyone knew someone wasn't casting."

Rylee shakes her leg violently. "Pam thought it was Izzy because she had to run into the house to pee. I think she was nervous."

Norm rolls on his back, guffawing, and leaps to his feet. "Lucky for you, my witch."

"I'm elated you're so entertained by my failures, familiar." I swipe my hand down my face.

"It's fine," Nana says. "We only have to hide your issue for a short time. Just until we build solid friendships with them."

"Because it's better to use your friends than strangers?" I roll my eyes at her.

"I've gotta get home," Cam says. "Catch you tomorrow at the store, Fortune."

Rylee taps my arm. "Me too, Blondie. I'll call you."

"Night, guys." My friends walk through the gate and Nana heads up the steps to the porch.

"Are you coming, Fortune?" she asks, opening the door.

I gaze at the flickering stars. They waver like my future. "No, I'm gonna rest out here for a minute with Norm and soak in the universe."

The door shuts as I sit on the top step. My loyal morkie levitates on a haze of green next to me and I run my hand along the back of his head.

"I was petrified tonight. I thought Pam would figure out it was me."

"What will you do next time, my witch? I doubt her daughter will have the sudden urge to pee again."

I peer at my diminutive familiar and smile. "Norm, I have an idea."

FIFTEEN

Thursday morning, it's near eighty again, and the intense SoCal sun beats down on the back of my arms as I cycle to meet up with Zara Harris. The skies are the color of blue California lilacs. There isn't a sign of a cloud in sight. I hop off my racer, lock it to the bike rack, and pull my tee down over my linen dress shorts.

When I enter Java House, Joey tosses a friendly smile. "Good morning. Zara is at the back table in the corner. What can I get you?"

"I may need the rush from both sugar and caffeine. Give me a mocha latte."

After a couple of minutes, he slides the mega cup to me and I insert my credit card into the terminal. "Did she tell you why she wants to meet with me?"

"Well, it's hardly a secret. Zara is vying to be coven leader one day, but now..."

"Oh..." I pull out my card. "Why talk with me about it?"

"You're kidding, right? Your ancestral history. She already has

Izzy to contend with, and now you show up. She's probably trying to get ahead of the extra competition."

"Well, that's ridiculous." If he knew how much. I throw a dollar into the tip jar. "Thanks for the latte."

"You're welcome. Have fun with that." He gestures toward the back.

I pick up my over-priced mocha and head to the table. Zara waves when she sees me. I sit down across from her and take a sip of my latte. She takes a swig of her coffee from a portable mug.

"Thanks for coming. I have a session with a client in thirty minutes, so I'll try to be succinct."

"You usually are. I'm gonna be honest here because you're giving me the benefit of the doubt. Joey filled me in a little on your concerns, and I understand."

She peers over my shoulder at him and flips him the bird. "Words slide out of his mouth like a stripper down a dance pole."

"He's a good guy, though, and careful." I sip my mocha latte, recalling the time he hid me in the back room to avoid Malcolm Scott after our one-night stand.

She chuckles. "He knows I'm messing with him. I trust him with my life. We've been friends for ten years and harnessed our witchcraft together before accepting Pam's invitation to her coven. The question is, can I depend on you to keep this conversation between us? I am taking an enormous risk talking with you behind her back."

"You barely know me, Zara. Other than the visits to the store, you have last week's interaction to judge me on. You certainly didn't respond well to my outburst."

Her head bobs left and right. "Joey may have filled me in on your past with Jonathan. I told you he confides in me."

"What you say to me, I'll keep to myself, except for Rylee. I share everything with her, but she would never break my confidence. If you're good with that, then talk away."

She gulps down another swig of coffee and leans on the table. "Here's the issue in a nutshell. I agreed to join the coven and bring Joey and our level three abilities to the group based on the agreement I could take over as leader one day. Izzy had her Sweet Sixteen birthday party, and now Pam thinks she's ready to cast spells in the circle, which is a huge fucking mistake, if you ask me. I have no issues with her participating in spell castings to develop her skills. We all want her to thrive. But now her mom is pushing her, like the damn violin. She can't stand her daughter not being first at everything. What's stopping her from appointing Izzy to assume the position down the road?"

"And now I show up, a witch with a famous ancestry." I lean back. "You're threatened by me, too."

"Don't get me wrong. It's awesome we've added experienced witches to the coven. Joey says I shouldn't worry about you. Yet... Did you agree to join under the same premise? Did she promise you the leadership?"

Shit. With my curse, it never occurred to me any member of the coven would view me as competition. I crack up, nearly knocking my cup off the table. I grab a napkin to wipe up the spill.

She grimaces. "You think that's funny?"

If you only knew the truth. "I'm sorry. I swear on my mother's ashes, which are scattered in an East Coast woodland, by the way, that I have no desire to lead this coven. Pam begged me to join for years, and I refused." I hesitate. "Personal reasons. Nana convinced me to say yes this time."

Zara falls back against her chair. "Well, that's a relief because Izzy will never become a decent leader. Pam has indulged that girl, giving in to her pleas to join the circle before she was ready. Good leadership comes from dealing with hardships of some kind. You have to know how to make sacrifices."

"What do you want from me now that you know I have no aspirations for the job?"

Zara twists her mouth. "We need to convince Pam that Izzy's too young to take things seriously. Look at what happened at the circle. Too inexperienced to follow through on a simple renewal casting."

Except that was me. "She was probably nervous."

"True, but that alone proves my point. Will you back me should the situation get ugly?"

Would she ask me if she knew Nana's entire reason for joining the coven was to harvest their witchcraft knowledge? I don't think so. Plus, it wasn't Izzy. I shift in my seat.

"I doubt anything horrible will come of her participation, but sure. If it's an act that's detrimental to us or the community, you can count on me." I finish my mocha.

Zara slaps the table and stands. "I have to go, but I'm glad we talked. You're not what I expected, Fortune. I imagined you'd be... arrogant."

"That would require me to think highly of myself." I pick up my cup and place it in the dish bin.

"We'll see about that when you finally cast a spell on your own. We can see for ourselves whether the rumblings of your family history ring valid."

"Don't get your hopes up," I say.

"Talk to you at the festival." She heads out of Java House, slapping hands with Joey before exiting.

I smile at my favorite barista on the way out and head to work, thinking I could have avoided all this drama by remaining a solitary witch.

Customers flow in and out of the store all afternoon until I'm ready to squash the chime on the door. You'd think the time would pass quickly, like the blink of an eye. Instead, every time I glance at the vintage clocks on the wall, only ten minutes have passed. By six, the shoppers have dwindled to nothing.

"Gabby, why don't you head home?" I glance out the window. "I think the deluge is done. You'll still get your hours. Spend some time with your family."

"Thank you, Fortune. The problem is…if I show up early, Carlos may not cook dinner." She chuckles and picks up her purse. "We can make it together."

"Enjoy your day off tomorrow. Remember, I'm closing the store for the Summer Solstice Festival. A paid holiday."

"And I appreciate it. Have a wonderful evening, Cameron."

"Bye, Gabby," Cam says, moving behind the counter.

"No, you don't. You should pack and log out, too. No one is gonna come now. It's empty on the sidewalk. If you want to practice the craft, go to the house and work with Norman. I'll let Nana know you're coming. I bet she even finds her way out there, too."

"OK. That sounds lit." He grabs his backpack from the hook. "Where does she think you're going? In case she brings it up, I don't want to blow your cover."

"I hate asking you to lie for me. It's not fair. I told her I'm spending the evening at Rylee's discussing what she needs for her new art studio Rhys is funding."

"Oh, I don't mind. But aren't you a little old to keep this up? Just tell her. Let her have a tantrum and move on. What's the worst that could happen?"

"Her response won't be pretty and isn't worth the argument if this ends up being a couple of dates. Have you or your brother told your parents you're a witch?"

He laughs as he opens the door. "Fuck no. Have an awesome time, Fortune."

"Thanks, Cam. Good luck with your training."

The cuckoo clock finally strikes seven and I turn the sign to closed. Ollie pulls up in his SUV. I set the alarm, lock the door, and hop into the passenger side, adjusting my crossbody bag. He's dressed casually in a tight T-shirt and jeans, revealing his toned muscles. That alluring smile appears and a warm, fuzzy feeling rushes over me. He checks his mirrors and heads toward downtown.

"How was your day?"

"Busy. Had a steady stream of customers all afternoon. Good thing because the store is closed tomorrow. Cam and I will be at the Summer Solstice Festival. I thought about renting a vendor spot, but I'm helping a local pagan group with the activities."

"Actually, I've never been, despite the festival being an annual event. I hope you have a cracking time."

Part of me wants to tell him they're also a coven, but I'd have to answer all the questions that would ensue. Lots of people who identify as witches don't actually have supernatural skills. Without divulging the reality about our magic, pagan and witch are synonymous to Unremarkables. They imagine we play with crystals, herbs, and tarot cards or light incense and candles to meditate—make-believe in their eyes. If I told him the truth, he'd contact mental health services.

Once we arrive at the waterfront and park, we get a table outside with a coastal view. It's not as fabulous as the view from Rhys's luxury beachfront property, but who cares?

We order our meals and sip our wine while we wait. I watch a large boat pull out of its slip, wondering if Rhys has purchased a yacht, too.

"You appear to be elsewhere in thought?" he asks. "Care to share?"

I return my gaze to his expressive cognac eyes. "Admiring the boats, but you're more intriguing."

"Me? I can't imagine what you find fascinating."

His hair flits in the ocean breeze, and I soak in his humility. Is he actually this modest? I slump back.

"Really? You're a head detective. You search for clues to solve crimes. It must be rewarding to help people find justice for their family members and to make this city a safer place to live."

"Except when it's beyond your control." He takes another sip of wine.

"Are you referring to the recent drownings?"

"And the attack last night. We can't get a break in this case. Even with the most recent victim."

"I read the article in the newspaper. Couldn't she identify the person?"

"Well, yes. But it's not reliable. Her description made no sense."

"What do you mean?"

He leans forward, folding his arms on the table. "I shouldn't be discussing this with you, but...I can't stop thinking about it."

"You can tell me, Ollie." I reach across the table and clasp his hand. "I won't share it with anyone, not even Rylee."

He scratches the back of his head with the other hand. "I think the attack traumatized her so much she can't recall her attacker's description correctly."

"What makes you think that?" I ask, pulling my hand back.

"She said when he first spoke to her, he was an extremely attractive man with long dark hair. Then he removed his hooded black cape. She remarked he was covered in seaweed, and, all of a sudden, his face morphed into something grotesque."

Oh, fuck. "You mean like...shifted into a new face?"

"Yes, actually. Completely bonkers, no?"

Not if you knew about shifter fae. But why would a selkie commit murders like this?

"Sure sounds like trauma."

"And there are rumblings of a new criminal organization forming in the city. Corruption of the rich never ceases."

Is he referring to Rhys Davies and the fae? "Like who?"

"I'm sorry. That I absolutely cannot share. For your safety if for no other reason."

"That's alright. Better I not know." *Or should I find out?*

"Oh, I'm just knackered from it all." He tousles his hair and exhales.

A soft chuckle breaks free, and then I laugh out loud. "I'm sorry."

He cocks his head, grimacing. "You find murder and other crime comical."

"No," I say, clawing back my inappropriate outburst. "Your choice of words. Knackered made me chuckle."

His head falls back. "It's bad enough my buddies on the force torment me over my proper English. 'Et tu, Brute?'"

"You see, I never get that kind of sophisticated humor from American dates. I'm lucky if they can quote a TV show."

He grins at me and my insides turn to mush. I like this guy way more than I should. Our dinner arrives and we lay our napkins across our laps.

"Enough of business. I ruined one relationship by obsessing over work. I don't want to ruin this one before it has barely begun." He downs the rest of his wine.

"It's alright, Ollie." I reach across the table and clasp his hand. "If you can't share your distress with someone who's supposed to care about you, then what good are they?"

He squeezes my hand back. "I don't want to fuck this up, Fortune. I've had such a difficult time finding someone genuine like you."

Oh, shit. My gut twists into knots as I sit across from him, hiding a secret life. "I think the murders are horrible, and I hope you find the person. Vent to me as much as you want."

We exchange affectionate glances of understanding while we enjoy our meal. Although the topic of discussion shifts to tomorrow's festival downtown, I can't rid my head of his comments about the collaboration of the rich and corrupt. After dinner, Ollie suggests we take a walk on the beach trail to work off the effects of the wine. Being a do-things-by-the-book police officer, he won't drive until the alcohol has passed through his system.

Hues of orange and yellow streak the sky, topped with midnight-blue above. We stroll along the water and he entwines his fingers with mine, occasionally nudging me and chuckling at my corny jokes. When the trail becomes empty, he stops and pulls me to him. He strokes my cheek and bends down to kiss me. I urge him on as I slide my hands to his back. His jeans swell against me, and I wish we were at his house so I could drag him to his bedroom.

Is this why Ivy fell in love with my father? Did she crave this simple life without the trappings of magic? Because I'm ready to jump in headfirst and not look back. Ollie clasps my hand again, and we continue down the trail. It's been so long since a man shared his affection with me so subtly, yet it says everything about him.

By the time we've made it past the lifeguard station, the sun has set and an ominous marine layer has rolled in early, darkening the path. The moon weaves in and out, struggling to pull back the murky clouds, and the lampposts on top of the bluff in the park cast the only light. Over a mile away from the shore, the THUMS Islands, created to house oil drilling, illuminate the gloomy sky.

The normally gentle waves of Long Beach become choppier as the wind picks up. A man screams from the shoreline, but it's garbled by the breaking of the swelling surf. The ocean's edge is nearly two hundred feet from the trail, and the darkness obscures the area.

"What was that?" I ask, squinting.

"Probably a fight breaking out; drunks having a row."

"Do you need to go check it out?"

"If I stopped to break up every brawl in this city, I'd never get home. Let them work it out themselves."

We take a few more steps and the man yells out again. "Heeelp!"

"Stay here, Fortune." Ollie darts toward the water.

The adrenaline sends my heart into a raging tachycardia. "Not on your life!"

I run on the sand after him as my surroundings grow tenebrous. Obscured by the misty haze, bodies wrestle, and I can't discern who is who. A person nearing six feet in height shoves the man into an ocean wave. When their arm submerges into the saltwater, they roar in pain, and a shimmering light emanates from their extremity. I finally recognize Ollie as he attempts to yank the assailant off the victim, but the attacker in the hooded cloak smacks their hand against my date, sending him flying.

"Ollie!" I run to the water and beat the aggressor on the back. They whip their arm toward me with similar force, but I end up on my butt a few feet away. My copper band illuminates like a glow stick.

The attacker stomps toward me, their shoes sinking into the wet sand, and flings their hood back, revealing a woman of astonishing beauty. Her arm glistens where she appears wounded. In seconds, her face morphs into a monstrous visage of evil, her eyes gleaming a brilliant white. She roars at me and takes off down the trail in the direction of the peninsula.

Oh, shit.

SIXTEEN

I dash to Ollie where he's rolling to his side to get up. As he moans and rubs his torso, I drop to the sand.

"Are you hurt?" I inspect his face in the blackness.

He grunts as he stands. "Bloody hell." He motions toward the ocean's edge. "The victim. We have to get to him."

"You shouldn't walk. I'll go."

"Got the wind knocked out of me, but I'm fine. What a swing from a woman. She must be strung out on meth. Unfortunately, I didn't get a proper gander at her face."

"Yeah, probably." The easiest explanation for now.

Ollie pulls out his cellphone and enters 911. "This is Detective Oliver Prescott off duty. There's been an attempted drowning. Send an ambulance and a unit to Toyon Avenue. Follow the trail north past the lifeguard station. I'm assessing the victim now. I have a friend with me." He ends the call as we discover the victim lying face down but out of the water. "Help me roll him over." After moving the young man onto his back, he leans close to his mouth. "Shit. Step away, Fortune."

I do as he asks and give him the space he needs to perform

CPR. He pinches the man's nose and blows into his mouth several times, then switches to his chest, pumping his arms vigorously as sweat drips down the side of his face. Sirens blare in the distance, and I raise my head. Red, blue, and white lights flash at the bottom of Toyon Avenue. I feel helpless. If only I could tap into my magic. But would I use it in front of Unremarkables? I stare at my bracelet and recall the symbol emitting a glow. Did it save me? And the time before?

The young man coughs, water and vomit escaping his mouth. Ollie rolls him onto his side. "Fuck. I thought I'd lost him." He rubs the man's side. "What's your name, sir?"

"Jimmy...James Smith. She said she liked me."

"Remain still, James. An ambulance is on the way."

I squat next to Ollie and caress his arm. "That was amazing. You saved that man's life."

"Maybe. I hope he's able to identify the woman, because I doubt I can." He takes his phone out and texts someone. Shortly after, he receives a notification. "I sent a message to Manny. He was already on the way here."

The emergency medical technicians arrive with a stretcher that has all-terrain wheels for the sand. Police officers trail them from behind. Ollie shares what actions he used to revive the young victim and leaves them to their work. His colleagues approach him—a woman in her forties and a man in his thirties.

"You'll need to share what you remember," he says. "Do the best you can."

"It's dark, Ollie. I didn't get a good look at her." I hate lying to him.

He caresses my arm. "Share what you can. Sometimes memories come back to you later. This was a traumatic event, and you should talk with someone."

"I lost my mother as a child. Nothing will ever top that,

Ollie." Although tripping over a dead body comes close. But I can't tell him that.

The two officers take my statement and Ollie's as the EMTs load Jimmy onto the stretcher and roll him toward the trail. I stretch the truth, telling them it was too dark to identify her characteristics. It wasn't a complete lie. She had no facial features—just a blob for a face. While we're finishing our statements, a forensic team arrives and sets up portable spotlights to inspect the area. What started as an intimate date has ballooned into an all-out investigation with uninvited guests. His partner Manny arrives, panting. He grabs Ollie and hugs him, patting him on the back.

"You just can't stop working, can you, dude? The motherfucker could have killed you." Ollie winces, clutching his ribcage. "I bet you didn't let the EMTs look at you, did you? You probably cracked a rib. Makes me wanna crack another."

Ollie laughs and grabs his torso again. "You remember Fortune Whittle?"

"Yeah. Wish we were meeting again under better circumstances."

"Me too, but I'm glad you're here," I say.

My date caresses my arm. "Fortune, I'm going to be here fairly late. Manny, could you drop her home for me?"

"Sure thing. I'll be waiting on the trail, Fortune." He kicks up sand as he plods toward the path.

Ollie embraces me, moaning. "I'm sorry I put you through this. You could have gotten hurt. I should have let it go. I wouldn't be surprised if you never wanted to see me again."

"No. Then that young man would be dead." I peer up at him. "You're a good person. One of the best I've ever met. Please go to the emergency room and get checked."

He grins. "So, now I have two mother hens? Manny is bad enough." He leans down to kiss me. "I'll talk to you tomorrow."

"Goodnight, Ollie."

I catch up with Manny and follow him to his four-door sedan as reporters descend onto the beach. I stare out the window on the ride to Carroll Park, mulling over the events of this horrendous night. Nana is going to read about the attempted murder in the morning. If my name shows up in the news, what do I say? I text Rylee and fill her in, in case my grandmother talks to her.

RYLEE

That's horrifying. Do you think Rhys knows who this being is?

You can bet your ass I'm gonna ask him Saturday night.

"Fortune, that was some pretty ugly shit to witness," Manny says. "Would you like to talk to a professional? I have the phone number of the Trauma Center."

"Thanks, but I'll be alright. I have someone I can vent to when I get home."

"I have a card if you need it." He pulls his car next to the curb. "Ollie hurt something awful when his ex took off. I haven't seen him this happy since... All I wanna say is, don't string him along. Oh, and I've got a gun." He lifts his hoodie, exposing a holster.

I chuckle. "I promise I won't do that. Make sure he gets to the ER."

"If I have to drag him in there kicking and screaming."

"Thanks for the ride, Manny," I say, exiting the car.

I run up the driveway to the house and sneak in, avoiding the creak in the hallway flooring. What a relief. Nana went to sleep early. When I enter my room, I collapse on the bed and moan. Norm recites an incantation and levitates to my mattress.

"Well, did you do the deed tonight?" He waggles his whiskers.

"No, did you not hear the sirens in the past hour? My date turned into attempted murder."

His eyes bulge out like a chihuahua's. "You tried to kill the detective? There was surely an easier way to avoid sleeping with him, my witch."

"For fuck's sake, Norm. No." I slap my hands on my face. "We have a big fucking problem..."

I spend the following fifteen minutes sharing the night's tragedy, the reaction of my copper band, and the revelation of a murderess shifter fairy in our midst. Norman's ears stick straight up. When I'm finished, he shifts next to me.

"Your bracelet most likely gave you protection. What will you do, Fortune? Surely, you must tell the detective."

"How? I'd have to expose all the fae and the true nature of the witches living here. Ollie would never believe me." I sit up on the edge of the bed. "We have to solve this ourselves."

"How do you propose *we* do that, my witch?"

"I mean, we as in the coven, which includes Betty." I bite my lower lip. "She can't know I went on a date with Ollie, especially since I lied and said I was going to Rylee's. This incident will be in all the papers tomorrow. Luckily, I didn't speak to any reporters."

I grab my phone from my crossbody bag, still hanging across my chest, and open my contacts. I tap on Rhys's name.

"What will you tell Betty, then?" He leaps to the floor, floating partway, and scuttles to the door, resting his alert ear near the frame.

"I'll say I took a walk along the beach to get some steps in. She knows how obsessed I am with getting my exercise in. There will be some scolding. It's not a complete lie."

He recites his levitation incantation once more and lands next to me. Peeking at my phone, he reads the screen. "Are you going to call the Tylwyth Teg?"

I close the app. "No, I'll wait until I visit him next. Calling him now only encourages him to contact me."

"Do you think he's involved? Could he have a reason to send a shifter fairy after humans in the city?"

"I don't know, but I'm gonna squeeze it out of him if I have to."

"That may require more than asking questions, my witch. Are you prepared to...entice him?"

I amble to the patio door and stare at the threatening clouds. "I'll do whatever I have to do. That being could have killed Ollie, and it's already murdered so many. No more sleeping in. I'm going to get up early and perform the cleansing ritual every day and practice with Ivy's runestones. I may have merely a few minutes to use my magic, but that's more than zero."

Norman scuttles over to me. "It's about fucking time, my witch."

By eleven on Friday, the marine layer gives way to another perfect sunny day with a temp in the low 70s. Could it be any better? Yes. It would have been more pleasant not to wake up to a newsfeed article about an attempted murder by a deranged woman on drugs—especially because I know she wasn't. At least my name didn't appear in the story. I'm energized from my cleansing ritual, but the runestones were vague as always. All I can do is keep trying.

All the vendors for the Summer Solstice Festival have set up on both sides of the bike path that cuts through the Japanese-style park. It contains a man-made body of water with a pedestrian bridge and lots of ornamental trees. In the distance, people ride in the swan boats, pedaling.

Surprisingly, the Summer Solstice Festival is a well-attended event every year, sponsoring rituals, workshops, and local stores. It gives the community an opportunity to experience what we're all about in a family-oriented setting and shows them we aren't that different. We eat, sleep, and go to work like anyone else. Unremarkables don't need to know we hide magic up our sleeves. I attended many times in the past but never volunteered to help. Nana decided it was best to lie low and not bring attention to us. That philosophy of isolationism changed after the incident at the lagoon.

I steer clear of Pam most of the day. She decided to rent a booth for her store at the last minute, and Izzy is with her. Joey is working the Java House vending truck, and Cam is turning pages for Heather while she performs with a trio under a nearby tree. The rest of us take turns running the information table and handing out pictures for children to color.

Izzy wanders by and I chase after her. "Hey, Isabella. How are you doing?"

"OK, I guess. Why are you talking to me?"

I peer back at Pam's booth. "You seemed upset at the circles. I wanted you to know if you ever want to talk to someone, I'm a good listener. Moms can be demanding."

Her eyes inspect my face, checking for sincerity, I suspect. "She wants me to be the best at everything. It's impossible without using witchcraft. It's why I asked to join the coven early."

Ahh, that explains a lot. "When did the push to improve your violin performance begin?"

She frowns. "In May after the spring concert. She found out I'm in the second violin section." A notification rings on her phone—a short melody from a classical symphony. She reads it and smiles. "I found someone to teach me at the end of May. I'm improving quickly."

"The person in your high school orchestra?"

She hesitates. "Yeah. He plays so well. And he's so cute. I really like him." She has a crush on this boy. That explains a lot. "I have to go. Mama wants her lunch."

"It was great chatting with you. Call me if you ever need to talk."

"Thank you, Miss Whittle."

"You can call me Fortune, Isabella."

Izzy runs toward the food vendor truck and I return to the information table. That girl is going to snap if Pam doesn't let up. You can't push the acquisition of witchcraft skills. At least the violin lessons are going well and she's made a new friend.

After two hours of constant questions from patrons, Rylee motions to me. "I'm getting tired. Let's go grab a coffee. Anyone else want one?"

"I'd love an iced vanilla latte," Zara says.

Jonathan shakes his head. "I'll pass. I've met my quota for today. The caffeine will make me tense."

I quash a laugh. The man was born wound as a clock. This demeanor didn't help our past relationship either. It's not a shock he's a financial broker and advisor. "How about you, Nana?"

"No, the weather is too warm out for me to drink coffee," she says. "But you go ahead."

My grandmother nods toward Zara as I walk out of the booth, reminding me I need to divulge to someone what I witnessed last night. I catch Zara's attention and wave for her to come closer where Jonathan is out of earshot. She drops fliers onto the table and strolls over.

"What's up? Do you need money? I thought the coffee was on the house."

"It is. I'm not ready to share this with the entire coven yet, but I had to tell someone. Since we have a mutual agreement, I'll disclose something to you."

Zara's head tilts to the left. "Sounds important. Are you sure you don't want Pam to join us?"

"No," I say. "Not until I know more. Do you agree with that?"

She squints at me. "Sure. This must be damn good."

"Once you hear her, I think you'll agree it's not," Rylee says.

"You heard about the commotion on the beach last night?" I ask.

Zara nods. "Yeah. They think some woman was drugged out of her mind on meth. What's that got to do with us?"

"I was there and witnessed what happened. It wasn't a woman. I believe it was some kind of shifter fairy."

She grimaces. "What makes you think that? Because she was near the water?"

"No," Rylee says. "Because Fortune said her face melted."

Zara's face twitches. "What the fuck? Are you sure that's what you saw?"

"Yes," I say. "And her arm was glistening weirdly. I think she was wounded after shoving her hand in the water trying to drown that dude."

"As far as I know, the fae have been living with us peacefully. This sounds like one of them needs to get with the program. You need to tell the others now, Fortune." She glances back at the information booth.

"I'm having dinner with a prominent Tylwyth Teg in the community. Let me see what I can glean from him."

"OK, the coven doesn't meet again until the first Thursday in July. That gives you time." She crosses her arms. "But why would he cough up information about his community to you?"

Rylee jumps in to save me as usual. "He's the same guy who is sponsoring my art studio. We've known him for a while. If he knows something, I think he'll tell her."

"Thank you, Zara," I say. "I'll let you know what I find out."

"Why were you down on the beach?" she asks.

I gulp and glance at my best friend. "I left Rylee's and took a walk to clear my head."

My defender crosses her arms. "I told her it was a bad idea, but Fortune never listens to me."

"That tracks. I'd better get back before they suspect we're plotting something." Zara heads toward the information booth, shouting, "Don't forget my iced latte!"

"Do you trust her?" Rylee asks as we stroll to the Java House truck.

"I have to, or I'm fucked every which way."

"Facts, Blondie."

We arrive at the truck and put in our order. Joey is busy as ever. After filling the order, he pokes his head out.

"I saw you chatting with Zara. What was that all about? And don't tell me you were chatting about lattes."

"You'll hear about it at the next circle in July. Too much to share now, and we have to get these coffees back."

"Sure, but I know when I'm getting the runaround." He gestures at the booths. "Hey, don't look now, but Mr. Hot Stuff Detective is strolling this way."

Rylee grabs two of the coffees. "What?"

I turn around to find Ollie winding through the bike path between the vendors and walking straight toward us, dressed in sweats. As he passes the information booth, my heart thumps against my ribcage. "Oh, fuck my luck."

"Yeah, your luck is definitely fucked," Joey says, snickering. "Betty has an unobstructed view. Why is he here, though? Didn't you say he cracked a rib?"

Ollie searches the crowds until he makes eye contact with me at the truck and waves. He continues to stroll at a laborious pace, a hand nursing his torso, and my heart rate increases with each step he takes toward me.

"What are you going to do, Blondie?" Rylee asks as the ice in Zara's drink melts.

I peer over at the information booth where Nana is preoccupied with a visitor. "She's busy. We're good."

Ollie finally arrives, winded and in obvious pain. "I felt as if I were moving in slow motion walking to you. Nice to see you again, Rylee."

"You too," she says. "I'd better get this to Zara. Sorry about your injury."

"Thank you. You should have dinner with us sometime."

"Sounds good. Later," she says, walking away.

"What are you doing here?" I ask, snatching a glance at Nana.

"It won't be announced for a couple of days, but it appears we've caught the female attacker from last night. I thought it best to tell you in person."

"What?" I flinch and coffee spurts out the top of my cup. "You said you didn't get a good look at her?"

"No, but James identified her. He wasn't one hundred percent sure, but she confessed. The woman who was attacked at the lagoon identified her assailant as a man, but now she isn't certain. It was dark and she was traumatized by the incident. So, this case may or may not be unrelated." He caresses my arm. "I was worried about you."

When I peer at the information booth, Nana's eyes are locked on us. "I'm alright." I step back and wipe the top of my cup with a napkin. "Are you OK? Shouldn't you be home resting?"

"I'm on the way there. Left the urgent care clinic." He moves closer. "I'll call you later."

"Oh, I may not answer. I have a business meeting with someone." I take a sip of my latte.

Joey shouts from the truck, "Hey, handsome! Want a coffee for the road? You look like you could use one." He winks at me.

"Sure." Ollie grabs the large cup from my savior. "Thanks, Joey." That should keep his hands full.

Nana is watching us like a hawk, or a controlling grandmother. "You've been up all night. You should go home and sleep. Please take it easy?"

"I don't have a choice because I've been put on light duty. I may be out of commission for a few weeks, but I'll be in touch. Manny is handling this case while I heal. Enjoy the rest of the festival, Fortune."

"Thanks for coming to check on me, Ollie."

He smiles and makes his way toward the bike path.

"Shit. Thank you for distracting him, Joey. I worried he might kiss me goodbye."

"You're welcome, hon. But maybe you should fess up and stop all the secrecy. Take it from me. There's nothing to be gained by hiding in a closet."

He's never had to live with Betty.

SEVENTEEN

As I complete my cleansing ritual, Norman shuffles back and forth on the table, clearing the surface of the bowl, used herbs, and other tools of the craft. I lay the crystal wands aside and breathe deeply. For the first time, I don't tremble removing my suppression band. I set it on the altar within my grasp and pick up my mom's runestones carefully stored in their velvet bag.

"I feel naked without my bracelet but also...free. By the way, Rylee told Betty that Ollie showed up at the festival to follow up on what I had witnessed the night before."

"Quick thinking on her part, but that was a close one, Fortune."

"I'm going to tell her, eventually. My mind can't fit one more thing in there right now. I have dinner with Rhys tonight and I have to leave space for that. Talk me through how Ivy would prepare the stones, Norm."

He scuttles to the end of the table and raises a paw. "If I remember correctly, it's the small grimoire on the top shelf, the one Betty has buried under a mountain of regret."

"I wondered why that tome was shoved under those boxes." I slide a step stool to the shelf and pull out the grimoire. "What now?"

"Open it, my witch."

Norman waves a spray of faint green over the tome and it flies out of my hands, landing on the table with a thud. Pages flip one after the other as holographic words and symbols glow in bright yellow. They spring from the parchment, swirling and dancing in the air.

"What the fuck? What is this, Norman?"

He grins and his whiskers shimmer. "It was your mother's, Fortune. Ivy's incantations and sigils. Her short lifetime of witchcraft exists in this journal."

"All these years, and it's been collecting dust on that shelf? Why didn't you tell me about her grimoire before?"

He gazes at me, his eyes tearing up. "Because you weren't ready. You let your grandmother define you from the time you were a child. Although you professed to make decisions on your own, you acquiesced to her demands. I knew one day you would find your center. I knew you'd find the confidence to tackle your curse on your own—and push back Betty. How I lived for this day."

I approach my mother's living journal, mesmerized by the dancing images. I extend my hand to touch them but jerk it back, fearful of what my cursed magic will spark.

"Don't do that, Fortune. Do not return to your insecurities. You must move forward."

I breathe in, suppressing my fear, and grab at the holographic symbols. They fall like tumbling dice as the pages settle flat. I slide a finger across the ink of my mom's handwriting. A faint voice rings out.

"Fortune..."

"Mom? Is she in there, Norman?"

"No, my witch. But the essence of her is. Her personal spells are contained within the bindings. You will begin with the one she used for divination with the runestones. It was her secret to deciphering their messages."

I flip page after page, passing spells of protection, healing, enchantment, and transfiguration, with obvious influences from Nana. An entire section contains incantations for the erasure of curses and hexes, scribbles marking through some of the words—failed attempts at removing our family affliction. The last entry is dated around my fifth birthday.

"Ivy's handwriting is sloppy here, as if she were frantic. Do you remember her working on these spells, Norm?"

He moves next to the grimoire and sits on his hind legs. "She knew she had two years left before your innate witchcraft could reveal itself, and every spare minute counted. She also learned that if you lived in an Unremarkable household where no one practiced the craft, your magic could be suppressed."

"You mean if she had left Nana and gone with my father, I could have lived a normal life?"

"Yes, but for that to come to fruition, Ivy would have had to give up witchcraft forever."

I pet his hairy head. "Was she going to run away with my father, Norm?"

He pats my hand with a paw. "I do not know, my witch. She did not confide in me."

"If she had fled with me to go away with my dad, she would have had to leave you behind. I wouldn't even know you exist."

"And for that, I am grateful you are here, Fortune. Unfortunately, both destinies would have left me without Ivy. But you would have had an Unremarkable life with your mother."

I tear up, imagining a life without Norman. Yet, I long for the life with my mom that could have been. I flip back a few pages in the tome. "I found her divination prep and incantation. Can you help me prepare?"

He salutes me with a paw. "At your service." He reads the instructions and nods. "Ah, yes. I remember now. Cleanse the runestones by burning garden sage and allow the embers to die out while you work. Light a yellow or blue candle."

"Blue would help clear my mind." I read on. "To trigger their effectiveness, I should apply my energy to the stones in a bowl and ask a question, focusing on an intention. Then I choose or cast the stones."

"I recommend choosing first, three at the most. Are you ready?"

"Yes, I'm more able than ever before."

After dumping the stones into a wooden bowl, I raise my right hand and recite a question as I summon my magic. "What is my path in this world?" The amethyst crystals shine briefly under the amber rays emanating from my fingertips. I call them back.

"That's the first time I've felt completely in control. I like it."

Norman sets a paw on the rim of the bowl. "Draw three and set them on the cloth in order."

I dip my hand into the bowl and select them, one at a time, placing them on a divination cloth Nana uses sometimes. I lay them in order: Nauthiz, Perthro, and Hagalaz.

"You must focus your intention on their meanings," Norman says.

I breathe deeply several times and focus on each symbol, referring to my mother's handwritten notes. "The first is my state currently. Nauthiz: need and endurance. There's a struggle. That is the definition of my life right now. The second refers to my inner emotions. Perthro: mystery and fate. I must brace for the unknown. Well, that's obvious. The last one represents external influences. Hagalaz: disruption and uncontrollable forces of nature like hail or..." A wave of dread overwhelms me, and I lose my balance.

"What, Fortune?" Norman taps his paw on my hand.

"Chaos and destruction. I don't feel good about this." I throw the stones back into the bowl.

The garage door opens and Nana walks in, a crinkle digging in her brow. She's still in her nightgown, robe, and slippers. "I thought I sensed magic in the air out here. You're up early."

"Yeah," I say, throwing the divination cloth over my mom's journal. "I'll be getting up at the crack of dawn every day to perform the cleansing ritual and practice with the runestones. If I maintain consistent improvement, I could cast spells with the coven."

"I don't think that's a good idea, Fortune. It's only been a couple of weeks since your mishap at the lagoon."

Norman emits an audible sigh. "Now, Betty..."

"Don't you cause trouble, familiar. I know what's best."

We'll see, won't we? "I am making progress, Nana." Amber radiates from my fingertips, so I grab my bracelet and shove it on. "The control lasted about fifteen minutes. I bet I could bank it, too. I'm going to ride to the store and sift through some boxes of clothing now. Norm, can you put stuff away?" I point to Ivy's journal behind my back.

"Of course, my witch." He winks, scuttles across the table, and blows out the candle.

"Why don't I cook us breakfast, Nana?" I ask.

"That would be wonderful. I'll get the pan out."

My grandmother exits the garage and I follow her out. That last runestone left a dent in my newfound confidence. I sense chaos ahead.

Deciding a T-shirt and biking shorts is probably not the best way to influence a Tylwyth Teg at dinner, I put on a sundress that matches my baby blue eyes. I pull a tan crochet cardigan off a hanger and grab my white espadrille wedge sandals.

"Don't forget Cam is coming by tomorrow for training. I'll perform my daily cleanse and you can assist Nana."

"Noted," Norm says. "I have high hopes for Cameron. He's a fine young witch."

"You like that he won't put a leash on you. I'm leaving now. Wish me luck."

"Don't let him break your will, Fortune. If you know what I mean." He bats his eyelashes.

"I already told him I won't sleep with him."

"But can you control those primal urges, my witch?" He wags his tail.

"Bye, Norman...the Conqueror."

He sticks his curvy tongue out. "Now you're just mocking me."

My morkie familiar points his butt at me and blows a string of rainbow bubbles as he struts away. I chuckle and head out the door.

My dress and high heels make cycling problematic, so I take the bus to Beach Boulevard. When I arrive at the iron gate, the guard lets me in. A luxury sedan sits on the other side of the fountain in the driveway. As I stroll past the pond in the courtyard, a man approaches in my direction—scratch that—a witch, Jonathan Walker. This is *not* good. He stops when he sees me.

"Fortune. What are you doing here?"

"I'm discussing...business with Mr. Davies." I nearly laugh calling him that. "Why are you here?"

"He's a new client. Is he going to invest in your store? Because he didn't mention it."

"It isn't related to my shop." I can't tell him how I know this Tylwyth Teg. It would complicate things. "He's sponsoring Rylee's art studio. She asked me to go over the financials with him."

"Yes, he shared that with me. Well, enjoy your dinner."

My former lover walks past me, but I call out. "You should know he's a Tylwyth Teg."

He peers back over his shoulder and smiles. "I am aware."

Then anything I share at the next coven circle shouldn't shock him. He continues past the fountain and gets into his car. I ring the doorbell and soon after, Rhys swings the door in. The universe is testing me. He's dressed in a loose linen short-sleeved shirt and worn jeans. His feet are as bare as a baby's bottom, and his waist-long blond hair flows over his chest.

A corner of his mouth curls. "I suspected you might change your mind, but I'm glad you didn't." He steps back. "Come in, Fortune."

I follow him into the dining room and drop my crossbody bag and crocheted cardigan on the table. He has set out plates and cutlery for two. Goblets are filled with ice water, but the wine glasses are empty. An internal voice whispers I should avoid the alcohol.

"Can I help? You know I don't do well sitting still."

"Yes, I know how your body moves." He shifts close to me, his cobalt blue eyes drawing me to him. "I have a handle on dinner."

Rhys steps back and a neon-green luminescence emanates from his hands. The eel-like fingers extend into the kitchen and swim about. Within minutes, fancy entrees resembling chef-prepared cuisine float through the air and make a soft landing on the table. A bottle of wine trails behind, twirling. As he wraps his hand around the bottle's curve, his magic dissipates to a mirage of sparkles.

"Please sit." He gestures at a chair perpendicular to his at the head of the long table. "I'll pour the wine."

"Filling me with wine won't make a difference. I'm not going to sleep with you." I take a sip of the water.

"So you wrote in your text reply." He sits and picks up his fork. "Eat. The food is authentic and I prepared it myself." He takes a bite of his salad.

I follow his lead and find the dressing delicious. "It's good. I didn't imagine you could cook."

"I'm resourceful. You should have learned that about me by now. Look around you."

"Yeah, I'll give you that." I peer up at Rylee's painting and chuckle. "I'm sorry, but that picture of you staring down at us while we're eating...it's a bit much. Unremarkables who come here must recognize the resemblance."

"Any Unremarkable who sets foot in this house is *in the knowing*."

"Including the crooked politicians that were here the other night?" I remove my salad bowl and dig into the ziti layered in tomato sauce and mozzarella.

Rhys's guard, who is also his driver, enters the dining room and whispers something to his boss. The self-professed fairy in charge checks his phone and sets it back on the table. "Tell the selkie leader I'll meet with him sometime this week." His employee nods and leaves.

"Sounds like you're running things now. How many fae have crossed over into LB?"

He chews his ziti slowly and swallows. "A fair amount."

I shake my head. "Great. You said you had information about the portal and the lagoon."

He drinks a significant portion of his wine and sets the glass down. "Why don't we enjoy our dinner? We can discuss business after."

"Alright, but I won't forget. It's the only reason I came."

That mischievous smile of his appears, the one that prompted me to strip him bare every damn time. "Is it?"

I claw at my wineglass and down half of its contents, trying to distract myself from the warmth marinating between my legs.

"Fine. Let's finish this meal because I have other commitments."

My plan is to gobble up dinner without uttering another word. But time flits by like the life of a butterfly. Rhys is charming as usual, recalling memories of the first night we went to his tent and the series of times after. To my relief, he avoids mentioning the myriad of sexual acts we engaged in. Instead, he prattles on about the time a cop flashed a light into the tent, and I screamed like a banshee. He bursts out laughing and finishes his wine, then pours himself another.

"To be fair, I was buck naked and thought he might recognize me." I consume the last morsel of chocolate mousse—my favorite, and he knows it.

"When I turned around and you saw me standing there... I wish I'd taken a picture of you with my cell phone." He leans back against his chair, chuckling.

"First of all, it wasn't funny. Second..." I knew in that moment he had a plan to win me back, but I keep that to myself. "I've been amiable. Tell me what you know about what's happening at the lagoon."

His laughter fades and his mouth falls flat. "Why don't we take our wine onto the back balcony?" His Welsh accent has an edgy tone to it. "We can view the sunset from there. And I shall respond to all your questions."

"Alright. I'll do that. But then I expect answers. Or I'm leaving."

Rhys carries his wineglass toward the patio doors. I grasp

mine and follow him onto the balcony. I lean on the iron railing, but he stands an arm's length back.

"My first question. Why the fuck did you buy a house with so much iron railing, Rhys?"

He laughs again and sips some wine. "Once I established myself as the leader of this multifaceted fae community, I needed a residence that would deter the uninvited."

"You mean those who want to challenge your leadership. Sad that you can't rest your arms on the railing and soak in the view."

My former Tylwyth Teg lover squints at me, sets his wineglass on a side table, and waves his hand at a folded blanket on the chair. I stand up as holographic fingers lower the cloth over the iron. He rests his arms on the padded material, and I join him.

"A simple solution, but I'm over the moon you're concerned about my welfare." A hint of sarcasm seeps through his Welsh voice.

"Don't read into it, Rhys. We're over but I still care what happens to you." I tilt my head. "Since you're the de facto leader now, are you outlawing the use of glamour by the fae?"

"Yes. Unfortunately, like humans, not all will comply."

"That requires enforcement. Do you have something in place?"

"Not yet. Running a new kingdom requires patience."

A cool breeze blows, playing with my hair and prompting goosebumps to rise on my skin. Rhys unbuttons his shirt and removes it, exposing his ripped arms and torso. He wraps the linen around my shoulders. *Oh, universe, hold me back.* I turn my head and scan the trail on the beach. I spot the lifeguard huts. Did he witness the incident? Could he observe Ollie and me from the balcony?

"Did you read about the attempted drowning Thursday night?"

He turns his gaze toward the water. "I didn't need to read about it. I had a front-row view."

Shit. "The Long Beach Gazette said they caught the female who did it."

"A woman nearly drowned a young, vibrant man?" he asks, returning his attention to me. "Sounds implausible, no?"

I slide so close to him, the heat of his body warms me. "Not for shifter fae. I saw its face transform into something hideous. Will you ask this selkie leader if it's one of his?"

"If you desire it." He caresses my arm. "Fortune, I promise you. I do not know where this being is."

"It's responsible for all the drownings, isn't it?"

"I believe so." He bends to kiss me, but I shift left.

"We have to do something. They're going to charge that woman with murder. She was strung out on drugs and needs help, but she shouldn't be a patsy for a supernatural killer."

He pushes away from the padded railing. "I'll put my workers on it. See what they can fish out of the selkies first."

"What about the lagoon? You still haven't told me what you know."

Rhys walks to his wineglass and finishes the last drops. "When the rumors started, I went there and examined the area. Someone transformed that section into freshwater."

"Yeah. Jonathan Walker, your new financial advisor apparently, figured that out. So did my familiar, Norman. Who in your community would do that?"

"Fortune, it wasn't fae magic that affected the change."

I push off the railing. "You could sense that? The coven put a filter on that portal. What witch would want to mess with it, and why?"

"The correct questions." He sets his glass down. "Search for the answers and you will find your witch."

"I need to go so I don't miss the next bus." I walk into the house with him close behind and return his shirt. "Here. I'll grab my cardigan and bag."

Rhys escorts me to the front door, sliding his arms into his shirt as we go, but his firm pectorals and abdomen poke through. I peer up at his gorgeous, bearded face.

"Thank you for dinner. I'm glad I came. It was fun."

He steps forward and I get a whiff of the sweet wine on his breath. "I want you, Fortune, but I won't beg." He slides a finger along my jawline, and his touch gives rise to a yearning more intense than before. "I'll be here waiting for you."

"You shouldn't rely on that. I have to be honest. I don't know what you're involved in, but I doubt I'd approve."

He draws his hand back. "Do not judge me based on the unknown."

"I have to go or I'm gonna miss my bus."

"William can take you home." He opens the door and motions to his driver.

I exit the house but turn back. "Did you tell Jonathan I slept with you?"

"No, that's not for me to share, Fortune. Sleep well."

I climb into the black SUV and William drives me home to Carroll Park. That dinner left me with more questions than answers, and my head is spinning. I trust my gut and send a group text to Zara and Rylee.

> My source tells me a witch cast a new spell at the lagoon, not a fairy.

ZARA

> That's disconcerting. Do we have a renegade in LB?

RYLEE

No freaking way. Who could it be?

Good questions.

EIGHTEEN

Over a week has passed, and I haven't missed a day of performing my cleanse. It's time-consuming but appears to be working. I cast minor spells without a glitch, and my power is growing. If only I had figured this out sooner in my life. Nana still isn't aware Norman showed me Ivy's spell journal. In time, I will confront her.

Ollie and I exchange a few flirty texts back and forth while he's confined to the house, but I'm itching to visit him. No more attacks or murders have been reported, so I make plans to take off early and surprise him with dinner. But first I have to survive this hectic afternoon, buzzing with customers. Cam is working, but it's way past 2:00 p.m. before we get to the new stash of estate sale finds I picked up on Monday.

Gabby strolls into the store waving a fan at her face. She's wearing a loose floral blouse over white cotton pants. "The sun is brutal today. I love clear skies, but those rays burn like a fire on my skin."

"Thanks for coming in," I say. "I'm making dinner for a

friend who's recovering from an injury, but I didn't want to leave Cam here alone."

She stuffs her purse under the counter. "What a nice thing to do, Fortune. You are a good person."

"Sometimes I fail miserably, but I appreciate the support." As I move from the cash register, I pull my pink tee down over my skinny jeans.

Cam walks in from the back of the store in a Cal State Long Beach tee and denim pants. "Now that Gabby's here, can you show me what boxes you want me to start with?"

"Sure. I'll be back, Gabby."

She flings her hand up. "Take your time."

I follow Cam to the storage room and open a couple of boxes full of mixed items, mostly clothing, jewelry, and knickknacks from the seventies. He pulls out a pair of metallic red shoes with four-inch platforms and seven-inch heels, snorting.

"Oh, my gods. You expect someone to buy these?"

"Platform shoes are back in style. They'll be gone in a week. But first, we have to sort through all of this. Some won't be worth selling. I bought the lot and gambled. Do you mind going through some today? Grab an empty box and throw out the bad stuff. I'll do a second sift through tomorrow."

Cam nods and sets the shoes to the side.

"So, you and Heather seemed to hit it off," I say.

"Yeah, we went to the movies and hung out at a couple of brewpubs. She showed me around campus, too. I've never dated a musician. I think she's an amazing cellist, but what do I know?"

"Sounds like you found a friend. I hope it works out."

"Thanks." He glances at the storage container full of my great-aunt's old music boxes. "Do you mind if I take a few minutes to tinker with a couple of those?"

"Sure, but be careful. They're old. Your training seems to be progressing well with my grandmother."

"Yeah. But thanks for staying in case she got bossy."

"Dude, that woman was born bossy. But she cares."

His eyebrows draw together. "I'm worried about what's going on. A renegade witch messing with the lagoon, and now we know there's a shifter being killing people. They have to be related."

I rub his back. "Most likely. It's another reason I'm headed to Ollie's. I need to poke around the case, but he may not feel comfortable sharing. We'll discuss what I learn with the coven and come up with a plan. I'll clean up the merchandise after that frenzy of afternoon buyers."

"Gotcha. Thanks for not making fun of me. Sometimes I wish I didn't know about the secret society in our city."

"You and me both, dude. But normal can be overrated, too. I'll check back to see how you're getting along later."

"Thank you, Fortune."

Cam opens the box with my great-aunt's collection, and I go back to the front of the store. When I walk through the doorway, Rylee is chatting with my other employee at the register, dressed in her usual attire except for the addition of high-top sneakers.

"Great to catch up with you, Gabby. Don't let Fortune work you too hard."

"She's a wonderful boss and friend, but you know that. Have a nice day."

Rylee heads my way. "Hey, Blondie. What's up? Have you spoken with Rhys since your dinner?"

"No, I doubt I'll hear from him before Thursday's circle."

"There's gonna be drama around you accusing a witch of tampering with the existing spell there."

"Zara will support me, I hope."

"You know that Tylwyth Teg won't stop until he gets you back."

"I'll cut him off for good once he tells me what his underlings found out."

Rylee snickers. "Where have I heard that before? It's OK to admit he has a hold over you. I mean…" She leans into me and mutters, "I had a date with that selkie. Did you know they have webbing between their toes? But it was the best sex I've ever had."

I crack up. "I'm happy you finally got past Erin."

"Who?" she asks, grinning. "Isla was a lot of fun to hang out with. I may see her again. Don't write off Rhys completely."

"Red, I'd be a hypocrite to tell you not to date a fairy. If you find happiness with her, then I support your choice one hundred percent. I just need more in a relationship than a satisfying sex life, and I don't think Rhys is capable of providing that. Especially since he took on this persona of a rich man. I have a deep hunch he made a lot of deals with the worst humans here, including those sketchy city councilmen who were at the party the other night."

My friend rubs her jaw. "Is it a bad idea I accepted his sponsorship?"

"No," I say, squeezing her arm. "That's one awesome thing he is doing. Yes, I don't doubt he is giving you money to get on my good side. But he told me how much he admires your work, and I believe him. I'm confident he's never lied to me, except about being fae. As soon as he saw my magic seep out one night, he fessed up—thankfully. I thought I'd revealed myself to an Unremarkable."

"Yup, I remember. But you kept going back."

"Well, you know why now." I attempt to squash a smile. "Like your selkie friend, I enjoyed our time together. Back to your sponsorship, I think he already had the money because he bought your painting. He became Mr. Davies, wealthy entrepreneur, for other reasons."

Out of nowhere, screams erupt from the storage room. We dash to the door. I yell back to Gabby, "Stay there! We'll find out what happened!"

"I hope Cameron isn't hurt!"

We run to the room and dart in. Cam has a broom in his hands and he's running around batting it at a flying object.

"Shut the damn door!" He swings again at something flying near the ceiling. "And lock it!"

Rylee does as he asks. "What is that?" She pinches her nose. "It stinks like a sewer!"

"I think it's a bat!" At least the wings resemble one, but its face and bright red skin tell another story.

The tiny flying animal zips from one side of the room to the other, laughing. "Hahaha! You can't catch me now! I'm free and I won't go back! Free, free, free!"

"What the fuck?" Rylee runs into the powder room and comes out with a plunger.

"Oh, shit. It's an imp." I rip off a flap of cardboard from a box and run after the mischievous being, panting. "Cam, what happened?"

"I pulled out a carved wooden box. I figured it had musical innards inside. But that thing leaped out at me when I opened it." He points to the open vessel.

Rylee swings the plunger at the prankster. "You need to get back in there, and now!"

We all flinch when someone bangs on the door. "What is going on in there? Why is the knob locked? Is Cameron OK?"

"Yes, Gabby. Go back to the register. Customers could come in. A bird got in here, and we're trying to catch it."

"Oh, OK. Good luck!" Her footsteps trail away.

The naughty imp throws a miniature fireball at a cardboard box, setting a section ablaze, and cackles. "You'll never put me back in there!"

Rylee swings again. "Fortune, what are we going to do?"

"I can't do anything. After my cleansing this morning, I used my magic to practice with the runestones. One of you has to put him back in there." I dart to the fire and smother it with a fiberglass blanket I store for accidents.

My friend jumps up at the imp. "Don't look at me. I haven't been going to training sessions with your grandmother."

"Cameron, you have to do it," I say, flapping the cardboard at the magical jerk. "Nana said you're doing great."

"What if I fuck up?" he asks. "Gabby is right out there." He bats the imp as it flings another fireball at us.

I grip his hand and stare into his eyes. "It's you or we chase this turd around the storage room until Gabby tries to knock down the door."

He peers up at the imp and drops the broom. He raises his hand, chanting. "Object of my heart's desire, come to me, it's time to retire!"

He faces his palm at the imp, his fingers radiating an amber glow, and repeats the chant. The imp stops flying mid-air, like a fly getting stuck in a flytrap, and Cam pulls him down an inch at a time.

The prankster whines. "Nooo! Let me gooo!"

With a tug and a push, Cam shoves the imp back into the carved wooden box and the lid slams shut.

Rylee and I scream and jump in unison. "You did it, Cam! You did it!"

He stands frozen, staring at his hand. "I can't wait to tell Spence."

I hug him. "Yes. You've got bragging rights now, and I'm sure he'll be proud."

"Fucking awesome, dude," Rylee says. "Time for me to begin training sessions again."

He picks up the imp in its container. "What do we do with this?"

"Put him in the cardboard box with the rest of my great-aunt's collection. Who knows what else is lurking in there? I'll take it back to the house and tell Nana. She can figure out what to do with him. I'd better get to the front before Gabby calls in the fire department. Take a break, Cam. You earned it."

He chuckles. "I won't argue with you."

Rylee and I head toward the door and she opens it. "Did you tell Betty you're going to be with me tonight?" she asks.

"Yeah, is that alright with you?"

"Sure, but at some point, she's gonna ask what the studio looks like, and you won't be able to describe shit."

"I promise I'll come by to check it out." I give her a hug. "Thanks for always being there for me."

"Have fun with Detective Prescott. Let me know how the surprise goes." She winks at me and exits the store.

I plan on it—fun with a side of subtle inquisition.

AFTER PICKING up groceries to make dinner, I store them in my basket and ride to Ollie's. When I arrive, I hang my bike helmet on the handlebars and grab the paper bag. I knock on the front door, but he doesn't answer. His SUV is in the driveway. Is he sleeping? I check the doorknob and find it's unlocked, so I enter.

Voices travel from the kitchen. I walk through the living area and pass through the doorway to discover Anwen Beddoe dressed in a bright red midriff shirt, black leather skirt, and matching spike-heeled sandals. She's holding a spatula and cooking cod and fried potatoes in a pan while Ollie leans against the counter in a tee and lounge pants, a hand resting on his abdomen. His face lights up, grinning.

"Fortune, you didn't tell me you were coming."

I set my paper bag full of food that won't get prepared tonight on the counter. "Because I wanted to surprise you with dinner, but I guess I'm too late." I glare at the devious Tylwyth Teg.

"Anwen noticed I was home. When she found out I'd been injured, she kindly offered to cook me dinner."

"That was nice of you, Anwen," I say, forcing a smile.

"It wasn't a bother. Ollie's a smashing landlord. Never bothers me."

"You're a brilliant tenant...and neighbor." He grunts, bending over. "I've got to sit down."

I caress his arm. "Rest on the sofa. I'll bring your dinner on a tray."

"That would be cracking." He moves toward the doorway. "Anwen, your help was truly appreciated today."

"Anytime, Ollie. It was worth the conversation."

He exits the kitchen and I approach Anwen. "You can go home now. I'll clean up your mess."

"You're fucking rude, you know. I was being a friendly tenant. He's a nice bloke, too. With my occupation, I want to keep the detective happy."

"All you fae are so transactional." I'm reminded of Rhys's recent demands to get me to his house alone.

She grabs her keys from the counter. "We've had this conversation before. Humans are no different. We're just honest about it." She opens the back door. "By the way, is the lovely detective aware you had dinner with Rhys on Saturday evening?"

My jaw drops slightly but I don't answer.

"Rhys and I go way back, probably three or four hundred years. We even fucked for a few of those. He tells me everything, Fortune Whittle. You might want to remember that."

"Evening is approaching. Don't you need to go to work?"

"Oh, fuck off, witch." She turns her nose up at me and leaves, shutting the door behind her.

That Tylwyth Teg burns my herbs. After putting away the groceries I bought, I inspect the cabinets, find a tray, and load it with dinner for two, utensils, and glasses of iced tea. Anwen cooked enough for a couple of people. She must have planned to eat with him. Am I sorry I kicked her out? Not one bit. I bet she was going to pick his brain about criminal cases in the city. Or glamour him, even though Rhys has forbidden it. When I get to the sofa, I set the tray on the coffee table and hand Ollie his plate and utensils.

"Anwen left. I told her I'd clean up."

"You do realize I'm not interested in her." He sets his plate on his lap and grabs the utensils.

"Yeah, but I don't want you to think you can't date other women. I know we're in the dating phase."

He flashes that alluring grin. "I like that you're so open and understanding. But at the moment, I'm incapacitated and good to no one. So, there's that."

I chuckle. "I was afraid to call and wake you up. When you didn't contact me, I…"

"Sorry I failed to phone or text. I've been sleeping a lot during the day because I chase slumber during the night like a lost cause." He cuts into his cod. "Since you were here on Friday, I have been ruminating about the woman who was attacked at the lagoon. Manny believes her case can't be related to Jimmy's because she said her attacker was a man."

"But you don't think so?" I chew my cod one chomp at a time.

He swallows a bite. "I shouldn't be discussing the case with you. It goes against everything I live by."

"I understand, but if you need to vent, you know I would never do anything to jeopardize your case." *Because you will never capture this shifter being.*

"The reason I am a competent detective is that I rely on my gut feelings when investigating. But I always back those hunches with facts. Although I'm on light duty, I interviewed James with Manny. The description of his attacker was exact, down to the long dark hair and attractiveness. But how could they be the same person? Or did the woman present herself as a man to that jogger?"

"I don't know, Ollie."

But I do fucking know. How I wish I could tell him his instincts are correct. We eat our dinner without saying much more about the subject, but I can sense the lingering questions consuming his brain. I finish my meal and set my plate on the tray. He leans forward to add his dish but winces. I hand him his iced tea.

"Thank you, love," he says. "Manny is out investigating a possible new crime ring that's emerged in the city. Some wealthy Welsh entrepreneur who popped up out of nowhere. Bought a beachfront estate and set himself up as a philanthropist. It's dodgy, I tell you, and I'm stuck in this fucking house."

I nearly choke on my iced tea. "You have a different job right now—recovery." If I had better control of my magic, I could prepare a healing spell. But I'd have to confess I'm an actual witch with supernatural powers.

"There's something else as well," he says.

I shift next to him and stroke his shoulder. "It's alright to talk about it, Ollie."

He caresses my face and pulls me close. I lean over and kiss him passionately, offering him my tongue. As he cups the back of my head, I reach for his manhood, which is swelling in his thin lounge pants. But he clasps my hand and leans his forehead against mine.

"I want you, Fortune. I'm ready to take this next step, but the timing is not with us." He kisses me again. "The desire is most definitely there, but the pain is a bit distracting. I am so chuffed you understand why I can't get work out of my head. My ex never grasped how much it affected me."

"I absolutely do." More than you realize. "What else is rattling your brain?"

"Both of the victims said the faces of their assailants morphed into something not human. Manny suspects it means nothing. It was dark and they were frightened. But my gut says..."

"Says what, Ollie?" I stroke his drawn face.

"It tells me they are the same individual, but that's not possible unless...it's not a person. And I cannot reconcile that feeling."

My stomach turns watching him struggle with his astute assessment. How I wish I could tell him. Yet, how would it help? An Unremarkable can't battle a supernatural being. He's safer for not being *in the knowing*.

I embrace him and caress his back. "All you can do is wait. If no more attacks occur, then you'll know your hunch was misguided."

But what if the homicidal being shows up again?

It's a clear July night and every witch in the coven is in attendance, dressed in short sleeves and shorts for the warm weather, including Pam's daughter, Izzy. As we gather in the back corner of her yard under a half-moon, I survey the faces of my fellow witches. Could one of them have sabotaged their own spell on the portal? Certainly not Nana or my friends. Joey? No way. Pam wouldn't trash her own witchcraft, and Jonathan put on a convincing act at the lagoon if it was him.

Izzy is texting back and forth with someone. She can barely hold it together in a circle without the need to pee—no chance she's capable of that level of witchcraft skill. There's no way it's Zara who's standing across from me, eyeing my every move. She's going to beat a hole in the ground with her foot tapping. For a psychologist, she doesn't have much patience. I nod once at her and inspect Heather's aloof expression. The young witch is new, but what would her motive be? Cam has been hanging out with her. Wouldn't he have suspected something?

Pam begins. "North, East, South, West, I call this circle to order. We will perform our ritual in a few minutes. I want to share that the other covens in our region were overjoyed with the reception of our festival this year. Pagans and witches came together to celebrate, and the visitors enjoyed all we had to offer. I hope everyone here feels the same. Do any of you have anything to add?"

Joey enters the center. "I want to thank Heather for playing with her trio. It was amazing to listen to period music while the community participated in friendly rituals. I hope you're here to play again next year." He steps back.

"I heard lots of visitors commenting on it," Cam says, smiling in her direction.

Heather smiles affectionately at him. "Thank you, but you're biased."

Rylee shoots a hand up. "That was the first festival I actually attended. I gotta say. It was gnarly. Can't wait until the next one."

Pam lays a hand on her chest, grinning. "I'm so happy to hear that. If we can keep this number of members in the coven, we will be stronger. Capable of making changes in our community, both on a human level and a magical one. Thank you to our new members for lending assisting this year. I worried you wouldn't attend this evening, but I'm elated you are here." She glances at her daughter, who continues to pull out her phone and text. "Izzy, if you're going to take part in this circle, you must put that cellphone away."

Isabella sinks in her seat and stuffs the phone back in her pants pocket. Nana nudges me and I make eye contact with Zara. As I step into the center, I glance at my grandmother. "I hadn't planned on returning, Pam. I never wanted to be in a coven. But I returned because we need to pool our resources after what I've discovered."

Jonathan's eyes narrow and he crosses his arms. The rest of them stare at me, squinting, except for Zara, Nana, Rylee, and Cam. They know what's up.

"You're aware of the murders and assaults that have occurred over the last few weeks. Well, a human isn't responsible. There's a shifter being, most likely a type of fairy, that's killing people—drowning them. I think it's connected to the lagoon and the portal somehow."

Heather throws a hand up. "Do you have proof of that? The fae I know can be untrustworthy, but I've never met any who would kill."

"Yes, I do." I don't want to betray Ollie, but they need to know. "Two of the victims were able to identify the assailant. They said the person's face transformed into something vile. Does that sound human to you? Besides, I had a view of the last attack. I was walking home along the beach when it happened. The being's face morphed like a shifter."

Joey's eyes grow wide. "That's fucked up. So, some selkie has turned into a psychopath?"

"Sounds like a winner to me," Zara says. "More likely a sociopath."

"Well, you would know, but they're both ghastly. I don't want to meet them in an alley."

Jonathan peers at me, skepticism oozing from his eyes. "How do you know what the victims saw? Isn't that information kept confidential while they're hunting for the suspect?"

Rylee jumps in. "Does it matter how she knows? The question is, who messed with the water in that area of the lagoon?"

"Exactly," Zara says, staring Jonathan down.

The others scratch their heads, rub their jaws, and shift in the gravel, except for Izzy. She has pulled her phone out again and is texting like a stenographer.

"Do you know which type of fairy tampered with our spell?" Pam asks.

"No," I say. "But it wasn't fae magic that changed the water's composition. A witch did it."

My answer prompts everyone to scan the circle. The same question is going through their minds, I'm certain. *Is the renegade witch one of us?*

"Who told you this, Fortune?" Jonathan glares at me. "Rhys Davies?"

Rylee, Nana, and Cam lock eyes with me. "Yes. He's checked out the area. He says the fae aren't responsible."

"Who the fuck is Rhys Davies?" Heather asks.

"He's a Tylwyth Teg," Nana says. "A rich one."

You're not helping, Betty. I mouth "stop" at her, and she purses her lips.

Rylee interjects. "He's a philanthropist, though...sponsoring my art studio. I asked Fortune to go over the finances with him for me. I'm not great with money." *Nice save, friend.*

Jonathan stares directly into my eyes, as if he's attempting to trip me up somehow. "He told you this the other night at his house?"

"Yes," I say. "He offered the information."

"But can you believe him? He's fae, a rather important one in their growing community."

"Enough of the accusations," Zara says, huffing. "We need to go to the lagoon and try to cast a spell to return the water to its original composition at the least."

Pam glances at Izzy and tries to snatch her phone from her, but her daughter jumps back. "If none of these issues concern you, dear, perhaps you shouldn't remain in the circle."

Her daughter huffs. "You all don't know what you're doing. You're guessing what happened in the lagoon." She pulls her flip-flops off and runs off toward the house, making eye contact with me as she passes.

The coven leader screams with an authoritative tone. "Isabella, come back to this circle!"

"Why don't I go talk to her?" I ask. "This has upset her for some reason." Pam seems to be more concerned with the actual outburst than with her daughter's reason for it.

"No," Pam says, scowling. "I apologize for her behavior. I've been having issues with her. Zara, we will follow your recommendation and meet late one night at the lagoon to remedy this now that we know something nefarious has occurred. I will discuss with Jonathan and contact you. Tomorrow is the Fourth of July. We'll have to wait until the weekend when the area is less likely to have people about."

"But aren't you forgetting something?" I ask, flashing my palms at her.

"What would that be, Fortune?"

"Don't we need to figure out which witch messed with your spell?"

Pam's gaze roams around the circle. "I trust everyone in this coven. Or are you suggesting one of the new members could be responsible?" Her eyebrows spring up.

"No." I glance at my friends and Nana. "I can vouch for them. Remember, I never even wanted to join a group. But I'm willing to remain to help you solve this."

"I recommend we perform our spell of renewal," Jonathan says, peering at me out of the corner of his eye. "Since Izzy isn't here, we should cast it with ease."

What is he doing? Is he deliberately trying to expose me? My heart thumps like an engine needing oil, but I prepared for this possibility. "Before we cast this spell, I need to confess something." I shift next to my grandmother.

Nana's head snaps up, her wrinkled face frozen with shock. "No, Fortune."

I pat her hand. "It's alright, Nana. They should know. They're gonna find out anyway."

Rylee crosses her fingers, but I've told her my plans. Cam's eyes are bugging out like a frog's because I hadn't shared my intentions with him.

"When we attempted to cast a spell of renewal at the end of the last circle, it didn't fail because of Izzy. It was my fault." I clasp my copper bracelet. "Pam, all these years you were under the impression I believed I was too good to join your little coven because of my ancestry. But that wasn't it at all. My father was an Unremarkable. You believed I was this extremely powerful witch, but the fact is..."

Nana leans forward. She's about to rupture a vein in her forehead.

"I'm an Unremarkable, too. So, I can't perform magic."

Jonathan arches an eyebrow. I pray to the gods he won't spill the beans. The rest of them chatter loudly among themselves while Rylee and Cam console Nana. I'm relieved my surprise admission didn't send her into cardiac arrest, but she would have pooh-poohed any of my solutions. Norman was right. It is time to stand up to her.

There's one witch who isn't speaking over the others about my revelation. Zara is chuckling and slapping her face. Her laughter evolves into a session of full-on guffawing and clutching her abdomen. I glare at her, frowning. I get it. You think it's funny I can't do magic. But the truth is far more complicated, friend.

"Quiet down, everyone," Pam says. "Jonathan, were you aware of this?"

He glances at me, and I'm sure he'll toss me into the ring. "I knew she had some issues, yes."

I can't believe he is covering for me, even if he is stretching the truth.

"Issues? Not being able to cast spells with internal energy is more than a simple problem. You've left me with very little choice,

Fortune Whittle. If you are not a practitioner, you cannot remain in this coven."

Nana pats her heart. "She is a witch in every other way. She prepares spells from grimoires, memorizes incantations. When I need help, she helps me cast the spell completely up to the point where she must summon her own energy. She has the knowledge. I ask you to keep her in the coven. If you want my skills, she stays."

Cam yells out, "That goes for me, too."

"Me three," Rylee says. "We're a package deal."

Jonathan shakes his head and smirks at me. "Let her stay, Pam. She's useful. Not only does she have a lifetime of witch training from a competent crone, she obviously has connections. Her knowledge is valuable."

I peer at Jonathan and mouth the words. "Thank you."

"I agree," Zara says, catching her breath. "Fortune is an asset to us." She glances at me with a twisted smile.

Pam checks her cell phone. "It's late, and I have to deal with Izzy. For now, at your request, I will allow Fortune to remain. I'll send a date and time to meet at the lagoon once Jonathan and I have discussed the parameters. Let us complete our renewal spell and close the circle."

I step forward again. "Pam, I'll set up the candles. The rest of you can join hands and prepare."

Our coven leader nods reluctantly and I go to the altar and grab the red, white, and black candles. After I set them all on the stump in the center, the others raise their hands in unison. I step outside the ring, where I've always existed in my magical life. For the first time ever, I feel alienated. They recite the chant of fire renewal and their amber magic combines, leaping to the candles like before. Fires ignite on the wicks and the flames shoot up, as they should. As my fellow witches lower their arms, expressions of a successful completion appear on their faces.

"Wonderful, my friends," Pam says. "After the candles have burned for two hours, I will extinguish them with the iron snuffer. It is done."

Rylee and Cam take off ahead to head home in their own cars while I stroll with Nana to ours. Pam stops us to talk, and I don't think it's about the weather.

"Betty Whittle, I am irate that you hid Fortune's magic deficiency from us. Did you think I wouldn't find out?"

Nana stands tall. Well, as high as her old body permits. "My granddaughter *is* a witch. She has trained and has all my knowledge. She may not have the ability to cast spells at the moment, but her time may eventually arrive. That has always been my hope."

"We shall see." Pam turns on her heel and heads toward the house. Joey joins us.

"You could have told me," he says. "I'd love you no matter what your power is. As far as I'm concerned, you're still a witch. Don't let anyone tell you differently."

Zara rushes to us. "Thank you, Fortune. That's the best laugh I've had in a looong time. Personal reasons, my ass." She lays a hand on my shoulder. "If you hear anything else, text me. Let's go, Joey. I'll drop you home."

When we finally arrive at the Rolls-Royce, Jonathan is leaning on the car. He helps Nana into the passenger-side seat and shuts the door. He approaches me.

"That was certainly a choice. What happens when they discover the actual truth?"

"Once we solve this mystery and save the town from this shifter murderer, I'll drop out, go on with my life as I was before. They don't need to know my secret."

"I thought Betty had plans to ask the coven for help with ridding you of your family curse?"

"If they find out I lied, I doubt they'll jump to offer their services. Betty will have to deal with the consequences."

"Sometimes the universe has a different destiny planned for us. Remember that."

As he walks away, I get in the car and turn the key. Nana releases a sigh that could power a windmill.

"What you said tonight fucks up all our plans," she says.

"*Your* plans, Betty. Yours. They were never mine."

"You did this to defy me." She gazes out the car window.

"Nana, the coven isn't the sole answer to this family curse. My daily rituals are giving me steady control over it, and the rune-stones are finally making a little sense. I feel powerful. Isn't that enough?"

She doesn't say another word on the way home or as we enter the house, going directly to her bedroom and shutting the door. When I arrive inside my sanctuary, Norman leaps from his comfy bed, hovering as I plop onto my mattress.

"Well, how did your plan go, my witch?" He lands softly and scuttles to me.

"I was certain Betty was gonna pop an aneurysm. I swear, a vein was pulsing on her forehead, preparing to burst and plunge us into a horror flick."

Norman belly laughs and rolls over. "I wish I'd been there."

"Oh, stop, Norm. Neither of us wishes ill to come to her. She is still my grandmother and gave up her life to raise me after Mom died. Soon, I'll have to confront her about a lot of things, and it won't be easy for her. Tonight was a test. We both survived it, although she was silent as a mouse when we got home. She's probably down there sulking...and scheming. Because she is Elizabeth Whittle."

He sits on his hind legs and lays a paw on my leg. "I am sorry. You know Betty and I have never gotten along. I want you to stand on your own, Fortune. Now that your control is increasing, that day will arrive. Will you follow through?"

A notification buzzes on my phone and I pull it out of my jeans pocket, smiling.

OLLIE

My kitchen cabinets are stuffed to the gills with food. Whatever shall I do?

I guess you need a cook to use them up?

Do you have a recommendation?

I'd rather not bother Anwen. It would most assuredly eat into her working hours.

I crack up. Ollie has never referred to her as a hooker outright. He's too proper and kind.

How about tomorrow for the Fourth of July?

That would be smashing.

Norman leans over my hand, attempting to sneak a peek. "Is that the Unremarkable detective?"

"Yeah. I'm gonna make him an early dinner. I can return in time to take Nana to the fireworks."

"This relationship with the detective is progressing rather quickly, my witch. Once it becomes serious, you must share your secret with him. Make him *in the knowing*. If he were to find out some other way, he would—"

"Never speak to me again. But if I tell him the truth, he'll say I've lost all sense of reality and take me to the psych ward for evaluation."

"Not prime choices, Fortune, but truth always wins."

I stare out the window at the half-moon and exhale. "Fuck my luck."

CHAPTER
TWENTY

When Ollie and I finish dinner, I take the dishes to the kitchen and divvy up leftovers for the weekend, placing them in the fridge when I'm done. I scrub down the counters and load the dishwasher so Anwen won't feel the need to help out any more than she has. The last thing I want is for that Tylwyth Teg to attach herself to her landlord. A notification sounds on my phone. It's Pam Barrera.

PAM

> We will meet Saturday after midnight around 1:00 a.m. Come prepared to cast a spell of water renewal. Dress in black.

I guess she's inviting me? I certainly can't participate, but I can help them prepare. The last time I even tried, I nearly set the area on fire. Will they do the same?

When I return to the living room, Ollie is lounging back on a pillow at one end of the sofa. One arm is resting above his head with his bicep flexed. He's wearing a T-shirt and athletic shorts, hardly sexy attire. But if he didn't have a cracked rib, I'd hop on him like a bunny. Fuck that shifter fairy for injuring him.

"You look relaxed," I say, flashing a flirtatious smile.

He sits up, moaning. "I had to lie back for a few minutes. Thank you for dinner, and for allowing me to so rudely suggest you come here to prepare it for me."

"Oh, Ollie, I didn't mind at all." After adjusting a pillow behind his back, I sit next to him and caress his thigh. "I'm so sorry you're in so much pain. I wish I could ease it."

My hand slips to his inner thigh and drifts upward. He pulls me to him and kisses me, but it's obvious he's hungry for more. When I find him, I caress his swelling erection and inhale his musky scent. He slides his fingers across the front of my loose V-neck tee, fondling my breast and nipple through my sports bra. His touch sets me ablaze, sparking a burning desire between my legs. Oh, how I want him inside me, but that intimacy will have to wait. He comes up for air and leans back.

"If we keep this up, I'll forget myself and this rib won't heal for another two months." He adjusts his bulge.

"I shouldn't sit so close, then," I say, sliding away. "I'm having a difficult time controlling my roaming hands. This is probably the longest I've ever gone dating someone and not done the deed. Does that admission bother you?"

He caresses my cheek. "Not in the slightest. I wish I were capable at this moment. However, if you recall, I'm the one who wanted to move at a snail's pace."

"Oh, I can wait, Ollie, for as long as you need to recover." I sit back and cross my legs. "I'm just sampling the goods. Like checking out the mangoes at the grocery store."

He guffaws, grabbing his torso, and groans. "I've never dated a woman quite like you. So blunt and genuine. I enjoy being with you because you don't play games. Even though we've known each other for barely a month, it's like we're old friends reuniting after decades, as if we met in a past life. Except I am a nonbeliever. This emotion is a little unsettling to me."

"I feel the same way, Ollie. But I'm a pagan. I also believe in karma."

My gaze falls to my shiny copper band and reality hits me like a clear prediction from a runestone. I have to tell him the truth, but now is a bad time to share the supernatural world with him. At the least, I should bring up the issue of children.

"This may be getting way ahead of our situation, because we haven't even committed to dating each other exclusively. I have to share something with you that's important." What can I say? I'm a cursed witch and shouldn't have offspring? That would go down like spoiled cod liver oil. "How old are you exactly?"

Tension wrinkles his brow. "Forty-nine. Are you concerned about my age?"

"No, of course not. I'm forty-six, and I have a birthday soon. Ollie, if you were hoping for children one day, that's not possible for me. Considering both our ages, I thought I should be honest about it...since our relationship is becoming more intimate. If you were hoping—"

He lays a finger on my lips. "No need to continue, Fortune. Although I would happily welcome children, it's not a deal-breaker. I'm looking for a companion for life, nothing more."

My angsty chest relaxes. "I am so glad to hear you say that." I lean in and kiss him. "Well, if we're not going to engage in back-seat bingo, we better find something else to do."

"Backseat bingo?" he asks with a titter. "Where on earth did you pick up that description?"

"My Nana. Whenever I'm out late, I get that old fifties slang flung at me like a softball. Mind you, she had my mom out of wedlock from a one-night stand."

"Your grandmother sounds like an amusing woman ahead of her time. I'd love to meet her."

My heart leaps into my throat. I was *not* expecting that request. "I'll introduce you when you're better." That gives me a few weeks at least.

He puts an arm around me and strokes my shoulder tenderly. "I've been staying awake recently—cut back on the medication. Would you like to watch a movie?"

"I want to but I can't. I told Nana I would take her to the fireworks. This is the last year since the Coastal Commission wants to protect birds and the water."

"Probably for the best. I think a drone show would be brilliant."

"How about we sit here and talk until I have to leave?"

"Nothing I'd like to do more." His cell vibrates and he checks the screen. "It's Manny." He reads the text and replies.

"Something wrong?" I ask, sitting up.

"He was filling me in on his research. Has us both dumbfounded."

"The environmentalists they brought in can't explain how fresh water is occupying part of the lagoon. To quote them: 'It's an unexplainable phenomenon.' He's also been looking into the man who has appeared seemingly out of nowhere, the one I mentioned last time you were here. He appears to be engaged in nefarious activities. I'm sorry, but I can't share his name or the specifics with you. I hope you understand?"

"Of course I do. I think I know who you're talking about, though." Oh, just tell him, Fortune. He is safer staying away from a powerful fae leader. Better if he thinks he's not as bad as he might be.

"Who do you think I'm referring to?"

"Rhys Davies," I say matter-of-factly. "You should know he is supporting some philanthropy. He donates to the Whatever Goes Gallery. And he set up Rylee in her own studio."

"Noted. Have you met him?"

I can't lie to him about this. "Yeah. The two of us went to his estate one night. The director of the art gallery invited Rylee to meet her benefactor, and she was told she could bring a date." There is no way I can tell him he was my lover. That might implicate me. I don't want him to suspect I'm the former mistress of a possible crime boss—in the police department's mind, anyway.

He chuckles. "You were Rylee's date?"

"Yeah," I say, trying to wrap this up. "So no one would hit on me or her."

"Brilliant thinking." He stares at me as if suddenly I'm in an interrogation room. "Did you recognize anyone else there?"

Shit. I've walked myself right into quicksand. My plan to remove interest from Rhys didn't take a fork in the road. It fell off a cliff. I have to lie to him, and my stomach does somersaults.

"The place was packed with people, so I hung out around the pool and on the balcony most of the time."

He nods. "Well, if any recollection comes to you, you'll tell me?"

"Sure." I check my cell phone for the time. "I'd better get home. As it is, parking will be a bitch."

"It always is in Long Beach. I'll walk you to the door." He moans as he stands and shuffles by my side.

"Concentrate on healing. Do your breathing exercises and go to physical therapy." I kiss him. "I put leftovers on plates in the fridge. They should take you through the weekend. I'll be back on Monday."

"You're spoiling me, Fortune Whittle. I could get accustomed to it."

"See you on Monday."

"Enjoy the fireworks."

He shuts the door and I hop on my racer. On the ride home, the conversations of the evening swim in my head.

I have to come clean, or he'll think I'm no better than his cheating ex-wife.

***

THE FIREWORKS DISPLAY glitters in the indigo sky, showering it in colors of red, white, blue, and a rainbow of others. Nana and I cover our ears as the explosions bang and whirl in the skies. The pungent odor of sulfur and a hint of vinegar permeate the air. The surface of the water reflects the vivid show, shimmering in the ripples. My grandmother smiles and points up as the embers trickle down.

As we enjoy the splendor of the July 4th festivities, I recall a time when I was five years old. Nana, my mom, and I watched fireworks set off over a farmer's field behind the elementary school in Milton, Delaware. We nibbled on hot dogs and popcorn we got from a vendor in the parking lot and sang songs while we waited for the sun to retreat into the horizon. It's one of my favorite memories, full of laughter, a surplus of hugs, and enough ice cream to add another butt cheek. I was magic-free and innocent of the family curse. I long for the normalcy of my childhood.

When Nana and I return from the fireworks, I lock the garage and we enter the house through the back porch. Light filters through the second-story patio door of my bedroom.

"I'm going to sleep early, Nana. I also want to check on Norman. He's a familiar but presents as a dog. I bet he took refuge under the bed."

"Your morkie is fine." She takes my hands in hers. "I am well aware you have a life outside the confines of this house and looking after me. I enjoyed the fireworks, and I'm glad I got to watch them one last time. Thank you for taking me to view them with you tonight."

"You're welcome, Nana." I hug her and she squeezes me back.

"My frustration with your way of dealing with things often clouds my underlying emotions. But I still love you."

"I don't say it often enough, either. You're my pride and joy, and I love you, Fortune. I am so lucky to have you. Goodnight, dear." As she chants, she waves her hand, turning off the lights in the kitchen with a glimmer of magic.

I stand back, smiling. "You too, Nana. Sleep well."

My grandmother goes to her bedroom and I head upstairs to check on my morkie familiar, who's probably curled up under my bed. When I swing the door in, I find him floating in the air, blowing a rainbow of bubbles. One paw throws a blast of moss-colored holographic bombs to pop them one at a time and the remaining illusion trickles down like sprinkles of glitter. He's holding a joint in the other paw, taking a hit after each glorious explosion. I stand with a judgy expression on my face and my hands on my hips.

"And here I was worried you were frightened and shaking like a chihuahua under my bed. Looks as if you're having fireworks of your own." I collapse onto my mattress.

He blows purple smoke rings. "No concerns here, my witch. I'm as happy as a cat familiar with a ball of yarn." He cracks up and lowers himself onto his padded bed. "Betty had a wonderful time, I assume."

"Yeah. We both did, actually. Brought back a lot of memories of when Ivy was alive. Before the...accident."

Norm rolls over and scuttles to me. "You're ruining my buzz, Fortune." He chants and levitates to the bed.

"Sorry." A notification shows on my phone. "It's Ollie."

OLLIE

I hope you and your grandmother had a wonderful time.

> We did. Thank you for checking. The fireworks were enchanting.

OLLIE

> I'm gutted you had to leave so early.

> Me too. Goodnight, Ollie.

> Sweet dreams, love.

"What did the detective have to say, my witch?" Norman asks, his head swaying back and forth.

"He wanted to know whether we enjoyed the fireworks." As I rub my temples, knots tighten in my stomach. "I don't know what to do, Norm. I've never felt so conflicted. We're becoming a lot closer, and I'm hiding all these secrets about myself and the supernatural world. I didn't expect to like him so much."

"Definitely lost my buzz now." He pats my hand. "This is a question for the runestones, don't you think?"

"I can't worry about that now. The coven is meeting at the lagoon tomorrow to attempt a solution to the water composition. And Rhys Davies—Rhys of Dyfed—hasn't contacted me. He has to be up to something. It's the only explanation."

"Then you must confront him. Asking him face to face is the course of action to obtain direct answers."

"Yeah, I realize that." I ruminate on the party at his estate and all his guests: selkies, Tuatha Dé Danann, Tylwyth Tegs like himself, and Unremarkable politicians who are *in the knowing*.

What are you up to, Rhys?

TWENTY-ONE

Saturday arrives, bringing another hot but clear day, which bodes well for a clandestine spellcasting in the wee hours of Sunday. Though a misty night with a thick marine layer would mask our activities. I hope the coven's water renewal spell is successful, or it's onto Plan B—and there isn't one. I still haven't received a call or a text from Rhys, and that's disconcerting. Is Ollie's partner right? Has the fae leader started some kind of nefarious collaboration with the criminal elements in the human world?

After dinner, Norman assists Nana in the house while I use the solitude to prepare for a divination with the runestones before I have to leave. I open my mother's journal and symbols fly off the pages as I flip them. I understand her enchanted book is merely a source of her words, but I sense a connection with her I never had before. The memory of her visage forms clearly in my brain, the blurred image finally in focus again. I can't explain it, but it's as if she's speaking to me through the tome.

Since I don't need to use my magic to cast a spell with the

coven, I energize my mom's runestones after cleansing. I take the plunge and ask the specific question I've been avoiding. "Should I date an Unremarkable?" I pull three stones, setting my intention.

I lay the stones in a row from right to left and refer to my mom's notes. "Ansuz says a message is at hand. Be wary and focus on channels of communication." Alright, Mom. "Gebo calls you to be happy. Accept the new relationship in your life." Well, that's positive, but what if it's not referring to Ollie?

The final one is Hagalaz again. I swallow my trepidation and read my mother's notes more carefully, hoping for an alternate interpretation that doesn't involve chaos and destruction. "This may not be general pandemonium. A dangerous situation may be approaching. Take steps to protect yourself." My stomach churns. This last rune keeps popping up. What is going to happen? And how is this connected to Ollie?

I pour the stones from the wooden bowl into the velvet bag and set them aside. I have to address these riddles another day. After cleaning up, I dust off embers from my T-shirt and jeans and go back inside. When I enter, Nana is sitting at the table, rinsing a dish in the sink, holographic amber hands doing her bidding. With a wave, the dish slides into a slot in the dishwasher and her magic dissipates, leaving a trail of sparkles behind. I close it and press the button.

"I could have done that from here, Fortune."

"Yeah, I know. Sometimes it's easier to push a button, don't you think?"

"Suit yourself." She pushes up from her seat.

"I'm gonna head out now. Catch you later at the lagoon."

She crosses her arms. "I don't know why you have to go so early."

"Because I need to clear my head in the stillness near the water. I can't do that with you there, chit-chatting along the way. Also, I may not be casting the spell, but I should be prepared for whatever happens. We don't want to set off an explosion and wake up the nosy neighbors across the street. Rylee and Cam will pick you up in a while in Rylee's car. I'm riding there on my bike."

She flips a hand up. "Fine. Don't forget to take your hoodie. I hope I can stay awake. My middle-of-the-night spell castings are buried back east under a pile of what could have been."

"Yeah, everyone knows you miss your former life there, Nana. But it got me away from my dad, didn't it?" I can't believe those words slipped out.

"You know very well why we moved. It had nothing to do with your father. The neighbors became suspicious of your unusual behavior. Your bracelet slipped off."

"Nana, you made the band big enough for a man's wrist. How was I supposed to keep it on?"

"I tightened it after. Besides, this gave us both a fresh start. You flourished here, and we could be more open about who we are. I need to change."

Nana exits the kitchen as Norman comes scuttling in with his dog leash between his teeth like he's playing fetch and drops it on the floor.

"When are we leaving, my witch?"

"It's a relief you're finally accepting the existence of the dog ordinance, but I can't take you with me tonight." I bend down to whisper. "You would be extremely helpful to the coven. I just need some time alone to figure out what I should do. You understand." I stroke his back.

"Of course." He peers down the hallway. "You have much to decide. I hope the answers reveal themselves on your journey."

"Thanks, Norm. Wish me luck."

"May good fortune find you." He winks at me. "See what I did there?"

I chuckle and snatch my hoodie and crossbody bag from a kitchen chair. "Bye, Norm."

The uneventful ride to the lagoon takes longer than I expected, which will give me little time to sort out my complicated life. I lock the wheel of my bike to the rack at the head of the trail on the other side of the causeway because it's closer to the portal. I stuff my hoodie through the strap of my crossbody bag and start down the trail. The sultry air is oppressive even for Southern California, and my shirt sticks to my skin like tape. As I approach the water, the aroma of salt and seaweed permeates.

It's pitch black except for a spray of light from a lamppost in the distance and the sliver of a beam from the partial moon. The homes across the lagoon sit lifeless like blocks of timber. I plan on hiking past the portal and over the causeway to get some steps in and ponder solutions for my dilemma. How do I tell an Unremarkable detective there is a supernatural world—and I'm part of it?

As I approach, I discover two figures crouching at the water's edge. Damn. Who showed up early? There goes my introspective stroll. I don't call out to them for obvious reasons and continue toward my fellow witches. A violin plays in the distance and my head swims with the melody floating across the lagoon. When I get closer, they stir but don't raise their heads. The divination of the Ansuz rune speaks to me, bringing my mind back into focus, but its message is unclear. Yet, I sense they don't belong here.

"What are you two doing here?" I ask.

The person on the left keeps their head down, but the one on the right turns toward me, their face coming into view under a ray of moonlight.

I flinch. "Izzy?"

Isabella gapes at me, jumps up, and sprints like an Olympic runner down the trail. I take off after her, testing my running skills, and nearly trip over my own feet. My longer stride does the job, allowing me to catch up to her. I grab the back of her hoodie and she tumbles to the ground.

"Please don't tell my mom." She rolls onto her back. "He's been teaching me how to perform better on my violin. That's all. He's been teaching me how to play so well, but Mama found out I stole money from her purse to buy a pay as you go cellphone for him. He needed one. I had to let him know I couldn't add any more time to it."

I stand and help her up. "In the middle of the night?"

"She told me I couldn't see him for lessons, so I had to sneak out when she was asleep."

"Oh, Izzy. I understand the pressure your mom has been putting on you, but this isn't the answer."

Footsteps kick up gravel on the trail in the distance, and she peers past me. "Please don't tell her. I beg you. I've gotta go."

"Aren't you staying to cast the water renewal spell?"

"You do *not* understand. I can't."

Isabella takes off across the causeway. I stare after her for a while, pondering how much I should share with Pam before I return to the portal. By the time I get there, the rest of the coven is already preparing the area. The boy is gone.

"Where were you, Blondie?" my best friend asks.

"Weren't you supposed to wait for us here?" Nana steps over the short fence with Rylee and Cam's help.

"Yeah, but I ran into Izzy," I say, catching my breath.

Pam's head snaps toward me. "My daughter? She was here?"

I hesitate, not wanting to tell her the entire story. Even though Pam has been harsh with her daughter, she deserves to know. "Yeah. Izzy has been meeting that boy to continue her violin lessons at night because you told her she had to stop."

"I don't know what to do with her. I told her she couldn't see him anymore."

"And you thought that would work? She didn't have her violin, though…must have borrowed his."

Heather steps over the fence. "Every string instrument has a different feel. If she's trying to improve her performance, she should have brought her violin."

"Well, she didn't have it," I say, hopping over to join them.

As if summoned by our conversation, mystical music travels across the lagoon, originating from who knows where.

Cam raises his head. "Do you recognize it, Heather?"

She closes her eyes and her head rolls around. "No, but it sure is soothing. Sounds like Fauré or Debussy, but it's different."

Zara clears a section of sand and draws a pentacle with a stick. "We really don't have time to be distracted by a free concert, witches. We have a job to do."

"Why can't we do both?" Joey says, swaying back and forth. "Oh, it's serene. I could listen to it all night."

Pam moves next to me. "Could it be that boy? I should go to his house and speak to his parents about this."

"At 1:15 a.m.?" I ask, grimacing. "I don't think so."

Heather chimes in. "That's not a high school senior playing. The person performing that music is a professional."

"Must be that creepy violin dude who lives on the other side of the causeway somewhere. I ran into him the night Jonathan and I came. I wonder if Izzy's tutor friend is his son?"

Rylee gathers dry kindling for a small fire to enhance our energy. "He was playing pretty late the night we came, too. Gotta be the same dude."

"Ignore it as best as you can," Jonathan says. "It's fogging up my concentration as well. Let's join hands to focus. Fortune, since you tried something similar before, will you stand by to assist us?"

"Sure." I don't know what he expects me to do because taking off my suppression band to help would add to the problem. I stand ready for…a catastrophe.

The coven huddles together, joining hands, and Pam recites the chant of renewal. "With solid mind and hollowed heart, I conjure up this blessed art. With healing magic and enchanted speech, I transform this water on the beach."

They set their intention and summon their combined magic. An amber glow seeps from each of their hands, slithering like snakes into the center, and the pentacle radiates its power. I stand in awe, wishing I could do more. For the first time in my life as a witch, an empty sensation guts me inside. They bend their joint stream toward water and lower it until it makes contact, then... BAM! White beams resembling lightning appear and bounce off the surface, crashing like thunderclaps. I grasp my suppression band and run into the circle, trying to warn them without divulging what happened to me.

"This can't be right! Stop the spell now!"

The coven breaks its link and Zara stamps out the fire nearby. Rylee scrapes her sneaker over the sand and obliterates the pentacle as lights illuminate the windows of the homes across from us one by one. The violin music echoes undisturbed in the distance, as if white rays of lightning are a daily phenomenon. He's dedicated. That's for sure.

Pam waves at us with both hands flapping. "Disband, witches. Quickly."

Our coven leader, Zara, Heather, and Joey skedaddle down the trail. The rest of us rush over the fence, but Nana gets stuck. Jonathan sweeps her off the ground and carries her over, planting her softly on the gravel.

"Thank you," she says. "You're a wonderful man and witch."

Sure, Betty. Butter him up.

We continue on the path until we arrive at the trailhead off the street. "Nana, Red and Cam will drop you home. Don't wait up. You need to get to sleep."

"Be careful riding back, dear. That thing is still out there."

"Catch ya at the studio after lunch tomorrow," Rylee says. "Don't forget."

"I won't, Red. Later, Cam."

"If I can drag my body out of bed." He chuckles as he gets in the car.

Jonathan hangs back while I unlock my bike. He kindly lifts it off the rack for me and lays a hand on my shoulder.

"I'm sincerely proud of you, Fortune. I would never have guessed you would commit yourself to a coven and its witches. Despite your deficiency, you strengthen the circle in other ways. One day, you could cast magic with us."

"That doesn't appear to be an option any longer."

He lowers his hand. "If and when the time comes, I will pressure the coven to find a solution for your family's curse. I at least owe you that."

"Thank you. That's a dilemma for another day. What will we do about the vise grip on the spell?"

"We have to identify the witch who put a lock on it. After tonight, I'm fairly certain none of our witches would have done this."

"I agree. How do we find this renegade witch who messed with the portal?"

He moves close and caresses my arm. "I don't know yet. We'll discuss it on Thursday next week at the circle. Meanwhile, Pam and I will check with the other local coven leaders about any suspicious members. As your grandmother said, please take care getting home."

Jonathan heads to his car and I roll my bike off the gravel to the street. There are thousands of practicing witches in Los Angeles and Orange County, all with their own agendas. Where the fuck do we start? Most practitioners abide by the rules to do no harm. What if they were attempting to do that? What if this action was a misguided spellcasting that resulted in an unexpected consequence? Would they be afraid to ask for help?

As I hop on my bike, a few residents exit their homes in their bedclothes. The music from the violinist still resounds across the lagoon.

"Go to bed, dude."

TWENTY-TWO

On my ride home, my mind spins like a top, whirling and twisting into a million permutations. I'll never sleep with this topsy-turvy brain. Norman's words are as clear as a sunny day in SoCal. I can't wait for Rhys to contact me on a whim. So, instead of continuing home, I turn left and head toward the beach. When I arrive at the gate of Rhys's estate, I search for William. He's nowhere to be found. What was I thinking? It's almost 2:15 a.m. I'm here now, though.

"Hello! Is anybody there?" I find the call box and push the buzzer. Rhys will probably be pissed as hell, but I don't give a fuck at this point. When he was pretending to be homeless, he stayed awake all night and slept during the day like a vampire. Oh, he has to be awake. I press the buzzer again and William comes out of the house rubbing his eyes.

"What do you want at this hour?" he asks.

"I need to see to Rhys." I shake the iron bars. "Open the gate."

He shakes his head. "Mr. Davies is busy at the moment."

"Ha! He is awake. I can wait. He would be angry if you sent me away. I wouldn't chance it if I were you."

William frowns and passes his hand over the lock with a shimmer of lime-green, releasing the latch. The gate rolls back. "When we get to the house, you need to wait while I tell him you're here. He's in the middle of a conference."

A meeting in the early hours of a Sunday morning? *What is he up to?* I park my bike and follow Rhys's bodyguard, driver, henchman—whatever he is—to the front door. He walks down the hallway to the living area, where male voices echo in the immense room. The laughter and bold flashes of color bleeding into my line of vision tell me there are other fae there that aren't inhibited at displaying their magical skills.

After five minutes of foot-tapping that could rival a jackhammer, I stamp down the hallway and crash some kind of fae-human meeting. Malcolm Scott is there along with a few other selkies I recognize. From the trails of the varying hues of magic, I surmise there are Tuatha Dé Danann as well. Several of the city council members are there again, but I'm surprised to see the Chief of the Long Beach Police, Henry Bloodworth. His name brings all kinds of imagery to mind, but now he's in attendance at this clandestine gathering. Disgust builds in the pit of my stomach. This isn't good.

As I approach Rhys, he notices me and whispers to his body-guard and Malcolm, who winks in my direction. *For fuck's sake.* I'll be paying for that one-night stand for eternity. The Tylwyth Teg leader heads my way to cut me off. Judging by the frown lines between his eyes and his tense jawline, he's far from delighted I'm there. He faces his palm toward me and his eel-like green magic wraps around my bicep, leading me to the balcony as he follows. When he shuts the patio door behind him, I shake my arm, but it's a failed attempt to wiggle out of his grasp.

"You don't have to fairy-handle me. Pointing toward the glass door would have been enough to direct me."

"I apologize, Fortune," he says, retracting his magic. "What are you doing here? You should not have come. There are important people here who will be offended you witnessed their presence."

"Too fucking bad. It's been two weeks, Rhys. You said you would contact me, but I haven't heard a single word from you."

A teasing smile replaces his annoyed expression. "I'm moved by your longing and affection."

I growl. He's so fucking arrogant. "Did you forget to have your fae minions search for the shifter that was killing humans?"

"No, I did not. They have been scouring the city, especially near the water. I believe their presence must be suppressing the being, or it has returned to the Otherworld through the portal."

"The coven was there tonight. It's why I'm up so late. They attempted to change the water composition back to a salt base. They failed miserably. Their magic rebounded off the surface like what happened with me when I tried to perform witchcraft on the dead fish there one night."

Rhys's head drops. "Was that a rational decision with your issue?"

"I've been performing a daily cleansing ritual to remove as much negative energy as possible. It's been working for short time spans. That was the only time I tried to perform witchcraft there, and it messed me up for a week. Nana had to re-energize my suppression band. After a couple of weeks, I started them again. My control is progressing. But I told the coven I can't perform spells because my father was an Unremarkable."

"It's not a complete lie. That was brilliant on your part. However, attempting to change the water composition back to its original state was a bad idea, Fortune."

"Why? We have to fix it, Rhys. I've heard the city has environmentalists investigating. What if they discover the portal poking around in there? That's not great either."

He clasps my hand and squeezes. "This being may need freshwater to rejuvenate itself."

"An outstanding reason to change it back."

"If you find the witch who transformed the water and they return it to its salt composition, the being would be stuck on this side with nowhere to go and no way to refresh. That would be one irate shifter destined to lash out."

"Or it's already crossed back over to the Otherworld, and we cut off its access to pass through here." I pull my hand from his. "Are you keeping something from me, Rhys? I saw the chief of police out there."

"I am the leader of the fae. No matter what behavior individual fairies exhibit, I must protect them, Fortune, with whatever means possible. Like your kind would do for yours."

"Not for all of them." I shove my hands in my jean shorts pockets. "Henry Bloodworth should have told you that. But then...he shouldn't be meeting in the middle of the night with a fae leader, should he?"

Rhys squints at me. "You should go now."

"Yeah, I think I've got my answers."

I barge into the house and head to the foyer. Rhys follows me to the front door. When I grasp the knob, he wraps his hand around mine. Surprisingly, it's tender. I peer up at him. His expression has softened—dare I say, a yearning that shows more affection than lust.

"I care what happens to you, Fortune. Think of me what you will. I am a fairy adapting to live in your world, and I wish you were part of it." He bends his head down, barely touching my lips, and kisses me. "I am here if you need me."

Blood pulses through my veins, sending my heart aflutter. "Goodnight."

As I meander through the court garden toward my bike, the thumping in my chest intensifies.

Rhys has changed.

As I stroll along the water's edge in the wet sand, I'm mesmerized by the moon's reflection on the ocean's rippling waves. A stunning man with long blond hair, bulging biceps, and an abdomen worthy of the hottest underwear commercial appears as if he's risen from the sea, and I can't stop staring. His body glistens under the moonlight, revealing his abs aren't the only thing he's packing. As he approaches me, his blue eyes radiate in the dark, locking with mine. He offers his hand and I go with him willingly...

When I wake, I struggle to lift my head from the pillow and give up. I roll over, and Norm pounces onto my torso.

"Ugh. You could have warned me, Norman." I rub my aching temples.

He sits on my abdomen. "Dreaming about the detective, my witch?"

"No. I was recalling a memory before I met him, actually. Must have been sparked by last night's events."

His ears stiffen at attention. "Where were you? Did you stop by the detective's abode for a late-night snack? Betty has been humming all morning. She has the idea you were with Jonathan, your old witch flame."

"Oh, for fuck's sake." I wipe my face with my hands. "She saw me talking to him when she left with Red and Cam. And before you ask, no, I did not go home with him. I was on the way to the house and decided to stop by Rhys's and confront him. I didn't sleep with him either. He was meeting with other fae leaders, and some Unremarkables were there. Council members and, get this, the chief of the Long Beach Police Department."

"That's alarming. If your detective knew about this revelation, he would surely start an investigation of his activities."

"Oh yeah, Ollie would flip out. That's not all. I get the impression Rhys won't divulge the location of the shifter even if he figures out where it is because it's fae."

"Self-preservation works for both worlds, does it not?" He throws up his paws.

"Apparently. Did Betty tell you what happened at the lagoon?"

Norm slides off my stomach onto the mattress. "The Fortune Whittle disaster repeat? Yes."

"What time is it?" I grab my phone from the nightstand. It's 11:25 a.m. "I have to get cleaned up and dressed. Gabby opened the store today because Cam and I knew we'd hit the sack late. I have to stop by Red's studio, too." A notification shows on the screen—a local news article about the odd flashes of lightning at the lagoon. "The coven's shenanigans made the news."

Once I'm done getting ready for the remainder of this Sunday, I head downstairs to the kitchen to make a smoothie. Betty is in rare form as she chants incantations and juggles plates, her hands glowing a bright amber. Norman's paws radiate green halos, supporting cups on each side as he helps on the counter.

"What are you doing, Nana?" I ask, noticing a freshly made smoothie in my bottle. "Thanks for making my quick brunch."

"You're welcome, dear. Norman helped. I woke up and had so much energy. Did you enjoy your time with Jonathan?"

Norm pinches his doggy lips, suppressing a laugh, but his round eyes aren't hiding anything.

"I wasn't with him, Nana. We're civil to each other now, and I'm happy we can both accept this progression in our friendship."

"I saw you together and thought—"

"You need to get the idea of us as a couple out of your head. He's not who I want. Ever."

Her concentration falters and the dishes wobble. "I suppose that wealthy Tylwyth Teg can make you happy, then?"

"I'm not sure I want him either."

Norman's hairy head quivers a warning at me while he balances the teacups.

"Why can't you be happy with the men you've gone with, Fortune?" she asks, scowling. "You are too picky."

Maybe it's the sleep deprivation or I have no fucks left. The pent-up words spew out like vomit. "Because I cut off so many choices to stop this family curse from passing on—not anymore."

"Whatever are you talking about?" The plates sway back and forth while she attempts to stabilize her magic.

"Not a good time, my witch!" My morkie familiar lowers the cups to the counter.

"I think it's the perfect time, Norm. Nana, I'm dating an Unremarkable. And there is nothing you can do about it."

Betty gapes at me and loses control. As her magic dissipates, the kitchen dishes tumble to the floor and crash into several pieces, sending shards flying across the room. When silence captures the moment, she stands there with tears welling up.

"I'm sorry, Nana. This isn't how I wanted to tell you. But I couldn't keep it from you any longer. I don't enjoy lying to you."

"How long have you been seeing this man, whoever he is?" With a chant and a sprinkle of amber from her hands, the broom in the corner sweeps up the ceramic pieces.

"For a few weeks. He's the detective who came to talk to me on the day of the Summer Solstice Festival, but I met him the night I crashed my bike."

She crosses her arms. "I remember him now. He appeared to be hurt."

"The shifter being injured him the night it attacked that man on the beach. He's recovering at home."

"I bet you knew about this, you traitor familiar."

"I'm her assistant, Betty. You merely borrow me." He sits on his hind legs and wiggles his whiskers.

"Are you in love with this Unremarkable?"

"We're dating and getting to know each other. I've been spending a lot of my time there to help him with his recovery."

"Good. Then it's not too late to end it."

I cackle like an evil witch. "Betty, I won't stop seeing him. I like him...a lot."

"Just like your mother. She ignored everything I told her, and now—"

"I am not Ivy. She was a young woman following her heart. I'm older and know exactly what I am doing."

Norm's head flips back and forth, like he's waiting for an opportunity to chime in.

The broom empties the broken dishes into the trash and Nana returns it to the corner with a wave of amber glitter. "Have you thought about the consequences?"

"Nana, I haven't even had sex with him yet. I'll be careful, as always."

"Ivy said she was cautious. Look what happened."

"Yeah, she had me and passed on the family curse. Boo-fuck-ing-hoo." I grab my smoothie and open the back porch door. "The thing is. I don't care about the curse because I've learned to live with it. You know what I do regret? Growing up without my father."

She throws her palms up. "He could have seen you anytime."

"Really?" I scoff. "You think I have no memory of that time? It replays in my head like clockwork whenever I remember my dad. After he saw me on the playground that day, you dragged him away and screamed at him. What did you say to my father, Betty?"

Norm rubs his paws together. "This is getting good."

She stands there, tight-lipped, glaring at my mom's familiar.

"You have nothing to say? Well, someday you'll tell me."

I step onto the porch and shut the door calmly even though

the temptation to slam it tugs at me. If I'm going to claim to be a mature woman, I better act like one.

The ride to Rylee's art studio on East Broad Street takes about two minutes. When I get there, I lock my bike on the rack nearby and enter. Shelves line one wall and store paints, brushes, books, buckets of rags, and more. A drafting table for sketching sits in one corner, while her massive painting easel faces the front toward the natural lighting. My best friend ambles in through a door, her clothes covered in a rainbow of splotches.

"Hey, Blondie!" Her hair is clipped up and flopping all over. "What do you think?"

"That I've been a rotten friend by not coming by sooner. Red, this place is awesome."

She grins, scanning the room. "I keep pinching myself that I have this studio. I know you have your issues with Rhys and what shit he's stepped in, but I'm so indebted to him."

"When I spoke to him last night, he seemed different. He may be involved with some sketchy people in order to exist here, but he appears to be softening in some ways."

"Yeah, it's weird. He came by here the other day to make sure I had everything I needed. Fortune, he didn't ask me anything about you. Or to influence your feelings about him in any way. Could human emotions be rubbing off on him?"

"I don't know. He's doing right by you, so that makes me happy."

"One more thing you should know. He didn't rent this place. He bought the building."

"What? That must have cost a couple of million."

"Yah," she says, clenching her teeth. "He told me I could live in the apartment above, and I wouldn't need to pay rent. What should I do?"

"You know what, Red? Move in. You deserve it. Worst case, he pisses you and me off, and you scram."

"OK, I'll do it. How was Betty this morning? She couldn't stop chatting in the car about Jonathan after she saw the two of you together."

"About that…"

I recap what happened in the kitchen before I left. Rylee's ears hang onto each word without uttering a response until I'm finished.

"Wow." Rylee sits on the stool in front of her canvas. "I can't believe you blurted it out like that. On the bright side, you don't have to lie to her anymore."

"I feel bad about how it went down, but sleep deprivation kills my patience. Red, I have to give this relationship a chance. Ollie is the nicest guy I've ever met, except for Joey."

She chuckles. "And he's not on your dance card."

"Exactly. Listen, Rhys wouldn't cough up any information. I'm thinking I should talk to Malcolm Scott directly. Do you think your selkie girlfriend, Isla, would set up a meeting?"

"I can ask her, but do you really want to talk to that selkie dude after avoiding him all night at the cocktail party? It would def piss off Rhys. I mean, it's your funeral," she says, clenching her teeth.

"You're right, and I'm sorry. I shouldn't have asked you to jeopardize your budding relationship with Isla. I hope we can find the witch who messed up the lagoon. There have been no reports of attacks since the night it injured Ollie. I think the shifter crossed back over. If it needs fresh water to pass through, it's imperative we change the composition of the water soon."

"You know, I've been thinking about that night we visited the lagoon when your magic went haywire. We saw someone in a hoodie messing at the water's edge."

"Yeah, we suspected they poured chemicals into the water and killed the fish."

"Do you think that was the shifter?"

"Nah. Too small. I mean, that person was about Izzy's height."

Red's eyes grow wide. "You think?"

The fuzzy memory of Izzy from the prior night, crouched by the water, drifts through my head, and I compare it to my vague recollection of the night of my mishap. "Fuck. It could have been her."

"Why would she cast a spell there, though?" My friend shakes her head.

"Pam has been so hard on that girl. She would absolutely mess with the coven's spell just to push back at her mother."

"Yo, Blondie, if we show up accusing Pam's daughter of being the renegade witch without good reason, she'll kick all four of us out. Besides, what does it have to do with the shifter?"

"I don't know." I pat her shoulder. "If something comes to me, I'll let you know. Later, Red."

When I arrive at my store, Gabby is behind the counter. I roll my bike past the register.

"Hey, Gabriela. Thanks for opening up. Is Cam in the back?"

"Yeah, where did you all party last night? He's got the worst hangover ever."

I force a smile. "Students, right?"

Let her believe what she wants. The truth would have her marching out of the store thinking we've lost all our marbles. I push my bike through the storage room door and shut it. Cam is sitting on a box and sorting through clothes.

"Thanks for coming in at noon," I say. "I staggered in way later than I expected. I spoke with Rhys and got nowhere. When you're rested, could you and Heather go to campus and do research in the library for me?"

"Sure. I don't have my ID card yet, but she has hers."

"Great. I want you to dig into all folklore containing beings that thrive in fresh water."

His eyebrows leap. "That could take days, Fortune."

"Yeah, I know. If you have to skip work to do it, I will gladly pay you for the hours."

"I'll send her a text now." He types with his thumbs on his cell phone screen.

"Thanks, Cam." I lean my bike against the wall and head to the front of the store.

If Rhys won't divulge what kind of shifter this being is, we'll have to figure it out ourselves. I send a text to Red and explain my plan, remembering my ally in the coven.

I have to talk to Zara.

TWENTY-THREE

Monday morning after my daily cleansing ritual, I text Zara and explain my theory. She's not shocked and believes Izzy would have had the balls to defy her mother, especially with the pressure she's been under.

> Should we approach Pam before the circle convenes next week?

ZARA

> No, she will be defensive. We need the others there for support.

> Alright. We wait then.

> Thank you for confiding in me. You didn't have to.

> Part of me hopes I'm wrong because Pam will lose her shit.

> And I pray to the gods you aren't. That would put us one step away from a solution.

I've never confided in anyone other than Rylee, sometimes Joey, but certainly not my grandmother. She would always begin her response with a *but*. I'd become accustomed to burying my curse from everyone, witches and Unremarkables alike. Not anymore.

I remove my suppression bracelet for longer periods each day, and I'm up to one full hour. Although I've cast few spells in the garage, my confidence is building. Nana could be wrong. In time, I could possess the skills to live out my life as I am—as a competent witch.

When I finish cleaning up, I enter the kitchen to make my smoothie. Nana is washing dishes in the sink by hand. What a martyr. I roll my eyes at Norman, who's resting on a chair and juggling three apples within a halo of green glow. My grandmother hasn't spoken to me since my big reveal, and I honestly don't know what to say to her to bridge our rift. I can't give in this time.

I pull out the blender and fill it with the ingredients for my power drink. The heat is intense today, so I grab a piece of junk mail to fan my face while I push the button to mix. A loose tee and cotton dress shorts are the least amount of clothes I can wear without appearing unprofessional. How I'd love to work in a bikini.

"I'm heading to the store, Nana. You should turn on the AC for a few hours. The heat index is gonna be a burner today. After work, I'll stop at Ollie's house to prepare dinner for him and do some cleaning. I plan to return around nine."

She raises her hand and water drips from the sponge. "Suit yourself."

"Norm, can you stop entertaining yourself for a minute?"

"Of course, my witch." The green halo splinters into several sections and the apples tumble onto the kitchen table.

"Can you pull out Ivy's spell journal and search for water

element spells? If any apply to the situation at the lagoon, let me know."

He salutes me with a paw. "At your service."

Nana drops a pan into the water with a splash and peers at me.

"I thought that might get your attention," I say. "Norman showed me where to find Mom's small grimoire. I understand why he waited to show me, but you? It's unforgivable you didn't share it with me years ago."

She glares at Norman, her chest heaving. "I should have never let Fortune take you as a familiar. You've been nothing but trouble."

He chants and levitates up until he's opposite her face. "Unlike you, Betty, I have always had Fortune's best interests at heart."

"Nana, don't blame him for your poor decisions," I say. "Still, I forgive you because I want to move on. You can choose that path with me, or go yours alone. It's your choice. Later, Norm."

"Have a productive day, my witch."

I grab my purse and smoothie and exit the house with renewed vigor. It's freeing not to cover up my dating an Unremarkable to Nana, but I'm still hiding my secret from the coven... and from Ollie. *One step at a time, Fortune.*

The store is busy all afternoon, with customers flowing in and out like fish through the saltwater lagoon. To avoid running the air conditioner, I prop open the door to catch the ocean breeze pushing through Long Beach. Cam is tinkering in the back, attempting to repair one of Great-Aunt Miriam's music boxes, a peace offering, if he can get one to work.

I can't stop smiling as I help the buyers, even the ones who complain about the state of the clothing being *old*. It's a vintage shop, people. By 4:30 p.m., the number of browsers drops off, but my cheerful temperament doesn't go unnoticed.

"Come again," Gabby says as she bags a shopper's vintage clothes. "We have new clothing put out every couple of weeks." The young woman leaves and my employee squints at me. "Fortune, you must tell me what is going on with you. That beautiful smile of yours has found a permanent parking space on your face today."

My mouth blossoms into a full wide grin. Should I tell her? Oh, why not? "I'm seeing someone new."

"Oooh," she says, her eyebrows jumping. "Is he the friend who was injured you've been helping?"

"Yes, actually. He's a detective with the Long Beach Police. He got hurt the night someone tried to drown that man in the ocean."

"How terrible. They didn't mention that in the paper. Thank goodness they caught the person."

"Yeah." My grin fades abruptly as the sound of high-pitched, metallic-like bell tones trickles through the store. "I'll let Cam know he needs to relieve you soon."

I walk toward the storage room with hope in my heart. Presenting Nana with at least one working music box could soften the rift between us. When I enter, Cam is cleaning the innards of one of them with a tiny brush and blowing dust off.

"Did I hear music?" I ask.

"Oh, yeah. Gobs of dust on this one, but it called to me. I don't know why."

He turns the tiny hand crank and enchanting music fills the room. It's a familiar tune. After a few seconds, it stops.

"Can you wind it more, so it lasts long enough to hear the entire melody?" I ask. "I've heard it before."

"Yeah, I recognized it, too, but I couldn't remember where."

Cam turns the handle around and around to bank some time. After he finishes, the metallic melody fills the room. As I hum along, the image of the amorous violinist surfaces in my memory, performing the mystical tune.

"Isn't that the music we heard at the lagoon?" I ask.

His lips part. "Maybe? I can't remember much about those late-night excursions."

In an instant, I can. Once I direct my attention to this piece of the puzzle, it becomes vivid in my mind, as if it was obscured before, buried under some sort of fuzzy enchantment.

"You and Heather went to the library yesterday, right?"

"Yeah. We spent the day sifting through various mythologies with shifters, some fae, others not. Didn't find anything significant yet, so we're going back tomorrow."

"I want you to focus on shifters that may involve music in some way."

Cam's eyes narrow. "You think the violinist is involved?"

"It's just a gut feeling. Ollie may be rubbing off on me."

"I think it's weird, but it makes sense if Izzy is responsible for the spell tampering. Pam Barrera will *crash out* when you tell her, if you know what that means."

"No need for an explanation, and you're absolutely correct. Which is why I'm waiting. By the way, I would stay away from the house for a while. My grandmother and I are in a bit of a rift right now."

His brow puckers. "Oh, what happened?"

"Lots of things. She wouldn't get off my back about Jonathan, so I told her about Ollie."

"Shit. Thanks for the warning. I'll miss Norm, though."

"We'll get through this. Should have happened a long time ago. I've always pushed back but never all the way. She has to sulk for a few days. Thanks for closing up. Talk to you on Thursday."

"Have a good time, Fortune."

The ride to Ollie's house only takes a few minutes. When I arrive, I lock up my bike as usual and make my way up the front porch stairs. After knocking, I enter, and the frigid AC hits me like a block of ice. Goosebumps rise, but I'm loving it. My injured date isn't on the sofa, so I kick off my sneakers and amble through the dining room.

"Ollie, where are you?"

He peeks through the kitchen doorway. "In here, love."

I shuffle in to find him cooking fish and chips on the stove. "I'm supposed to be preparing dinner." He's dressed in a collared short-sleeved shirt and casual slacks, his tie loosened around the neck.

"I'm nearly back on my feet, actually. I went to work today—desk duty, of course. Breathing is still a pain in the arse, so cooking in a frying pan is best to avoid bending over."

"Did the doctor say you could return?"

He glances at me but directs his gaze to the stove. "On light duty, but yes."

I cross my arms. "Be honest with me. What happened?"

He turns the burner down and leans back against the counter. "Manny called on Sunday. They found a body face down in the lagoon."

Shit. "Is it similar to the other drownings?" My breathing becomes erratic, and I struggle to remain calm as my heart skips and jumps like an anxious cat. Instantly, the AC isn't enough, and sweat beads on my upper lip.

"It will be in the papers tomorrow. They're going to perform an autopsy, but suicide is suspected. The young woman had been seeing a therapist." A cavernous crease forms between his eyes.

"What does your gut tell you?" It's obvious he has doubts.

"I don't want to discuss it anymore. You're here, and my time is yours for the evening." He pulls me close to him, wrapping his arms around me. "Fortune, I've very much enjoyed our time together. I can't thank you enough for all you've done."

"I fear there's a but coming after that statement."

"The woman we had arrested and detained has retracted her confession now that she's sobered up. She was released."

"Well, it's a good thing, right? If she's innocent." I'm relieved, but now he's going to become obsessed with finding the killer.

"Decidedly so. But that means the case remains open, and I'll need to spend some time on the investigation."

He strokes my cheek and kisses me. While our tongues play, his groin swells against me. I pull away and caress his chest.

"You're telling me you won't have time to see me for a while."

"The next two weeks will be extremely packed. Manny and I have to talk with the victims again, search for more witnesses... I want my mind to be on you a hundred percent when we're together. Do you understand?"

"Yes, you have to do your job, Ollie. Call me when you're able."

"Why don't we plan on two weeks from now, the third Friday in July? Coincidentally, that's the same day my physician is clearing me for"—he clears his throat—"extracurricular activities. Then I can thank you properly."

I slide my hand across his firm pectorals. "I look forward to it." More than you know. This pent-up desire is testing every ounce of willpower I have.

He clasps my hand. "Your copper bracelet is quite distracting. Any chance you could remove it for a bit?"

I stare at my Thorn rune band. I haven't taken it off or cast a spell since my cleanse. It has to be safe. "Sure."

My heart pumps into overdrive and the veins in my hands bulge out. I slide my bracelet toward my fingertips as if I'm in a slow-motion film until it's off. The tightness in my chest eases. Thank you, universe. The cleanse is holding. My heartbeat retreats as I place the metal cuff on the counter.

I kiss him and he wraps his arms around me, pulling me against his body. As I close my eyelids, I brush my right hand along the back of his head, relishing the freedom from the shackle of my bracelet. He moves to my neck, grazing the skin with his lips, and I moan. I'm in a euphoric state I've never felt before. Oh, how I wish my life could be like this forever. While he plants soft kisses, I lift my lids and my heart takes off like a jet—amber is seeping from my fingertips! I grab my suppression band and shove it onto my wrist before he notices. I step away.

"What's wrong, Fortune?" Deep furrows spread across his brow.

I'm panting and can barely respond. "We should stop. Dinner is going to burn."

"Oh, shite." Ollie grabs the spatula and flips the fish.

I stare down at my Thorn rune bracelet and steady my breathing. Am I fooling myself into thinking I can ever remove this band for good?

I'm not ready.

TWENTY-FOUR

When Thursday winds around, Nana still isn't talking to me. The music box still sits in the storage room because Cam needs to work on it a bit more. And the research has to come first. My newfound balls are allowing me to take risks I never chanced before, despite the minor setback. My grandmother doesn't care to listen when I report my success, but I share the results with her anyway. On the way to Pam's in the Rolls-Royce, I throw her a bone.

"Nana, you should be aware of what's going down tonight."

"What do you mean? Do you plan to divulge your curse now?"

"What? Fuck no. I may never tell Pam or the others because I've found a workable solution." She doesn't need to know about the incident at Ollie's. "This is about the renegade witch. Rylee and I think we figured out who it is. It's someone in the coven."

Her wrinkled face contorts. "Jonathan? Is that why you won't go back with him?"

"Oh, Nana, you're so far off you're gonna slide down the bluff to the beach. He can be devious, but he didn't do it. Rylee and I think Izzy is responsible."

Her head quivers in surprise. "Pam's daughter? She's a neophyte."

"That may be true, but she has all of her resources."

"What in the world would have motivated her to cast such a spell?"

"Pressure from her mother. You've seen how she treats her. Izzy confided in me a little. I think she sabotaged the coven's spell to push back. Sometimes it's difficult to do that directly when it's someone you love and look up to."

"Understood." My grandmother lowers her head.

"If we're wrong, Pam will probably give us our walking papers. So, be prepared. Also, Norman didn't find any water element spells in Mom's journal."

Betty stares out the window for a few minutes. "I'm sorry, Fortune. You have a good reason to be angry with me. Ivy developed a lot of foolish spells in that tome. I thought it best to keep it hidden."

"Nana, I told you I forgive you. What I don't understand is why you didn't burn it or throw it out."

"Because that journal was a piece of her. I couldn't part with it." She wipes tears from her eyes.

"Well, I'm glad you didn't. Her directions for divination have increased my interpretation skills. Nothing to brag about, yet I sense I've made progress. I even believe I could practice witchcraft fully someday. You have to trust me."

She lays her wrinkled hand on mine. "I merely fear for you, child. Your daily rituals are working now, but that does not guarantee success in the future. I didn't expect you to improve this well. Still, you must remain cautious. It would be catastrophic if an Unremarkable viewed one of your mishaps."

"I hear you, Nana." I swallow my lie. "But how do I know

how effective the rituals are if I don't remove my suppression band for long intervals?" Obviously, the effects won't last the entire day. I proved that at Ollie's.

After I park the car, Nana and I meander to the backyard through the side gate. Heather and Cam are waiting for me, fidgeting.

Heather flags me down. "We need to talk to you."

"Nana, go ahead," I say. "Tell Pam we'll be there in a second."

"Don't take too long." She squints at us and continues on.

Cam leans into me. "We just came from the library. We ran out of time, but I took some pics of a few pages from a reference book on Norse folklore I came across right before we left. You need to check them out."

He passes his phone to me. I scan the pages, flipping through the photos until I arrive at the last one. "You think the shifter is a Nokken?" I ask, giving him his cell.

"Yeah," Heather says. "It presents as a gorgeous man or woman and plays music, often emulating a violin, to seduce and lure its victims into the water—to drown them."

Cam explains further. "When the Nokken plays music, it affects your memory. I remember hearing the violin in the distance the night we checked out the water at the lagoon but little else."

"Shit," I say. "Everyone complained about losing focus the night we went to cast a new spell, too. And the damn thing was there the night I met up with Jonathan. I was really attracted to him, but Jonathan's footsteps approached, and the man was gone. It must have presented as a young boy to Izzy. Shifty bastard. Perhaps it appeared when she haphazardly tampered with the coven's spell."

"But why didn't it kill her?" Heather asks.

"I don't know. What does it say, Cam?"

He flips through the pictures. "Says you can appease this type of fae by offering it three drops of your blood, but it's risky."

"Eww," Heather says. "Why would Izzy do that?"

A light bulb clicks on in my head. I take a breath. "I think I know." Joey and Zara wave to us, and I nod in their direction. "Let me confront her. Let's go."

The rest of the coven is gathered in front of the altar. As we approach, Zara catches my gaze and nods. I wave to Joey and Red and join my grandmother, squeezing into the tight circle. I scan the faces for Izzy. She's missing.

Pam motions to begin. "After the failure of our water element incantation, we must discuss a plan of action to root out the witch who damaged our spell of filtration and changed the composition of the water in that section of the lagoon. Jonathan has a suggestion." She motions toward him.

He pulls out his cell phone. "I've completed some research using a personal database I made containing the local witches in—"

"What?!" Zara steps forward to confront him. "You never told us you were collecting names. That's highly dubious at best."

"I assure you I haven't shared the list with anyone. When I started the file, I was gathering contacts in case we needed assistance under desperate measures."

"We can talk about this later, can't we?" I ask, blinking.

"Oh, yes," she says, stepping back. "Turns out, we may not need those names."

"Why are you saying that?" Pam asks.

Rylee, Cam, and Heather fidget while Joey goggles at us. Nana raises her head and pats my hand.

"Tell her your theory, Fortune," she says. "It's best to get it over with now."

Joey shakes his head. "I'm really confused." Zara must have kept him in the dark.

"You won't be in a minute," I say, facing our coven leader. "Rylee and I were at her studio and were chatting about the shifter. One other night we were at the lagoon, we saw a person in a dark hoodie near the portal."

My best friend interjects. "I mentioned it may have been the shifter, but then..."

"Recently I caught someone in a hoodie messing around at the water's edge who had a similar stature, except this time I got to look at the individual's face—a witch. I'm fairly certain she's the one who messed with the coven's filtration spell."

"You're not gonna be happy about it, either," Rylee says.

Pam steps toward me, her nostrils flaring. "Well, who is it?"

As the others mutter to each other, I glance at Zara before blurting it out. "I believe the witch who tampered with the water is your daughter, Pam. Where is she?"

"Izzy is in the house, but you're mistaken. She would never do anything to compromise the safety of this circle or of the city. That's not how I raised her." Our coven leader pulls out her phone and types on the screen. "I sent her a text. She'll be out here in a minute."

"Let's not jump to conclusions," Jonathan says. "We'll ask her directly. Give her a chance to defend herself."

"Defend what exactly?" Zara crosses her arms. "If she messed with the water and the portal, she has a mess of explaining to do. She's violated so many rules of the coven, I don't know where to start."

Pam huffs. "If any disciplinary action is needed, that will be left to me as the coven leader."

"Because that's worked so well until now?" Zara asks, flipping a hand up.

"I'm sure she has an explanation," Joey says. "She's a good kid."

"This is connected to the shifter, I believe. Cam and Heather did some research for me and found some answers. But I need to ask her myself, or she may clam up."

"That's ridiculous," Pam says. "You are wrong."

Rylee points toward the house. "There she is."

Izzy slows her pace as she examines the expressions on our faces. "What do you need, Mama? I have to finish practicing."

"Dear, one of our witches has accused you of tampering with the water at the lagoon. You're not in trouble. Tell us the truth—that you had nothing to do with it—and you can return to your session."

Isabella scans the circle and stops at me but remains silent. Fear oozes from her eyes.

"When did you change the composition of the water at the lagoon?" I ask.

She doesn't respond.

"My guess is it was late May, after the spring concert when your mom started pressuring you about the violin. Right?" Pam scowls at me, but I continue. "You wanted to play better, but it takes hours and hours of practice. You wanted to improve your skills quickly, so your mom would let up on you. I know about the Nokken, Izzy, and I understand why you did it."

The coven leader's daughter stands frozen, wringing her hands, and her eyes well up.

"What are you talking about, Fortune?" Zara asks. "What is a Nokken?"

"It's a shapeshifter from the fae realm," Cam says. "It can shift into anything to attract humans to the water and drown them."

Heather adds, "Often, playing violin music to lure you in. Messes with your memories, too, to cover its ass."

Chatter ensues among the coven. Isabella peers at her mother, tears rolling down her face. Pam stares at her daughter, gaping. "You actually did it?"

Joey puts his arm around the teen. "Better to come clean now, Izzy. Puts things right. We all make mistakes."

Isabella lowers her head, crying, and a few minutes pass before she's able to speak. "You were so upset I was in the second violin section. I read about the Nokken and hoped he could help me. It couldn't pass through saltwater, so I searched for an incantation in one of your grimoires that would remove the salt near the portal. He's just a boy—well, a fairy. I asked him if he would shower me with his magic so I could play as well as he did. He said yes."

"And you gave him three drops of your blood?" I ask.

She sobs again, gasping between breaths.

Pam approaches her, tearing up. "You gave him...your blood? Oh, Izzy." She embraces her daughter, stroking her hair. Isabella cries against her chest.

My heart aches for our coven leader. I hope she has learned from this experience. And I wish this life lesson hadn't involved innocent lives.

"Why didn't he hurt you, Izzy?" Jonathan asks. "Are you hiding him somewhere?"

Isabella raises her head. "He said he wouldn't hurt me if I brought him things he needed. I bought him a cellphone and some food. I don't know where he is living."

"Didn't you understand he would kill people?" I ask.

She shakes her head. "He promised me he wouldn't. He said he loved me."

"The first drowning victim wasn't long after she summoned the Nokken," Jonathan says. "The timeline tracks."

Zara gestures at Pam. "Now what?"

Pam wipes away tears. "I will take Isabella to the lagoon so she can remove her spell."

"No, that could kill him," Izzy says, shaking her head. "I love him, Mama."

"Oh, child." Pam cups her face. "He's a fairy. He does not care about you."

Isabella runs off, sobbing, and our coven leader scans our faces. "I apologize to you all. This is my fault and I will rectify it. Izzy shall not join us again until she's matured enough to understand the consequences of her actions—and mine."

Rhys's words ring in my head. "The fae leader told me it was a bad idea to return the water to its original state until we know for sure it has crossed back over."

"Fortune, there have been no reports of drownings for quite some time," Jonathan says.

"Except for the recent one that hasn't hit the newspapers yet. There was a drowning at the lagoon. So far, the police believe it's a suicide, but my source believes it may be related to the others."

"Who is this source?" Zara asks. "Why should we trust this person?"

The whites of Joey's eyes grow as big as billiard balls. "We should show her some confidence, Zara." Nice try, friend.

"Is it this Rhys Davies?" Pam crosses her arms. "Because we can't put faith in a fae leader who is corrupt."

"No," Nana says. "It's not a secret anymore. She's dating an Unremarkable detective with the Long Beach Police Department."

"What the fuck, Betty!" I gape at her, bewildered.

A mischievous smile crawls onto Jonathan's face. "Does Rhys know this?"

"I don't care." But I do. It could put Ollie in danger. The fae leader has hooked up with some nefarious humans to make a life here. Unfortunately, I'm certain he glimpsed us together on the beach.

Joey throws his hands up. "I tried, Fortune."

Heather chuckles. "I don't need streaming anymore. The drama in this coven is better than an evening soap opera."

Rylee and Cam join her in a short laugh fest.

"It's alright, Joey," I say, shaking my head. "Ollie and I are good friends, and thankfully, he's confided in me or we wouldn't know the specifics of the shifter's attacks. We have to consider the possibility that Rhys was truthful as well."

Pam closes her eyes for a moment. "I believe the safest path forward is for Izzy to remove her spell. However, I will take a vote. Who agrees?"

Every witch raises their arm, except me. A vision of the Hagalaz rune stone flashes in my mind—an H with an angled bridge.

Chaos is coming.

A WEEK HAS PASSED since the coven met, and the next circle isn't scheduled until the first week of August. Apparently, Pam dragged Izzy to the lagoon, kicking and screaming, in the early hours of Friday morning and forced her to remove the spell she had cast. Several of us have frequented the area and the beach trail since then. The eerie violin music has mysteriously disappeared. Could we finally be safe?

Meanwhile, the witches in the coven proceed with their daily routines while I stress over their decision. An unsettling concern has set up house in my gut that I can't seem to shake off. Red says I need to dismiss the emotion and continue with my daily rituals. At least her relationship with Isla is progressing, and her art studio has taken off thanks to Rhys.

I haven't told my former Tylwyth Teg lover about Izzy and the removal of the spell she cast. He'll likely flip out when I do. The touch of his soft kiss left an imprint on my lips. He never gives up so easily. Why hasn't he called or sent a text? Is he up to no good with Chief Bloodworth? Does Ollie know about their connection?

The detective has contacted me via text a handful of times, writing them in the most business fashion imaginable, as if he expected someone might view them. I reply with affectionate phrases, yet his flirty messages are long gone. Has he lost interest in me since returning to duty? Maybe his wife had good reason to leave, like he admitted. I think Nana has noticed because I've been hanging around home more after work hours. Even so, she hasn't mentioned the Unremarkable once.

Friday morning, Norman assists me in my daily cleanse ritual in the garage. He sets up as I retrieve Ivy's journal and runestones from the bookcase. It now rests openly on the third shelf.

"You have seemed aloof these last couple of weeks, my witch." Norman levitates and draws a green halo in the air. It breaks into tiny flakes of glitter and falls to the floor. "A sprinkle for your thoughts?"

I smile and pet his head. "You read me so well. I'm worried about so many things. About the state of the lagoon, the Nokken, Rhys's possible criminal connections and..."

He floats to the table. "Detective Prescott?"

A notification rings on my phone and I read the screen. "Speaking of the detective."

OLLIE

Are we still on for tonight?

That's up to you. I haven't heard from you in a while.

I apologize. Work has cluttered my knackered brain.

If you're still busy with the case, I'll understand if you'd rather postpone.

OLLIE

No, I want to see you. Does half-past six work for you for dinner?

Sure. I'll close the store a little early.

Brilliant.

I shove my phone into my denim shorts pocket. "That was Ollie. His messages have been far from friendly—more like a text to a co-worker. He's probably stressed. Since they had to let that woman out of jail, he's obsessed with finding the killer of the drowning victims."

"Is that why you're casting the runestones this morning?"

"Yeah. I was afraid of what they would show, but I can't avoid it any longer. Let's get started."

When I open my mom's journal, the letters and symbols float off the pages. I review her instructions and pour the stones into the wooden bowl. As I chant the incantation, I call on my inner energy to infuse the carved crystals with my intention.

"What will I pull out this time?" I lift a stone, the Thurisaz, which is puzzling for the present. "Although Nana used the Thorn rune to provide protection and suppression of my curse, like Thor's shield, my mom's notes interpret it to mean something important is on the way. I need to be patient and wait for the opportunity to arrive."

"A reasonable interpretation," Norm says.

After placing the Thurisaz on the divination cloth, I pull out the second one, Kaunaz, and read Mom's interpretation. "Ivy writes about wounds and healing your inner emotions by ridding yourself of things. Create a fresh start." I peer at my familiar. "Do I need to remove Rhys from my life completely?"

"You're asking me?" Norm points his paw at me. "You must glean the meaning, Fortune."

"I know...but I don't know. Forget it." I swish the crystals around in the bowl and grab the last one with my fingertips. "Oh, shit."

My morkie familiar scuttles over to the cloth as I set it to the left of the Kaunaz. "The Hagalaz."

A wave of dread washes over me like a tsunami. I clutch the edge of the table and breathe in and out, in and out.

"Are you OK, my witch?" Norman lays a paw on my hand.

"Something awful is going to happen, and I have no clue what it is. I'm scared, Norm. I don't have enough control of my magic to fend off what's coming."

He levitates up to my shoulder and pats my upper arm. "As I recall, your mother expressed the same emotions the last time she cast these runestones. You must go forth with caution, Fortune. I lost Ivy; I don't want to lose you."

I pour the stones back into the bag. "Caution could also get me killed, Norm."

TWENTY-FIVE

Throughout dinner on Friday evening, Ollie flashes courteous smiles but barely talks. It's as if he's going through the motions. The quiet isn't helping with the construction of the house in my gut, hammering away at the walls. Is it because of work? Or me?

"Are you alright, Ollie?" I tug at my tank top.

He takes a sip of iced tea. "I'm much improved—on the mend. A couple more weeks and I'll be back to a normal schedule. Thank you for asking, love."

"It's just that...you appear distant tonight."

He sets his glass down. "The investigation of the drownings over the last two weeks took a turn I wasn't expecting." He drops his gaze to his dinner plate. "I have conflicting feelings, and I'm forced to do some things that don't sit well with me."

Join the club, detective. "Do you want to talk about it?"

He peers up at me. "Unfortunately, I can't, Fortune. It concerns Rhys Davies."

"Oh, I understand." What has the Tylwyth Teg fae leader done?

"Why don't we take our iced tea into the living room? We can relax there. The dishes can wait."

I pick up my glass, shuffle to the sofa, and settle into the soft cushions. Ollie sets his iced tea on a coaster next to mine and lowers himself, grunting. I shift my body toward him and caress his arm.

"Can I look at the bruising?"

Trepidation appears in his cognac eyes. "You may."

He releases the top two buttons of his collared dress shirt and I reach for the material.

"I can do it." I tug at the cotton, pulling the bottom from his pants, and unbutton the rest. As I push the edges aside, I gasp. "Oh, Ollie. I had no idea the bruising was so bad."

His entire abdominal area is battered in hues of black, blue, and yellow. But underneath, the muscles are firm, like ripples in the sand. His pectorals are tight and defined. I slide my fingernails across his chest and lean down to kiss his recovering torso, moving from one side to the other.

He strokes the back of my head. "Fortune, we shouldn't do this."

I sit up and straddle him. "You can stay put. I'll do all the work." I kiss him, offering my tongue to his welcoming mouth. He slides his hands under my tank top and presses them on my bare skin. I move inch by inch to his neck and graze his ear.

"Fortune, have you been to Rhys's home since the party you attended?"

I shift my face opposite his. "Why are you asking me now?"

He caresses my cheek. "I need to know before we progress any further."

"Why?" I climb off of him and stand. "You're interrogating me, aren't you?"

"Not exactly. But I have questions that are eating at me."

"Sure, I've been there a few times to discuss some things with him, but I don't like where this is headed." I head to the door, snatching my purse from the nearby chair on the way, and put on my sneakers. "I'd better go." What does he know about Rhys that's prompting him to turn detective on me? Now who's playing games?

Ollie darts to the door. "Please don't leave. Let's talk through this."

"You want me to answer questions, but you can't share what's going on with the case with me. When you've sorted out your conflicting emotions, call me."

I step onto the porch, pondering my mom's interpretation of the second runestone I pulled that morning. Am I supposed to rid myself of Ollie? Betty would jump for joy. I've never been more confused in my life, and that's saying something. I should have left the fucking crystals in the bag.

On the ride home, the questions compete in my head, as if they're vying for a winner. The one burning like a bushfire in my brain is whether the change in the water affected the filter on the portal. I pass Carroll Park and keep pedaling down Toyon Avenue to Beach Boulevard and turn left. When I arrive at Rhys's estate, his guard is missing. I send my former lover a text.

> I need to talk to you. Can I come in?

Several minutes pass before he replies.

RHYS

> Sorry for the wait, cariad. I'm in the pool.

I wish he would stop calling me that.

> I gave my guard the night off. Enter the code 456321.

> That's fucking original and hardly a secure choice.

RHYS

> It's a custom code for you. 😄

> Oh, I'll be around as soon as I park my bike.

I meander through the house and exit through the patio doors off the dining room to the backyard. As I rush down the tiled steps to the concrete deck, Rhys is swimming laps back and forth. His bare butt protrudes above the water as his body generates waves in his wake. The moon's rays and pool lights barely cast enough illumination to pass safety laws, but they provide a romantic ambiance. I note the distinct lack of a chlorine smell.

As I catch my breath, Rhys stops swimming and stands upright, his muscles flexing as he wipes the wetness from his face and trimmed beard. He pushes his long, drenched hair to his back while the clear pool water undulates around his sculpted abdomen. I'm mesmerized by his fair skin glistening under the sparse light as droplets glide down his muscular torso. No one could ever deny this Tylwyth Teg is gorgeous, and I've never seen him in his full winged state—no room in his tent.

Rhys looks up and notices me at the edge of the steps in the pool. "I'm glad you stopped by. I was beginning to worry about you."

"The store has been busy. If William isn't here, are we alone?"

Footsteps click on the concrete behind me. I turn my head to find Anwen Beddoe wearing a halter top, a short skirt, and black platform shoes she bought at my store.

"I'm done, boss. Entered all the data on the new bank accounts. Now I have to get to my other job." She snarls at me. "What are you doing here?"

"Enough, Anwen," he says. "Return in a couple of days when I have more information."

"Sure, Rhys." She tilts her head and smirks at me, whispering. "Does Ollie know you're here? Wait. Didn't you have a date with him tonight? Why did you leave so early?"

"None of your fucking business, Anwen. Don't you have clients waiting?"

She wiggles her fingers in the air and a lime-green glow appears. With a swipe across her body, the clothes transform into shades of hot pink. "I'm ready for them now." She yells, "Bye, Rhys," and marches up the stairs to the house.

"She'll be gone shortly and it'll just be the two of us," my former lover says. "Join me in the pool? It's heated."

"I don't have a bathing suit with me, but I'll dip my feet in." I drop my crossbody bag and pull off my sneakers and socks. "Why no chlorine or bromine odor? How are you keeping the water clean?"

"UV sanitization. Chemicals and saltwater are damaging to the Tylwyth Teg fae."

"Like the shifter." Should I tell him we know what it is? Or does he already know? "It screamed when its arm shoved the young man into the ocean waves."

"Yes. On the other hand, selkies live in the sea. But I'm chuffed you are concerned about my welfare."

I frown and shake my head. "I came because I need to share something with you. With our history, I felt I owed you that much."

"Fair enough." He rings the water out of his hair and wades toward the pool steps. "I'll come there then."

With each step, the waterline covers less of his torso until his manly appendage appears. As he approaches me, I recall the night on the beach when he was walking naked along the ocean's edge and I melted at the sight of his perfectly sculpted muscles. His body shimmers under the moonlight the same way tonight. I freeze in my spot.

"Oooh," I mutter under my breath. "I'm in trouble."

When he's standing merely a few inches away, the heat of his body warms me as an ocean breeze cools my skin. I take a deep breath, and the salty air alters my mood. He lowers his head, his cobalt eyes radiating, and captures my baby-blue gaze.

"Would you like me to get dressed?"

My heart beats an unsteady rhythm, sending blood pulsing between my legs. I pant like a distance runner, except I'm not moving. I swallow hard. "No."

A slight curl curves a side of his mouth, and he bends his head until his lips are so close, I inhale his sweet fairy breath.

"Tell me the truth, Rhys. Are you glamouring me?"

"No, Fortune. I would never do that to you." He slides his thumb across my lips. "Because I don't have to."

He kisses me and I lose myself in his touch, like so many times before. I offer my tongue freely and he presses hard on my lips, but this time his ardor doesn't convey a lust for the blond human he obsessed over. His deep passion passes through me, titillating every nerve. He lifts his head, pulls off my T-shirt, and tosses it, chuckling as he throws. I don't remember him laughing during sex before. Our trysts were purely lustful. He reaches for my jean shorts button but hesitates.

"Do you want me to stop?" His breathing is heavy, his erection rigid and ready.

I can't believe he's asking me. Even more so, I'm surprised at my response. "No."

Rhys unbuttons my jeans and pulls on the zipper while I remove my bra. I push at my shorts, gripping my panties as I slide them to the ground. He passes his fingertips over my breasts, circling an areola, as if he's savoring every moment. I dart off, run down the steps into the pool, and plunge into the warm water. After running out of air, I jump up, gasping. Water splashes behind me as I tiptoe to the edge. When I turn around, he moves toward me.

"I've been dying inside without you, yet I waited patiently for you to come back. No human has ever had this effect on me, Fortune. I want you so badly." He presses his body against mine.

I stroke his beard. "You have me now."

He kisses me again but shifts to my neck, stroking my skin with his lips. His head falls to my breast and circles the nipple with his tongue. His soft touch raises a desire in me I hadn't experienced when we tossed our bodies around in his tent on the beach. He spreads my legs and enters me, and I wrap my limbs around him as the water slaps against our bodies. When I slide my hands to his back, I feel the bulge of new appendages readying to emerge from his skin. He rests his forehead on mine.

"I so wanted to make love to you in full transition, but the tent lacked the space. I want you to experience all of me, Fortune."

Pale-green wings sprout from Rhys's back, spreading into a silk-like texture, and the light from the pool shines through. His fae magic spreads throughout his body, extending his pointed ears further and giving his skin a soft white glow. It excites me more than I could have imagined. He kisses me again, and my body succumbs to his motions. I grip his arms when I reach the peak of pleasure, squealing and shaking in his embrace, but he continues to make love to me. Hours seem to pass. Yet he doesn't stop, and I don't want him to.

He slows his movements and focuses on my face, his eyes roaming as if he's memorizing every line and feature—the arches in my eyebrows, the curvature of my nose, the cupid's bow on my upper lip. With the next thrust, he releases everything he has been holding back, and his cries of rapture resound among the soaring palm trees. He collapses against me, laying his head on my breasts.

His wings retract gracefully, like the feathers of a bird, and the white glimmer on his skin fades, scintillating near the end. I stroke his wet hair, basking in my afterglow. Yet I still manage to ask myself...was this a mistake?

Rhys raises his head and kisses me tenderly. "I will never forget this night, Fortune. If a fairy has a soul, you have stolen mine."

"Oh, Rhys, sex was never a problem for us." But was this more?

"No, it wasn't," he says, grinning playfully. "I am elated you stopped by."

I chuckle and splash water at him. "I bet you are."

He slides a finger back and forth along the point of my jaw. "I apologize for distracting you from your evening's objective. You never said why you came."

I chuckle. "You're not sorry at all."

He laughs. "No, I am not. What did you have to tell me?"

"Well, first. You need to be careful about your collaborations with the humans you've befriended who are *in the knowing*. I think someone in the LBPD may be investigating your activities."

He slides off me and rests against the pool's edge. "I am aware. He will never give you what I can, Fortune."

Anwen has told him about Ollie. Fuck her. But he probably knew anyway. "It's not a competition."

He peers at me. "Isn't it? I'm not worried about him. You're here with me."

"I owed you one warning, but I won't share more with you regarding it. I'm already violating his trust."

"Understood. What else is burning deep in that mind of yours?" He taps my head.

"We figured out who the renegade is. Pam Barrera's daughter Izzy cast the spell to change the water's composition. She wanted the help of a Nokken to play the violin better—not very smart. Although she put up a fight, our coven leader took her to the lagoon and forced her to remove it. There's no way of knowing if her witchcraft affected the filter on the portal."

Rhys stands, his face flushing the color of garnet. "They shouldn't have done that."

"I know. I shared what you said, but they were willing to take a chance since there had been no more activity from the Norse fairy. The violin music has disappeared."

"That was a fucking daft decision. Now it has no way to cross back over. That's why you haven't heard its music. It has no fresh water to rejuvenate. And it *will* lash out." He heads up the pool steps to pick up his phone and types onto the screen.

I follow him out. "Are you saying you know where it is?" I grab his arm. "Have you been hiding the Nokken?"

Rhys looks away and I remove my grasp, huffing. I dart to my clothes and get dressed in record time.

"Don't leave, Fortune. We will figure this out together."

I throw my crossbody bag over my head and squeeze water out of my hair. "Where is that killer, Rhys?"

"My underlings have been watching the Nokken to make sure it doesn't harm any humans again. But now it will strike with a vengeance since it can't rejuvenate at the lagoon. I've alerted my fae subordinates and the other leaders. Give me time to secure it."

"You mean lock it up?" I head up the steps to the house. "No, I don't trust you to follow through with that. I'm telling the coven." When I get to the top, I peer back at him. "I realize the lack of rejuvenation has probably affected the Nokken. Yet, you somehow believed keeping it from killing would be sustainable? It lives to kill, Rhys, and you fucking knew it. If that monster murders again, it's your responsibility."

Rhys's nostrils flare but he says nothing. I exit the house and dart through the courtyard to my bike. The sound of items tumbling catches my attention and I turn toward the garage. I tap my kickstand and walk warily to the massive door to lay my head

against the glass. "William?" Only the whir of a generator rever-
berates inside. I must be hearing things.

As I ride away, an animal howls in the distance. Permutations
of various futures swim in my brain alongside distant thoughts of
wild coyotes. I sure wish I had the divination skills of my mother.

Where is the murderous Nokken hiding?

CHAPTER
TWENTY-SIX

I must break a cycling record to get home. After I lock up my bike, I enter the house, panting, and sneak upstairs, trying not to wake Nana. I don't have time to explain the events of the evening to her now. I send a text to Red on my way up the stairs.

> Don't freak. I had sex with Rhys tonight…in the pool.

RYLEE

> WTF? 😂 How did that happen? I thought you went to dinner at Ollie's house?

> I did. I'll explain tomorrow before the circle. I'm spent.

> 😴 I bet you are.

> Ha. Ha. Ha. Goodnight.

When I get to my bedroom, Norm levitates off his bed and flies like the wind to my side.

"You're home exceptionally early for the plans you had, my

witch. And your hair looks wet. Did you frolic with the detective and take a shower?"

"Not with Ollie, and it's wet because I went into a pool."

His hairy eyebrows fall. "Please tell me you did *not* go to the Tylwyth Teg's residence."

"I'd be lying if I did." I plop onto the mattress.

Norman settles next to me, hanging on to each word as I feed him the events of the evening. He nods and shakes his head up and down, then left to right so many times, I'm getting motion sickness. When I finish, he covers his mouth with his paw, snickering.

"Sleeping with Rhys of Dyfed hardly fulfills the interpretation of the second runestone, Fortune."

"I had no willpower. After Ollie started questioning me like a suspect, I got pissed and left. I stopped by to warn Rhys. We're still friends."

Norm snorts. "Friends with benefits."

"I asked for that." I pull out my cell phone.

"Who will you contact about the Nokken's presence?"

"Everyone. I'm going to send a group text to the entire coven."

My familiar rubs his head against my arm. "I am truly sorry about the detective. Your feelings for him were genuine. Nevertheless, attempting to straddle an Unremarkable and supernatural world as a witch never arrives at a road without a fork."

"I understand. Ivy discovered that as well. Because that path didn't work out for her doesn't mean it won't for me. I don't want to give up. I've worked too hard."

He pats my leg with his paw. "Your mother would be proud of your progress, Fortune."

I enter my password and several texts appear on the screen. "It's Ollie."

OLLIE

I'm so sorry. Please call me.

I understand why you're upset. I am a bloody idiot.

When you've cooled down, can we talk?

"I don't have time to deal with him now. I need to send these texts."

"No doubt the detective is conflicted. He must know you have visited Rhys's property and has doubts about your involvement in his apparent criminal ways. Certainly, there is no paper trail of his existence prior to June, which would be suspicious."

"What do I say to him? I don't want Ollie to poke around in Rhys's dealings. But Rhys is a friend. I can't turn him in. Plus, he's fae. I'll just end up telling the detective one lie after another."

"Then don't, Fortune. Trust your feelings for Detective Prescott and tell him the truth. He will believe you."

I pet his head. "I have to get past this next circle."

After sending a group text to the coven sharing the information I learned from Rhys, I receive a few replies.

RYLEE

Wow. You were busy tonight.

PAM

I call for a meeting Saturday night.

JONATHAN

Let's not jump to conclusions and react irrationally.

ZARA

There's a Nokken on the loose. Anything we choose to do is rational.

"My former boyfriend may be a problem. Rhys is a client."

"This circle could become a tense situation. What will you do, my witch?"

"Whatever I have to do, Norman."

———

"ARE YOU READY, NANA?" I ask, my hand on the kitchen doorknob.

"Coming!" she shouts from her bedroom.

Norman hovers in the doorway. "You should take me with you, Fortune. I could add some analysis to your decision making."

"That would not go over well with the coven." I adjust my crossbody bag over my T-shirt. "If it were up to me, I'd search for that Nokken alone. I've increased the length of time I can cast spells up to several hours of the day. I could do my daily cleanse later and be ready for a middle of the night attack."

"Alone? You aren't exactly at the proficient level. You're still learning, and I fear for you. Don't forget the warning of the Hagalaz runestone."

"Oh, fuck that stone. In fact, I'm better off not doing another divination. It confuses me and makes me second-guess my decisions." A notification dings on my phone—an additional text from Ollie. "It's our local Long Beach detective."

"I guess I should reply to him. What should I say? I don't have the headspace to deal with this right now."

"Do you like him, Fortune? Or has he pissed you off so badly you don't want to return?"

Nana pushes Norm aside. "Why are you in the way, familiar? You can hover anywhere, yet you choose the doorway?"

"In order to kiss you as you pass by, Betty." He blows rainbow bubble kisses at her face.

She chuckles. "You can be entertaining, I'll give you that." Nana grabs her purse. "I believe the morkie is waiting for your answer."

"You too, I bet. I don't know, Nana." I tap reply and type onto the screen.

I'm sorry I didn't reply. I had to think. There is some serious shit going on right now.

I promise I'll contact you when things settle down.

OLLIE

I understand. Let me know when we can talk.

I stuff my phone in my bag. "Let's go, Nana. It's gonna be a shitshow."

"Good luck to you both." Norm flies off, leaving a trail of green glitter as we exit.

On the ride to Pam's house, Nana is quiet as a pixie trying to loot your home. She's probably hoping my interest in the Unremarkable detective has waned. I ask myself the same thing.

"Do you have questions, Nana? I know you're ready to burst thinking about Ollie Prescott."

She glances at me. "What happened, Fortune?"

"Ollie started asking how I knew Rhys while we were kissing —very odd. I think he suspects I'm involved in Rhys's affairs." I shake my head. "Which I am not. Not financially, politically, or whatever else he's up to. I got mad and left. Went to the fae leader's house and...I can't talk about the rest. Suffice it to say, I question whether I can trust either of them."

"I understand, dear. However, Detective Prescott was doing his job. Rhys should have been more forthcoming that the Nokken was still on our side of the portal. Now we are in a terrible state."

"Yeah, I hope we can come up with a plan." I pause for a moment. "Nana, I'm not keeping anything from you ever again, but you may not like what I tell you."

She pats my hand. "Well, you've always spoken your mind, dear."

"And I expect the same from you. We don't have to talk about it now. There are more important things going on. But eventually, we need to have a discussion about my father."

She turns her head to the car window, returning to her silent demeanor.

"Whenever I bring up the topic, you clam up like this. I won't pressure you. I understand it's a touchy subject. But don't you think I deserve to know who he was—is—if he's still alive? I'm 46."

"I need to recollect that time period. My old crone brain is not what it was."

At least she isn't saying no. "Nonsense. You have the memory of an elephant. Or should I say, shark? We are in Long Beach."

"Go Beach!" She chuckles and pats my hand again. "I will share when I am able."

"That's all I'm asking, Nana."

I pull up to the curb and find Rylee, Cam, and Heather waiting. Cam helps my grandmother out of the Rolls and I dash to them. "What's up?"

"They're at each other's throats in there," Heather says. "Pam and Zara, I mean. Izzy was gonna sit in on the circle, but the psychologist lost it."

Cam chuckles. "For a minute, I imagined she might throw punches. We decided it was safer to wait out here."

"Where's Jonathan?" I ask as we move toward the side gate.

"Oh, he's in there trying to referee," Rylee says. "I'm betting Izzy is gone when we get in there."

Nana inserts her two cents. "Pam's daughter has no business participating at this juncture. Only functioning adult witches should meet in this circle."

"Well, that leaves Fortune out," Cam says with a chortle.

I gape at him. "Aren't you getting frisky? Must be your fault, Heather."

"Cam's finding the path," she says. "I'm just lighting the way."

"Actually, I'm returning that dig you gave me a while back." His nose wrinkles. "Fair is fair."

I laugh. "It sure is." We arrive at the gate and I take a deep breath. "Let's go, witches."

Clouds float across the crescent moon while we argue back and forth over a plan to find the Nokken and eliminate it—minus Izzy's presence, of course. With all the personal agendas of the witches in this group, it's a wonder they've stayed together this long. We can hardly complain about them. Nana had her own objectives as well, and I went along with her ulterior motives to join. Despite all my grumblings, I'm glad we joined. We may actually save this city from a malevolent being dumped on us by the coven leader's immature offspring.

"I have doubts we can remove this Nokken," Pam says. "Even with our collaboration, our magic is no match for this being—not according to Fortune's description."

Joey throws up his hands. "We can't let that thing run loose. It needs neutering, if you know what I mean."

"Pam, we wouldn't be in this predicament if you hadn't given Isabella free access to all your grimoires." Zara taps her sneaker like a perturbed mother chastising a child. "Some of us tried to warn you she wasn't mature enough to handle the level of skill you trained her in."

Our coven leader raises her head with a stiff neck. "I am aware of my mistakes, Zara. She has been reprimanded. My tomes are under lock and key—a magical one."

"A little late now. I hope you're keeping better tabs on her. We still don't know if there was any damage to the portal filter. She must experience consequences for her actions."

"Alright, Zara," I say. "You've said your piece. We should move on from this."

"I second that," Jonathan says. "Not that we follow Robert's Rules within our coven."

She nods. "Agreed. Can you trust what Rhys told you?"

"Not anymore," I say. "I thought I could, but he withheld information."

"That isn't entirely true," Jonathan says. "He has been forth-coming with me."

"Has he?" I ask. "Or you could be blinded by the fact that he's your client."

"You might be biased by the fact you've slept with him."

I gape at the witch bastard. He's jealous.

Joey snorts. "You hooked up with the Tylwyth Teg leader?"

"Is that true, Fortune?" Pam asks. "How are we supposed to trust you?"

"I have the same question," Zara says, squinting.

Nana chants and sparks fly from her hand at the wood stump, creating a minor explosion. "Because she is my granddaughter, and I vouch for her. Do you want our help or not?"

"Wow." Rylee's eyes widen. "You go, Betty."

Heather cackles. "There's nothing like a crone to remind you who is silently running the show." She high-fives Nana and we all crack up.

"Heather, you have been a wonderful addition to this coven," Pam says.

She shrugs. "Damn straight. Now let's get to our objective. Let's kill this fucker."

"Do we know how?" Joey says, grimacing.

Cam has been flipping through photos on his phone. "The lore says forged steel or iron can repel it."

I nod. "And saltwater damages it. The Nokken's arm was injured when it shoved that young man's head into the ocean. Since it hasn't had access to freshwater to rejuvenate, its power has weakened, too."

"That would require the use of forged metal items like hammers, chisels, and expensive knives to push it into the water," Jonathan says. "And keep it there until its remaining energy depletes, and it dies."

"Wouldn't we have to submerge it?" Cam asks. "Like, for a long time?"

Pam shakes her head. "It isn't possible. We aren't a full coven of thirteen. We don't possess enough power to fight a Nokken, even using forged steel. It will sense our magic coming."

"What if this shifter couldn't identify the path of the source?" Jonathan asks, peering at me. "What if a witch exists who has uncontrollable magic? When her power is released, its path is unpredictable. The Nokken could not defend itself against it."

Oh, shit. I glance at Nana and she nods, her expression becoming somber. Once I confess I've been hiding faulty magical skills, Pam and Zara will be livid. They'll never allow me to remain in the coven.

Zara flinches. "What in the universe are you talking about, Jonathan?"

"He's referring to me." I grasp my bracelet. "When I said I

couldn't perform magic, I didn't mean I wasn't capable. Only that I shouldn't try."

I slip off my suppression band and wait, hoping my inner energy will emerge. After a few seconds, amber radiates from my fingertips.

"That's dope!" Joey runs to me, examining my hand. "Are you silently chanting an incantation?"

Heather tilts her head, attempting to inspect my hands closer. "I'm not a level three witch, but that doesn't look normal."

"No, it isn't," I say, watching the yellow snakes slither out. "I'm able to control it some with daily cleanses, and only recently. Generations ago, a witch cast a heinous spell on one of our ancestors. If we procreate with an Unremarkable, our offspring's magic will be uncontrollable. My grandmother infused this copper band with the protection of the Thorn rune to suppress it." I slide my bracelet on and the amber glow recedes. "I'm cursed."

Zara glares at me, grinding her teeth. "You lied to us."

"Did you know about this, Jonathan?" Pam asks.

"I did." He glances at me. "What I said still stands true. I told you her skills would come in handy, and they are."

Cam steps into the circle. "I trust Fortune with my life. She can do this."

"Can she?" Heather waves her finger back and forth at me. "Because it doesn't appear very threatening to me."

"Oh, it is," Rylee says. "Without the daily cleanses, her magic has a mind of its own. Since she tried to implement a spell at the lagoon where Izzy messed with the water, it ping-pongs like a missile with no trajectory now. It's fucking scary."

Jonathan interjects. "Once Fortune's magic hits the Nokken, its power should be reduced. We will need to collaborate to force it into the ocean until it disintegrates."

Pam addresses me. "How long would you need to go without

the cleansing rituals to revert to your original unmanageable state?”

“A week, two weeks, longer?” I bite my lip. “I’m not sure. My interaction with Izzy’s spell at the portal affected it, and I don’t know how bad it will be.”

“You’re going to trust her after this?” Zara asks.

“We have to,” Pam says. “Once the Nokken is gone, we can discuss her indiscretions.”

My disgruntled ally glowers at me, but I deserve it.

“OK, witches,” Joey says. “How do we find the shifter?”

I frown. “We’ll have to wait for the next victim.”

“Well, that sucks.” He plants his fists on his hips.

Pam steps forward. “If anyone sees or hears anything regarding the Nokken, send an emergency group text. It’s most likely to appear deep in the night. Let’s hope we have the week before it does, so Fortune is ready. With that, I dismiss you.”

On the way home in the car, Nana tears up. “I feared all my life I might lose you to the curse, granddaughter. I never imagined it would be at the hands of a fairy.”

“Oh, Nana. I’m not gonna die. Because one badass old crone will be there to save me.”

She chuckles as she wipes away the wetness from her face. “I’m proud of you, dear.”

“Give me time to fuck that up, Betty. Give me time.”

TWENTY-SEVEN

Ten days have passed and not one sighting of the Nokken has crept into the news. I've gone to the lagoon nearly every night after dark, searching for clues, any hint at all that the shifter has returned there—yet nothing. Although the being appeared near the ocean a couple of times before, it makes more sense for it to search for the freshwater access at the portal where it crossed over. But then I recall the distant howl of an animal I heard at Rhys's the last time I was there and ask Rylee to visit the beach trail with me around midnight on Wednesday.

"There isn't a place for the Nokken to hide out here," my friend says, surveying up and down the water's edge.

I stop and gesture at the lifeguard hut. "It could take cover there at night. Even though the ocean is full of salt, it will search for freshwater access."

"Sure, but it's summer. The hut is used during the daytime. Could the Nokken exist like a vampire and find a place to crash during the day?" She kicks up the sand and snickers. "I doubt it has to be a coffin."

"No, just some place to hide. Let's check it out."

We climb up the stairs of the unit and try to peek in, but the windows have covers. I turn and look up at the houses and apartments on the bluff above. Rhys's estate is among them, and over a hundred steps lead up to the property from the beach. There's a fence with a gate along the property line.

"When I questioned Rhys if he was hiding the Nokken, he said his fae underlings were monitoring its whereabouts. He asked me to give him time to find it. Maybe he did, and he's keeping it as a pet?"

Red stares up at the Spanish-style estate. "You could just ask him?"

"Pfft, I'm not going back there anytime soon." I descend the stairs and she follows me. "I can't control my urges around that Tylwyth Teg. When I cut things off with him, his allure was based on pure lust. But the last time? He was different. Living as a human has made him more emotional or something. Dare I say he has deep feelings for me?"

"How about you? What do you want?"

"I don't know, Red. I've been single this long. Maybe I'm not meant to be with anyone, supernatural or Unremarkable."

"Sounds lonely, Blondie." She strokes my arm. "Isla and I are getting more serious. I didn't think I'd enjoy a relationship with a selkie, but she's great. She let me watch her shift into her sealskin last week. It was amazing."

I hug her. "I'm happy for you. Everything is going so great with your art career. No matter what happens with Rhys and me, you keep that studio."

"Speaking of Unremarkable, have you heard from the detective?"

"No. If I visit him, I will surely spill the beans...the entire fucking bag. He'll think I need a psych eval, and that will be that. Once we find the Nokken and, as Joey put it, neuter it, I'll call him."

We turn around and head up the trail to Rylee's sedan. I glance back at Rhys's estate. He's standing on the balcony, gazing in our direction. Is he watching me?

THE NEXT DAY, I stay late at the store to keep busy. I must pull out my cell phone a dozen times to message Rhys. He has to know where the Nokken is, but I don't think he'll tell me. He's going to protect his own kind before any of us. Sending him a text invites him into my space again, and I have to acknowledge my weakness around him.

Ollie has honored my request to let me reach out when I'm ready to talk, yet I find my fingers tapping on his prior texts and reading them over and over. I shouldn't have left the way I did. What did he discover about Rhys?

The shoppers dwindle to zip and Gabby leaves for home around five. By the time the clock hits seven, we haven't had a customer for an hour. I turn the sign to closed.

"Let's go home. It's dead now, anyway."

Cam shuts the register and walks around the counter. "I'm beginning to think we'll never find the Nokken at this rate."

"That being hasn't had freshwater to rejuvenate for a long time. It's gonna show, and when it does, it will be bad."

Cam checks his cell for messages. "Holy shit."

"What happened?" I glance at his phone. He's reading a headline.

"They found two more people floating face down in the lagoon."

"No shit." I locate the article on my phone and read it. "If the Nokken was responsible, it's back at the lagoon. But that still doesn't explain where the thing was hiding?"

Cam's brow furrows. "You don't think Izzy would—"

"No, she's in enough shit with Pam. Plus, where would she put the thing? Not to mention, the shifter would no longer appear as a cute fifteen-year-old boy who plays the violin to her. Its face is disgusting when it hasn't shifted."

I send a group text with a link to the article. Immediately, my phone dings one after the other. They say we should meet at the lagoon and wait, but I've already done that several nights in a row. I message back.

> Should we split up between the lagoon and the beach?

ZARA

> What makes you think it will be near the ocean?

> Because it's already killed at the lagoon so many times.

JONATHAN

> Fortune may be right. We should meet tomorrow. Develop a plan.

PAM

> Come by at nine. We'll leave for the beach by ten.

Everyone else replies, confirming their attendance, and I motion to the door. "Go home and rest tonight, Cam. We'll all need our sleep."

The short ride to Carroll Park takes five minutes as usual. When I arrive home, the front door is open. Nana appears to be talking with someone in the foyer—probably a salesman. I keep telling her she should put out a sign that says, "Solicitors will be hexed."

I quickly lock up my bike and enter through the kitchen. It's still hot from the intense afternoon sun. After kicking off my sneakers, I shuffle through the dining room toward the foyer, hitting cool on the thermostat as I pass by. Betty can bitch if she wants. A familiar British accent trickles into the parlor. As I turn the corner, I glimpse his face, and he sees me.

"Fortune, I hope this is a good time," Ollie says with a slight stutter.

I gape at him, speechless. I never expected him to show up on my doorstep without warning.

Nana glances at me. "Detective Prescott and I have been having a wonderful conversation about England. I told him we have ancestors there. But now, I'm on the way to Pam Barrera's house to...pre-plan an event." She's dressed in a cotton blouse, capris, and walking shoes for the trek there.

"What? Shouldn't I go?" I ask. "I would think I'm kind of central to the planning."

She smiles and taps my hand. "I believe you have plenty to take care of here, my dear."

Ollie fidgets with his tie as I grasp my bracelet.

"Wait, Nana. You aren't driving, are you?"

"No, dear. I don't have a license anymore." She frowns at me. "You made me turn it in, remember?"

"Yet it hasn't stopped you."

She grabs her purse. "I'm walking. It's no more than fifteen minutes."

"Alright. Please be careful, Nana."

"I'll be fine, dear. As you said not long ago, I'm one bad-ass old crone."

Ollie smiles at us. "I bet you are, Miss Whittle." *You have no idea, detective.*

"Nice to have met you, Detective Prescott. Thank you for the alert." Nana walks onto the porch and I close the front door. Damn, I wish I'd been here. Who knows what she said to him?

Ollie rubs the nape of his neck. "I hope you aren't angry I stopped by. I had your address and was in the neighborhood checking on a recent robbery. The owner of the home was assaulted. I'm parked around the corner."

"Oh, that's not good. Probably not anyone we know if it's on the other side."

"Most likely not." He glances into the parlor. "Can we talk in there?"

Tiny paw steps scuttle upstairs and I glance at the stairwell. "Sure."

I draw the curtains to block busybody neighbors from viewing our conversation. At least he's wearing a jacket and tie instead of police garb. I gesture to the sofa and we sit.

He removes his jacket. "It's fucking hot today."

"Yeah, I'm sorry. Nana doesn't like to pay for AC. I turned it on for a couple of hours. It should cool down soon. How are you feeling? Has the rib and the bruising healed?"

"Mostly back on my feet. Thank you for asking." He smiles, and I recall the first night I met him on the beach trail.

The scuttling of paws resounds in the stairwell. I peer over at the foyer. Norman is staring between the balusters, growling.

"Go upstairs, Norman," I say, waving at him. "Now!" He hurries up the steps as I return my gaze to Ollie. "Sorry. He doesn't know you that well. He's protective of me."

"No worries. I want to apologize profusely for my actions at the house when you were there last. My behavior was entirely inappropriate."

"Which part?" I ask, failing to quash a laugh. "The kissing, the grinding, or sliding your hands under my shirt?"

His face flushes. "Actually, not that part."

"Oh?" I sit back and cross my legs. This could be fun.

He unbuttons his shirt and loosens his tie. "You're not going to make this easy for me, are you?"

"No, but is there ever an easy way to apologize to someone?"

"That's fair." He shifts toward me. "I shouldn't be telling you any of this, but now you're involved. In fact, I should ask these questions in a room at the precinct. Manny has been conducting surveillance of Rhys Davies and his property for many weeks."

Oh, shit. My mouth parts, a sledgehammer pounding in my chest. "And?"

"He told me you were seen coming and going several times at all hours of the night, including two weeks ago."

I swallow. "What are you trying to ask me, Ollie?"

"We believe this incredibly wealthy man has criminal connections—perhaps even some in our own police department, unfortunately. Manny pushed me to ask you questions regarding your visits to him, but it didn't sit well with me."

"Yeah, you seemed upset." I face him. "Ask me whatever you want, Ollie. I'll be as truthful as I can."

He scratches his head. "I will question you straight up, then. Are you involved in any criminal activities with a man named Rhys Davies?" His accusatory stare doesn't flinch.

"No, Ollie. I'm not a criminal. Unless it's a crime to sleep with someone."

He collapses against the cushion. "You have a relationship with the man?"

I swing my head from side to side. "I had—have—had a relationship with him. It's complicated, but I'm not seeing him now."

"That's good." He averts his gaze for a moment.

"I'm sorry. I should have told you, but my friendship with him is convoluted at best." Like he's a Tylwyth Teg being from the Otherworld, and I have a weakness for him.

"No need to apologize. I understood we weren't being exclusive. You should know he may be involved with some wildly corrupt men, Fortune."

"Yeah, I know. But I knew him before all that...before he acquired all that money. Rhys is basically a good..." I can't tell him he's a Tylwyth Teg. "A decent being. I'm telling you the truth because I like you, Ollie." And I believe we still have a chance.

He caresses the back of my hand. "Perhaps this wasn't meant to be. How can I ever compete with a man like him, Fortune? He's young and has unlimited resources. I'm a police detective and will never own an enormous house or have unlimited funds to travel the world."

"I'm not asking you to. All of that wealth doesn't matter to me. And he's not as young as you think."

He leans into me and his musky cologne raises my senses. "What do you want, Fortune?"

I caress his firm jawline, my heart aching for his touch. "I want you."

He kisses me, and Rhys's overwhelming magnetism is absent, yet I yearn for this Unremarkable more than ever. He pulls me to him, and I straddle him, our tongues continuing to explore. I come up for a breather, and he cups my cheek.

"I was so worried you would never speak to me again." His chest rises and falls, panting.

"You are the finest man I have ever met, Ollie." And here I am, hiding a secret life from him. "I don't deserve you."

"You are so wrong." He nuzzles against my face. "I am so chuffed I found a woman like you."

He kisses me again, swelling beneath me. I can't move on without him knowing who I really am. I yank my lips away.

"Ollie, I need to tell you something. I've wanted to for weeks." A wave of emotions rushes over me. This could end everything, but he needs to know. "You see, I'm a—"

He places a finger on my lips. "We can talk later. Would you like to continue this at my house?"

If I wait, I may change my mind again. "No, we can go upstairs. Nana won't be back for a few hours."

That sexy smile of his appears. "Then lead the way."

I clasp his hand and drag him to the stairwell, then dart up the steps in anticipation. After stopping to kick off his work shoes, he runs after me, chuckling. I saunter through the bedroom door and shut it once he's in. Norm is lying on my bed pillow.

"This is a big mistake, my witch. I'm attempting to save you from yourself."

Ollie laughs as he removes his socks. "He barks at you as if he's carrying on a polite conversation."

"I promise you, it's not polite." I shove my copper band up my forearm and point at the bathroom door. "Get in there, Norman."

He jumps onto the floor and growls at Ollie. "You'll hate yourself in the morning, Fortune. Don't say I didn't try." He enters and slams the door.

"You trained your dog to close doors?"

I glance at him and clear my throat. "Yeah, he's quite talented. He'd better insert some earplugs now." I strip the sheets back, sit on the mattress, and remove my tee. "Where were we?"

He pulls his tie from his collared shirt and flings it to the floor while I undo each button. As he pulls his arms from the sleeves, I trace my fingertips over the remnants of his bruises and slide them up to his toned pectorals. I rub his nipples with my thumbs and he moans.

"Does your torso still hurt?"

"A bit, but I don't fucking care."

Then I panic. "Oh, wait. I need birth control."

"A proper Englishman always comes prepared." He pulls a condom out of his wallet and tosses it on the bed.

I stroke his chest. "Are you proper, detective?"

A mischievous grin appears. "Not tonight." He pulls off my jeans and panties but hesitates. "You're so incredibly beautiful, Fortune. How did I end up here with you?"

I sit up and unbuckle his belt. "Ollie, you're so attractive and don't even realize how much." I rip the strip of leather from the loops and drop it. "You have no idea how hot that is." I rub the bulge in his pants and pull down the zipper.

My eavesdropping familiar yells through the bathroom door. "I can hear that, Fortune!"

"Should you attend to your dog?"

"No, he'll shut up in a minute." I push his slacks to the floor, snagging his underwear on the way, and tug at his hips. "I was a fool for running away. Make love to me."

He crawls onto the bed and kisses me. Our bodies become tangled like vines, flipping from one side to another. As he grazes my neck, his hand travels down my front and slides between my legs. I moan at his touch.

"Is this OK?" he asks. "I'm not hurting you?"

"No, it's wonderful. Don't stop."

He presses his warm lips against mine, and I offer my tongue. When he comes up for air, he moves down my torso, stopping briefly to nibble on my nipple. He plants a trail of kisses until he finds me. I yelp as he feasts on me, trembling and bucking, not wanting it to end. When I can't hold back any longer, I shriek with my release and pass my fingers through his thick hair. I tug at him.

"Oh, Ollie. I want you inside me."

"Far be it from me not to fulfill that wish."

He rolls on the condom, creeps up my torso, and kisses me as I guide him in. I clutch his arms as he fills me with everything I've always wanted—a man pleasing me without the bells and whistles of magic.

We make love for so long I lose track of the time, savoring every movement of our bodies intertwining. The sole reminder of the outside world is Norman singing "la-la, la-la, la-la" from the bathroom to drown out the obvious. I lose myself again, and he can't stop, either. He rests his head on my shoulder and I stroke his hair. This is one reason Ivy fell in love with my father. My life could be as sublime.

He shifts to roll away, but I embrace him.

"Don't move yet." I caress his back.

"Can you remove your bracelet? It's scraping my skin."

I lay my arm at my side. "How's that?"

"Better." He leans up on an elbow. "My leg has a cramp. We went at that for quite some time."

I chuckle as Ollie rolls over. The sun has set and I don't want to turn on the light. Moonlight peeks through the window and porch door, casting beams of white haze through the room. My bracelet slides down my hand and I shift it above my wrist. He moves to his side and caresses my cheek.

"There are probably a dozen texts waiting on my phone from Manny. I'll need to check in a minute." He lays his head on the pillow next to me. "But he can wait a few."

His eyelids droop and close. Those texts will have to sit tight. I raise my arm up over my head and exhale. I can't hide it any longer. When he wakes, I have to tell him.

I am a cursed witch.

TWENTY-EIGHT

A man's scream jolts me out of a sound sleep. Amber rays boomerang from the ceiling to the walls to the floor, squealing and lighting up the room like a mini thunderstorm. Plaster chips fall around us as I catch sight of my hands.

"Oh, shit!" I search the room for Ollie. He's taken cover near the porch door and is pulling on his pants. I rummage through the sheets for my suppression band and shove it on. As my inner energy retracts, he stands up straight, staring at me as if I've got the bubonic plague. I hop out of bed and throw on my clothes.

"Are you OK?" I dart to him, but he backs away.

"What is wrong with you, Fortune? Are you radioactive or something?"

"No, that's not it at all." I reach out to him. "You don't need to be afraid of me."

He stands there bare-chested and barefoot, panting. "Then what is it?"

The bathroom door creeps open and Norman peeks his head out. "Is it safe, my witch?"

Ollie's eyes grow big as he gapes at my familiar. "Your morkie just talked—like a man."

"What the fuck, Norm? You exposed yourself to him?"

My arrogant familiar struts out, farting rainbow bubbles. "My bad." He sits on his hind legs. "I'm settling in for a front-row seat."

Ollie shakes his head. "Am I dreaming? I must be imagining all of this."

"You aren't. I'm so sorry you found out this way. I was going to tell you last night, but you stopped me."

"You're right. I did." He stares at me as if he's inspecting a crime scene. His gaze falls to my copper band. "He called you a witch."

"I told you I was a pagan and in a coven."

"So you said. I imagined that meant you collected herbs and burned candles. Threw salt over your shoulder." He wiggles his fingers at me. "Certainly not shooting whatever that was from your fingertips like a secret military laser."

I chuckle and lay my left hand over my band. "It's my innate magic; call it witch energy. I promise I'm not working for the military, but I do throw salt occasionally."

"What happened didn't appear normal? As if any of this is." He glances at Norm. My familiar grins at him, his canine teeth glistening.

"You're not helping, Norman." I move closer to Ollie. "Nana said an evil witch put a curse on one of my ancestors generations ago. We don't even know why. It manifested when I was seven. My grandmother charmed this bracelet to help suppress the uncontrollable nature of my magic."

"When she called herself an old crone, she meant she was a sorceress as well."

"Yes, an extremely powerful one."

"Was your mother also a witch?"

"Yeah, but the curse didn't show its ugly face until I was born." This isn't the time to share the reason. I clasp his hand. "I wanted to tell you so many times, but I thought you'd think..."

"You needed a psych evaluation?" He rubs his forehead. "No, but I may need one. How is it possible your morkie can talk?"

"He's my magic assistant. You must have read about them in folklore."

"Yes, but aren't they usually cats?" Ollie peers at Norman, examining him.

"Excuse me? I'm top-grade familiar stuff. And stop staring, detective. You're making me nervous." Norm chants and a green halo appears, floating him up. "Fortune, we must clean this up before Betty gets home."

The detective's jaw drops. "Bloody hell."

"Stop showing off, Norm. Ollie, there's more I need to share—"

The door swings open and Nana darts in, huffing. She gawks at the condition of my bedroom and at us.

"What in all the Otherworld happened here?"

Norm hovers over to her. "Fortune's suppression band slid off. Isn't that obvious?"

"I'm not talking about the damage to the room." She points a finger at the disheveled sheets and Ollie's barren chest. "This and that."

"Really, Betty, must you embarrass them? It's bad enough I had to sing to myself in the bathroom during all their shenanigans."

Nana gapes at him. "We'll deal with this later. Fortune, everyone has been sending you texts for the last two hours. The Nokken attacked an Unremarkable on the beach. Jonathan Walker is helping the victim. We must get there and kill the shifter now before anyone else stumbles upon them."

"What the fuck is she talking about?" Ollie asks, slipping his arms through his shirt sleeves. "No one is going to kill anyone." He pulls his phone out of his pants and checks the screen. "Manny has been trying to call me. He says someone downtown near the waterfront spotted a giant person in a black hooded cape headed in the direction of the peninsula."

"It wasn't a human, Ollie." I pull on my socks. "It's a Nokken, a type of shapeshifter fae, and that being is responsible for all the murders and the attacks on those survivors."

His brow tenses. "That's why the victims identified their attackers as different people."

"Yes. And we have a plan...to kill it. There's so much more, but Nana and I have to go."

I throw my crossbody bag over my shoulder and we head downstairs. Ollie follows, tucking in his shirt. "I'm going with you."

"You can't," I say. "It's too strong. You could get hurt again."

"I'm a police officer, Fortune." He shoves his feet into his shoes and ties them. "It's part of the job." He types on his phone. "I sent Manny a text. Told him not to call for backup and to meet me near the area we found the last victim. I'll explain all of this to him...oh, sod it...somehow."

Nana turns toward him. "I appreciate your bravery, Detective Prescott. But this is beyond your capabilities."

"Not to argue, Madam, but I have already defended myself against...this shifter." Ollie grabs my arm. "Fortune, I won't let you go without me. It has murdered so many people."

Norman flies down the stairwell, leaving a trail of green glitter in his wake. "If he's going, I am too."

"It's too dangerous, Norm," I say. "You should remain here."

He snaps his paws together and moss-colored sparks fly. "Danger is my name. Protection is my game. I can fight off a Nokken."

"My car is around the corner," Ollie says, snatching his sport coat from the sofa. "I'll grab it and come back for you."

Nana shakes her head. "We don't have time, Detective Prescott. We'll have to take my car."

I shove the vintage keys into his hand as we exit the house. "You drive."

"How old is this automobile of yours?" he asks.

I slide the garage doors. "A few years."

He stares at the vintage car. "You own a Rolls-Royce?"

"Nana inherited it from her sister. Everything came from my aunt."

We jump into the car and Ollie takes off, heading toward the beach. On the way, I tell him everything: about the portal in the lagoon, the fae who are living with us, the other witches in the city, and how the Nokken crossed over. His face flushes darker shades of red with a particular comment.

"So, you call humans like me Unremarkable? That's fucking rich, considering how so many of us put our lives on the line for you."

"I know," I say. "It's a terrible term some witch on the East Coast came up with. Nana spread it here when we moved."

"That term is not derogatory. It merely states the facts of their magic deficiency."

I can't blame Ollie for being angry. The revelation of a supernatural world was thrust on him with no preparation. And it's my fault. The adrenaline running through his body must be off the charts. His chest heaves as he takes the corners sharply. Nana and I grab onto the grips of the car doors, but Norm flies to the right, smacking against the vinyl.

"Whoa, detective! Where did you get your license?"

Ollie glances at him. "I refuse to answer a dog."

Norm takes refuge on my lap. "Well, fuck you, too, detective."

He continues. "And now that the supernatural is evident to me, I'm *in the knowing*."

"Yes," I say. "And I am so glad you are."

Norm grabs onto my leg as his head bounces. "I tried to convince her to tell you a long time ago. No one listens to me." He peers at Nana, who's sliding back and forth in the seat. "You're quiet for a change, Betty."

She's peering out the driver's side window. "I'm more interested in the state of the weather at the moment."

I look up at the gray sky, which has grown ominous in seconds. Gusts of wind blow, sending dust, trash, and sand across the road. Rolling dismal clouds fluctuate in spirals, and I swear the lines twisting through them reconfigure into the symbol of the Hagalaz rune. A sense of dread tugs at my insides.

"The Hagalaz sign appeared to me in the clouds, Nana."

Norman leans forward on the dashboard, inspecting the gloomy sky. "The chaos is here."

TWENTY-NINE

As we get closer to the coastline, a dense fog appears—thick like fluffs of cotton. Where did this come from? My weather app said to expect clear skies with no chance of precipitation.

Ollie parks the car on Beach Boulevard and we rush to the ocean as quickly as we can, but Nana can't keep up. Norman scuttles behind us and gets swept up by a blast of wind. I catch him before he's thrown against the concrete wall lining the parking lot. My grandmother falls to the ground.

"Miss Whittle!" Ollie stops and helps her up. "You should return to the car. You're too old to be fighting murderous beings."

"I'll have you know I've fought in more dangerous situations than this, detective."

"She'll be fine, Ollie. And we need her."

We plod through the sand and proceed down the trail, calling out Pam and Jonathan's names. The blasts of air blow hair across my face, obscuring my view, and Nana's bun comes loose. When we get closer to the area where the last attack occurred, my grandmother is huffing and puffing.

"You all go ahead. I will catch up. We must find the coven."

"I won't leave you here alone, Nana!" My hair keeps flying across my face, so I grab an elastic band from my bag and wrap it.

Norm chants, levitating to my side. "Time is pressing, Fortune."

"May I help you, Miss Whittle?" the anxious detective asks.

She nods. "Yes, I don't want to hinder you."

Ollie picks up my grandmother and flings her body over his shoulder, and we leave the concrete path. As we trudge through the sand toward the water's edge, a clearing materializes. My fellow witches have arrived and are preparing to combine their power in case the Nokken shows again. Zara and Joey are attending to the victim, a young woman who appears unconscious. Jonathan is here with two others: Rhys Davies and Malcolm Scott.

When we get closer, Ollie lowers Nana to the sand and she pushes against the wind toward the coven with Norman hovering by her. The detective follows me as I press against the gusts to join Jonathan and the fae leaders.

"It's about time you got here." My former witch lover gestures at the detective. "What is he doing here?"

"I'm here to help," Ollie says. "This is my case."

Rhys glares at him. "There's nothing you can do here, Detective Prescott. Go home."

"He isn't going anywhere," I say. "Jonathan, what are they doing here?"

"I asked them to come. We needed something to mask this area, or the entire city might view our activity," he says.

I glare at Rhys. "You manipulated the weather?"

"He caused all this?" Ollie asks, gesturing at the sky.

"Yes." An arrogant grin surfaces on Rhys's face. "One of my many attributes. Ask Fortune about the others."

I scowl at the Tylwyth Teg and grind my teeth.

Malcolm Scott snickers. "Don't you think it's a wee bit funny three of your former lovers are here to lend a hand? I do."

"I—we—didn't need your help," I say.

Ollie squints at me. "You've slept with all these men?"

I swallow, glancing at them. "Well, only Jonathan is a man, and he's a witch. Malcolm is a selkie, a type of shifter fairy, but different from the one we're after. Rhys is a Tylwyth Teg. So, technically two of them are fairies." When I finish talking, I realize how ridiculous that must have sounded to him.

Ollie wipes his shocked face with his hands. "We don't have time for this. Won't they stop you from executing your plan?"

Jonathan steps forward. "They're here to help capture, or if necessary, kill this Nokken before it murders any more humans."

The clouds above us rotate and thin out. Rhys rips off his shirt. "I need to revive the storm. Malcolm, can you spot me in case I lose control?"

They dart to the ocean's edge and the Tylwyth Teg raises his arms toward the sky. While his long hair slithers in the air, his pale-green wings sprout from his back, his skin shimmering in bright white. Fae magic erupts from his hands, extending up, and the clouds twist and turn once again.

Ollie's jaw falls open, his hair tousling in the wind. "Bloody hell."

Out of nowhere, Manny emerges from the fog. He spots Ollie and runs to him. "What the hell is going on here, partner? Why are all these people here?" He stops short, seeing Rhys's magical display. "What the fuck, man?"

"There's too much to explain, Manny. There is a supernatural world hidden in this city. Those people are mostly witches who have real magical skills." He points at Rhys and Malcolm. "I can't believe I'm saying this...they are fae."

"No shit." Manny eyes me up and down. "Fortune?"

"I'm a witch; not a fairy. And you can't tell anyone what you've seen."

"Fine, but I chased that murderer down here."

"Manny, the killer isn't human. It's a type of shifter fairy called a Nokken. Ollie, I need to tell the coven."

I run, pushing through the gusts, and the detective runs after me. "The Nokken is around here somewhere," I say. "We need to prepare!"

"Are you ready, Fortune?" Pam asks. "We have brought a bag of forged steel with us."

I clasp my copper band. "Yes. Get the coven in a circle."

Norman hovers next to me. "It is time, my witch."

Ollie grabs my arm. "What is your plan?"

"The only way to weaken the Nokken enough to kill it is to attack the being using our magic aided with forged steel. It repels this shifter. Since it can sense the source, I'm the one who has to go after it."

"Because yours is uncontrollable." He squeezes my arm. "I don't want you to do that, Fortune."

"There's no other solution, Ollie. Please do not help. You'll get hurt again. I'll be alright. The coven will combine their power and submerge it with the aid of the steel. The Nokken was rejuvenating itself in the fresh water at the lagoon. A misguided witch cast a spell that caused that. It's gone now, and the being is very weak. Saltwater should weaken it further to finish it off."

"Would the ocean kill Rhys Davies as well?"

"No, but it could injure him badly. Not the selkie, though. They live in the sea."

Manny shouts from the distance. "There it is!"

"Stay back, Ollie. Please."

The gigantic Nokken slinks near the water, shrouded in its black hooded cape. I run toward it, my heart leaping in my ribcage. Jonathan joins the coven and they grasp hands, raising them above their heads and chanting, amber illuminating the gray sky. I head off the shifter and prepare to remove my bracelet while it approaches, roaring. Malcolm stands off to the side, but the Tylwyth Teg leader inches forward. *Don't you dare stop me, Rhys of Dyfed.*

Manny runs to Ollie, who stands frozen, his chest rising and falling erratically. When should I yank off my band? The Nokken grows larger with each step. It closes in on me as I grip my Thorn rune bracelet. Once I remove it, all of its protection will be gone. I have no choice.

I shout at the top of my lungs. "Come and get me, asshole!"

The Nokken roars, its face morphing into a disgusting mutation of flesh, and doubles its speed toward me. I yank off my suppression band and chant a directional spell, knowing my magic will take it on a journey of its own. My bracelet flies off into the sand as beams of yellow-orange light expel from my fingers and ping-pong across the sky. They strike the side of a lifeguard hut, setting it on fire, and land on the shifter, stopping it only a foot away from me. It cries out, piercing my ears, and I slap my hands over them.

Nana and Rylee scream. "Run, Fortune!"

The Nokken raises his head at me.

"Oh, shit!"

Voices resound against the ocean as I turn and flee. "Run!" "It's right behind you!" "Don't look back!"

I race toward the coven, gasping, but my feet sink into the sand. The roar of the Nokken increases, louder and louder with each of my steps, until something grasps my hair from behind and flips me into the water. I fight back, pushing up for air, catching fragments of distress ringing in the voices of my friends.

Through the ripples, I spot rays of amber flashing above and the shifter fends off Ollie with his other hand, plunging him into the ocean. I chant silently to invoke another spell, yet my magic seeps faintly from my fingers. A green halo floats above the surface, flitting back and forth.

The Nokken's clutch on me releases as hands grab my arms and sweep me up. I cough up fluid as I'm laid on the wet sand and view the ocean through glassy eyes. Rhys is hovering over the shifter, his arm submerged, and howling in pain. A damp hand cups my face and I look up to find Ollie looking down at me. Droplets fall from his soaked hair.

"Are you alright, Fortune?"

I lay my hand on his. "Yes, I'm fine."

Rylee, Cam, and Nana arrive. My grandmother bends over and slips on my suppression band. The seeping amber recedes. "Oh, Fortune. I thought we'd lost you."

I stand with Ollie's help and peer back at Rhys. He's floating to the ground, his left arm glistening with a wavering light.

"He killed the Nokken," Rylee says. "And he may have sacrificed his arm to do it."

"I'm so glad you're OK." Cam hugs me, chuckling. "I would have had to look for a new job if you had died."

I laugh and slap him. "You won't get off that easily."

Nana pats my arm. "You did it, Fortune. Your attack weakened the Nokken, but the coven's power and the use of the steel weren't enough to submerge it into the sea. We owe Rhys thanks." She looks at Ollie. "And so do you, Detective Prescott."

His shoulders stiffen. "I need to help Manny. He's been trying to contain the fire." He squeezes my forearm, hands me the keys to the Rolls, and darts toward the nearby hut.

Jonathan, Pam, Zara, Heather, and Joey wave for us to leave. Malcolm slips into his skin and enters the ocean.

"Can one of you drive Nana home? Someone needs to make sure all of this is contained. That Ollie and Manny won't share any of this."

Nana hugs me. "Hurry home."

I hand the car keys to Cam, and he and Rylee help my grand-mother to the car. I rush to the hut. Rhys's wings retract and he puts on his shirt as he approaches. Ollie is drenched to the bone.

"Did the Nokken hurt you?" I ask.

"No, you weakened the thing." Ollie rubs his torso. "A few bumps and bruises. I'll be on the mend in no time."

Sirens blare, resounding in the distance, while the fairy storm dissipates. Clouds break and the sliver of a crescent moon peeks through. I want to embrace Ollie and thank him for all he's done. But an invisible barrier has crept between us. Rhys stops at my side and rests his right hand on my shoulder.

"We should leave, Fortune. Unremarkables will descend upon us soon enough, and I must hide this arm."

"He's right," Ollie says. "You need to go before they get here." He stares up at the Tylwyth Teg. "Thank you for doing what you did. I recognize the sacrifice you made. It saved the lives of count-less humans."

Rhys nods once. "I didn't kill the Nokken for you, detective. I broke a fae rule to save Fortune. Nothing more."

My lips part, but the words don't come. "Ollie?"

He peers up the beach at the oncoming vehicle. "Go, Fortune." His chest falls. "Please?"

Rhys clasps my hand and drags me across the sand toward the bluff until we reach the gate to his property. As we climb over a hundred steps to the top, firefighters assess the lifeguard hut. I peer back, searching for Ollie among the black dots, but he's indistinguishable.

When we reach Rhys's property, he grabs me a towel from a pool chair. We climb into his black electric sedan and he drives to Carroll Park. I stare out the window in silence.

As Rhys pulls up in front of my house, Nana appears at the door. She lays a hand over her heart. After waving to the Tylwyth

Teg leader, she walks away. He puts his hand on mine and I turn to him.

"Thank you. I know killing the Nokken was hard for you."

"I'd do it again...for you." He pauses. "He will never be able to give you what I can, Fortune."

"None of that matters now. He'll never speak to me again after tonight."

He caresses my hand. "I care for you more than a Tylwyth Teg can for a human. I want to give you and your grandmother a better life, cariad. Why won't you let me?"

I pull my hand from his and open the door. "Because there's nothing wrong with the one I have."

I get out of the car and never look back. As the sedan pulls away, its whine increases in pitch, and Rhys's words tug at my heart.

Could he actually love me?

THIRTY

The morning after Rhys killed the Nokken and my magic set the lifeguard hut aflame, the news was plastered with articles describing the freak July thunderstorm. Many people grumbled that we could have at least gotten some much needed rain along with the lightning that burned the entire side of one of the beach huts. The coven was relieved that the fae leader's faux storm masked the true breaking news of that night.

Three weeks have passed and I haven't heard from Ollie or Rhys. I'm not sure about the Tylwyth Teg, but I have no doubt about the Unremarkable detective. I'll never hear from him again. But he and Manny are *in the knowing* now. Will they keep the disclosure of the supernatural world to themselves?

Cam walks into the back of the store while I'm taping a cardboard box shut, the one containing all of Great-Aunt Miriam's music boxes. I've wrapped duct tape around the wooden container imprisoning the imp. He offers his hands.

"Would you like me to carry the box to my sedan? The working music box is at the top inside."

"Actually, I'd appreciate it." I raise my arm, flinching. "My arm is still healing from fighting the Nokken."

"I'm sorry about the detective. He seemed like a really nice guy."

"He was—he is. But I broke his trust. I don't think he can forgive me for that after his wife lied to him."

"It's not like this was the same thing. You can't go on a date with an Unremarkable and blurt out you're a witch, and we're living with a kingdom of fairies within the city."

I chuckle. "So, how do you do that? For future reference."

"Hell if I know. I'm dating a witch." He picks up the box and heads through the back door.

"I'll lock up and meet you behind the store." I walk to the front and discover Pam Barrera talking with Gabriela.

"Hi, Pamela," I say. "Gabby, you can go home. I'm gonna lock up."

She shuts the register and picks up her purse. "See you tomorrow, Fortune. It's supposed to be a gorgeous day. Nice chatting with you, Mrs. Barrera."

"You as well. Enjoy the rest of your evening."

My loyal employee exits, and I turn the sign to closed. "I'm sorry, but I'd like to close early tonight. It was a slow day, and I told Nana I would cook dinner."

"I'll be brief." She scans the store. "I've always loved your shop. So many old things to cherish. I love that you give them a fresh life—a new home."

"What do you want to say, Pam?"

"We missed you at the August circle. Why didn't you attend?"

"I figured you wouldn't want me there. What coven wants to expand its membership with a cursed witch?"

She approaches me and takes my hands in hers. "Every practitioner has problems, Fortune, and a personal agenda. Zara covets my leadership." She leans into me. "Jonathan joined to win you back. And you can believe he hasn't given up yet. Joey and Heather can't decide on their paths. Need I go on?"

"No, you don't have to."

"Oh, but I will. Betty Whittle joined with an ulterior motive, didn't she? She's hoping we'll help you find a spell to remove your family curse."

"You know and you're still asking me to return?"

"Come back and take your place in the circle. If we can find a solution for you, we benefit in the end, too. What do you say?"

I pull my hands back and pause. "See you in September."

She smiles. "Fantastic. I want to thank you for looking out for Izzy when I was obviously failing to. Our relationship is better now."

"That's wonderful. We all learn from our mistakes."

"May the rest of your summer be a bright one."

"Yours too, Pam." After my coven leader exits, I lock up the store, set the alarm, and head to the rear of the building.

I've never been part of something bigger than myself. I certainly never imagined I would enjoy it.

CAM DUMPS the music box container onto the garage floor and Nana wanders in right after. She stares at the unmarked package.

"Hello, Cameron. What is all this?"

"I'll let Fortune explain. I'm picking up Heather for dinner. Take care, Miss Whittle." He heads out the garage door.

"Don't forget to come on Sunday for your training! And bring Heather with you!"

"Thanks for spending time with them, Nana."

She shakes a finger at me. "Don't think you're getting off scot-free. You have to start those daily cleansing rituals from scratch. You have months of hard work ahead of you."

I sigh. "Yeah, tell me something I don't already know."

"So, what's in this box?" She opens the flap.

"Don't scream at me. It's your sister's music boxes. They seemed to make you sad every time you looked at them because you missed her, so I boxed them all up and took them to the store a couple of months ago."

Her eyes bulge out. "Did you sell any of them?"

"No, Nana. I stored them there. But Cam opened a wooden box in the storage room one day, and an imp escaped. Thanks to your tutoring, he was able to grab it with a spell you had taught him. He got the scoundrel back in there."

She clutches her chest. "Phew. What a relief. Fortune, I was sad because they collected dust and I didn't want to clean them."

"Oh," I say with a chuckle. "What do we do about the prankster?"

"That was Miriam's familiar. She preferred using an imp. I told her it was a huge mistake. I'll make sure it remains in its home."

"Aunt Miriam must have been a trip. I wish I'd met her before she passed."

"Me too, Fortune. She knew more about our ancestry. In the fall, we should really go through the rest of her things in the attic. I've put it off long enough." The faint sound of a doorbell travels through the back porch screen door. "I'll get that. You finish up here."

"By the way, Pam stopped at the store before Cam and I left. She wanted to know why we hadn't attended the August circle. She knows what your ulterior motive was, but still wants us to stay. I told her we'd go in September."

She pats my hand and grins. "I told you everything would work out. Good deeds are always rewarded."

My grandmother heads into the house and I place the music box container on a shelf. I pull out my mom's journal and flip it open. The wonder of the floating words and symbols amazes me each time. What an amazing witch my mother would have been if she had lived. But there's one thing I know for sure. The rune-stones will never speak to me the way they did to Ivy. I pick up the velvet bag of crystals, shove it in my denim shorts, and head into the kitchen to cook dinner.

When I enter, Nana is walking through the dining room doorway. "There's someone here to speak to you, Fortune. He's waiting for you on the front porch. Norman is keeping him company."

I knew the Tylwyth Teg would cave at some point. "I really don't want to talk to him, Nana. There is no future for us."

She clasps my hand. "It's worth a conversation, dear. I want you to know I'll support whatever you decide from here on. It's your life."

"Thank you, Nana."

I make my way to the foyer and hesitate because I don't even know what to say to Rhys. I step onto the porch and flinch.

"Ollie." My heart leaps toward my throat. I swallow. "I wasn't expecting you."

"Is this OK, coming here to talk to you?" He's standing at the top of the steps wearing a T-shirt and jeans.

"Yes, I'm so glad you did." I pull on the bottom of my V-neck tee.

"Norman and I have had a nice little chat while I was waiting."

I frown at my morkie. "Are you sure you didn't misinterpret him?"

"I was quite amiable, I'll have you know." Norm jumps onto the porch chair. I check for neighbors. He's being risky talking to an Unremarkable out here.

"He was. I must apologize for taking so long to speak with you. What happened that day was jarring. It took quite some time to process. You lied to me, Fortune. Although the circumstances differ from what I dealt with regarding my ex-wife, I have struggled with the secrecy of your...life. However, ghosting you was not appropriate or the action of a mature adult. So, I came to share my feelings with you."

My heart sinks. "I understand. I wish I could go back and change what happened, but even a witch can't do that. Thank you for stopping by." I turn toward the door, but Ollie moves forward.

"I wasn't finished. You have left me with quite a conundrum—two, actually. After what transpired on the beach, I will never not be...what was it you called it?"

"*In the knowing*, detective," Norm says.

"Ah, yes. I shall forever be aware of this supernatural world buried beneath an Unremarkable one, as you called it. And I don't know how to proceed with that knowledge."

"I'm sorry I've put you through all this. I wish I'd never said yes to that coffee date."

"Don't say that, Fortune."

"What's the second conundrum?"

"The problem is, I like you." Ollie shifts closer and that sexy grin appears. "A lot, actually. And that's what leaves me in a bit of a pickle."

"I like you too, Ollie," I say, smiling. "Quite a lot."

He caresses my cheek. "I can't compete with the power of supernatural beings."

"I'm not asking you to. You have way more to offer beyond anything they can."

"What could that possibly be?"

I clasp his hand. "Integrity."

He smiles and glances at Norm. "Perhaps we can start fresh. Get to know each other anew. Would you be amenable to that?"

Norman interjects, shaking his hairy head. "Here we go again."

"Shut up, Norm," I say.

He chuckles at my opinionated familiar and steps back. "Hello, my name is Oliver Prescott. I'm a detective with the Long Beach Police Department. My friends call me Ollie. And you?" He offers his hand.

I wrap my fingers around his. "I'm Fortune...Fortune Whittle. And—I'm a witch."

"A pleasure to meet you, Fortune Whittle...the witch. Perhaps we can meet for a cuppa tea sometime."

"I'd like that, Ollie. Very much."

He puts his hand in his pocket. "I'll be in touch." He peers at my familiar. "Take care of her, Norman."

"Yes, sir, detective." My morkie salutes him with a paw.

Ollie smiles at me one more time, heads down the steps, and walks through the gate to his SUV.

Norman leaps to the floor. "I like that Unremarkable."

"Since when? What did you say to him?"

His paw slides over his mouth. "My lips are sealed."

A car pulls up and Rylee hops out. She waves to Ollie as he pulls away and dashes up the steps to the porch.

"Well? What happened?" she asks, flashing a hopeful grin.

"He came to apologize for not talking to me. He's still coping with all the supernatural stuff."

"It was a shock when I found out. I still haven't recovered from the night you introduced me to witchcraft and Norman flew into the garage like a helicopter. And then he started talking."

"In my defense, Fortune didn't bother to mention to me you weren't *in the knowing*. I'll be in the house, relaxing. It has been a difficult day." He enters the house and the screen door slams shut.

"That familiar sure does complain a lot," my friend says. "What about you and Ollie? Is that over?"

"He said he wants to start fresh. He's going to call me."

She hugs me. "That's promising, isn't it?"

"Red, I can't ever lie about anything to him again. And I'll have to divulge everything about the family curse. I told him I can't have children and that's a lie. I just shouldn't."

"Cross that bridge when you get to it. As long as you come clean, he'll understand."

I inhale the aroma of Nana's rosemary. "I hope so."

A notification dings on Rylee's phone. "It's Isla." She reads her screen and grimaces. "Some kind of shit is going down in the fae community."

"What do you mean?" I ask.

"Isla said a selkie found the dead body of a Tylwyth Teg female on the rocks of a jetty." Her phone dings again.

"You're kidding?" My heart flutters. "What happened?"

"Damn. They say she was murdered. Iron knife straight through the chest. They're fucking pissed. They're all saying a human must be responsible."

"How would they know that? Did they identify who killed her?"

"I don't know." Another text dings on her phone and she looks up at me with wide eyes. "It's Anwen Beddoe."

A lump surfaces in my throat. "Oh, shit."

ACKNOWLEDGMENTS

Thank you again to my daughter for brainstorming this new series with me.

Thank you to my son for his continued help with my website and online store.

Thank you to Charles Clark for another wonderful book cover.

Special thanks to my editor Sarah Faeth Sanders. This book is so much better after your insightful recommendations.

To my ARC Team. Thank you for sticking with me so long!

ABOUT THE AUTHOR

J.C. YEAMANS is an international selling author of Romantic Contemporary Fantasy. A resident of Delaware for the majority of her life, she now resides in Southern California. She writes character-driven fantasy fiction that explores folklore and the supernatural through the elements of mystery and romance.

She has published multiple works of fiction and is the author of The Bearsden Witch and Witches of Long Beach series.

As the owner of Reed Shore Press, she also publishes fiction and nonfiction works for others. When she's not putting pen to paper (or more aptly, fingertips to keys), she spends time biking, hiking, and weightlifting.

Sign up for J.C. Yeamans's newsletter at jcyeamans.com to stay in the loop!

Follow me on social media:

ALSO BY J.C. YEAMANS